BETWEEN JOBS

The City Between: Book One

W.R. GINGELL

ALSO BY W.R. GINGELL

THANKS & APOLOGIES

There are many thanks I need to make on account of this book. Mostly those are to the amazing beta readers who scoured this book for mistakes, inconsistencies, and general weirdness (as opposed to my specific brand of weirdness).

Specifically, my thanks go to Elizabeth Brown, Georgia Webb, Charlotte Michel, Carly Salsbury, Dinah Owens, Rebekah Kreyling, Priscilla Márquez, and Ellen Sheffer; with special thanks to Intisar Khanani, who spent her precious time going over my work when she could have been doing her own, amazing writing.

There are also apologies that need to be made for this book. First and foremost is the apology for the Romanised Korean, which doesn't at all convey the feeling of the language but has to make do at a pinch; and any shaky grammar thereto attached. Any errors are my own fault for being so certain that my grammar was correct and didn't need to be checked.

The other apology is one I make grudgingly, since it's not something I feel I really need to apologise for. This book uses Australian spelling, language, and vernacular. Since I'm an Australian and the book is set in Australia, I reckon this is fair enough. If some of the slang is unfamiliar to you, I apologise and say a very hearty, "Welcome to Australia, mate."

(It's also usually Queenslander slang, so if any of you Australians out there think the accent's a bit thick—go and live in the *best* part of Australia, mate!)

CHAPTER ONE

HI. MY NAME IS PET.

It's not my real name, but it's the only one you're getting. Things like names are important these days.

And it's not so much that I'm Pet.

I *am* a pet.

A human pet; I belong to two Behindkind fae and a pouty vampire. It's not weird, I promise—well, it is weird, yeah. But it's not *weird* weird, you know?

Hang on, I'm getting ahead of myself. I'll go back to the first day I saw them.

When I woke up that morning there was a dead guy hanging outside my window. It's not like I was meant to be living where I was, so it wasn't a personal insult or anything. Just a bit of a shock.

I was up early as usual, brushing my teeth while I looked for a pair of clean socks. I don't open the shutters on my window as a rule—it's a bad idea when you're squatting in a place—but I like to have a look out, even if it's still dark. I could see the gold of sunshine around the slats; at six in the morning it's already bright and light in the summer.

I peeked through the slats with my toothbrush hanging from my mouth, and there he was, strung up from the power lines, slashed open from torso to well below the navel and trailing dark red stuff down into the front yard. His head wasn't drooping over his chest decently like it should have been, either; it was dangling over the back. There was a bit of breeze, so I could see it swaying out from behind him every now and then.

There was a kind of loud silence in my ears that I get two or three times a week when my nightmare comes, the air warm around me even though it was a cool morning.

Into that warm, heavy silence, birds suddenly chirped, and when I moved forward, the window glass was icy cold beneath my fingers.

Then that thing—that thing that was dripping blood and intestines outside my window—it must be real.

It'd be a lie if I said the first thing I did was call the cops. The first thing I did was throw up; a big mess of toothpaste and toothbrush and last night's dinner, all over the carpet. Then I threw up again because it was still there when I looked out the window to make sure I'd actually seen it.

I called the cops eventually, but when the questions started to get a bit too personal, I hung up. I couldn't—can't—afford to be part of an investigation. I might have mentioned I'm not exactly living in this house legally: I'm squatting in my parents' old house.

Just minding my own business and trying not to get caught sneaking in and out. That's easier when there aren't many people living at your end of the street. It's funny what it does to a neighbourhood, having double murders go down in one of the houses. The house across from us was always pretty creepy, what with the lights and smells and the crazy bloke that lived there, but this end of the street didn't really empty out until my parents were murdered.

Then it was only me and the bloke over the road.

I looked out my window once more, to be sure it was who I

thought it was. There was the tattoo on his shoulder that he always showed off by wearing singlets.

Yep. That was the bloke across the road, all right.

Looked like it was just me now.

I EXPECTED THE COPS TO GET THERE A BIT QUICKER. I MEAN, IT wasn't longer than an hour, but it wasn't much quicker than half an hour, either. Two of them arrived first in one car, and did the same thing I'd done: threw up and called for more cops. I'll give 'em this, they were pretty quick to arrive after they knew it wasn't a hoax. In another ten minutes there were more cops on the scene than I thought Hobart actually employed, and sheets of white plastic were hung across the street. Unfortunately, they didn't bother to cover it from my side; if there's no one in the house to see, why bother?

"I'm here," I said, fogging up the glass. "And I don't wanna see it, either."

My windows are well hidden behind those slanted shutters— the old-fashioned kind that everyone thinks are fake decorations —and the cops couldn't see me. I could see them, though. Worse, I could still see *it*, just hanging there, dripping and glistening in the morning sunlight, right where it would have been looking straight into my window if its neck hadn't been snapped, hanging its head over its back. I stopped looking at it and gazed down into the street instead, sitting very still in my usual spot. They might not be able to see me, but I was careful not to let my shadow fall across the shutters anyway.

Better safe than dead. That's what Dad used to say. He said it cheerfully, with a grin—something like a riff off *Better safe than sorry*—but now that he and Mum are dead I don't think it's funny anymore.

So while the cops crawled around below, I stayed still and quiet. I mean, the shutters stop anyone from seeing me from the outside and even if the cops came inside they wouldn't be able to get to my room anyway. My room—oh yeah, I didn't tell you about that, did I? The cops couldn't find me even if they did come inside because it's a secret room, hidden in the top end of the upstairs living room behind a bookcase.

That's why I'm alive and my parents are dead.

Let me explain.

The first floor of our house looks like the others along the street—all the older houses, that is. It has two stories, is the same length as the ones either side, and all the windows match up. If there was someone next door, they could see right in through our windows. Ours...I keep saying that like it's still true. Like Mum and Dad are still here, not dead.

On the front facing of the house, now; that's where things get interesting. There are shutters on the windows upstairs. They look fake; and as far as I know, the shutters on the rest of the houses on this side of the street *are* fake. You don't get any sun from that direction anyway. But the inside of the house—now that's where it's different from the others in the street.

On the other side of those shuttered windows is my room; blocked off from the rest of the house and forgotten. It was already blocked off when we moved in. We didn't even know there was a room there until Dad was doing that thing that Dad does—pacing the length of the floor to see how long it was, preparing to do improvements. We never actually *did* the improvements, but he liked to figure it out in his head and make calculations and plans on graph paper. Some people do jigsaws, some people do crosswords; Dad did floorplans.

It wasn't until he'd paced the floor upstairs three times, frowning more each time, then went downstairs and returned, that we found out the upstairs living area was two metres shorter than the downstairs. After that, it was just a matter of finding the entrance behind the bookcase.

When I first made that long, skinny room my bedroom, we

turned the bookcase on its side and formed a makeshift hall of it. It was tiny and cramped, but I didn't care; I had my spy room, and the light filtered through the shutters, pleasantly cool and green. A year or two later I went away with out-of-state friends for a few days, and when I got back the bookcase was where it had originally been.

At first, I thought they were trying to tell me in a diplomatic way that I'd outgrown my hidden room. Turned out that Dad had built another bookcase, and this one swung open; now I was the proud owner of a secret room, behind a secret panel.

Tell me you didn't want that when you were a kid.

That's why, when our house was invaded late one summer night when I was thirteen, nobody ever found me. The home invaders didn't find me, though they found my parents. I don't remember much about that night, or finding them, but sometimes I see things in my nightmares, along with the monsters.

I don't even know why I woke up that night, all hot and sticky. It could have been the warm scent of some heated metal, coating the air like honey, that woke me. The sheet was the only thing covering me, but it was still too hot. I kicked it off and it tugged at my sweat-dampened skin, tangling in my feet—but no.

You don't want to know about that right now, and I don't want to talk about it.

Where was I? Oh yeah. The cops outside my windows.

It took them a long time to take down the dead guy. I suppose they were trying to do things as thoroughly as possible; they cleared out the entire street, and anyone trying to look in from higher on the hill would have only seen white sheeting from power pole to power pole. Apart from a few reporters, no one was stupid enough to try and push through that many cops.

I was encased in a bubble at the centre of it, stuck in my room while uniforms talked and took pictures and measured stuff below. Even if I'd wanted to leave, I wouldn't have dared. It was an ant's nest down there, and all of those ants were crawling around one dead guy who hung where he was all day, his insides right outside my window.

That's why I noticed them; the three blokes. They didn't fit in with the general squall of cops, and they definitely weren't reporters. They didn't all arrive at once, either; they arrived one by one, each one in his own self-contained circle of aloofness. The effect could have been created by authority, but none of them were in uniform, and none of them had the same identification lanyard that the other plain clothes detectives had, either.

The first one to arrive was an elegantly casual man who looked like he was in his early forties. He strolled down through the crawling scene with his lashes lowered. Maybe he was looking deferentially at the ground instead of the shifting throng of police, but I didn't think so. And those policemen and women scattered around him, forming a circle of silence that moved with him until he was below the body. Below my window, too; the area clearing of cops and noise as soon as he took his position there.

It wasn't authority, and it wasn't respect. What *was* it? As if they couldn't see him, but were repelled anyway. Like iron filings being pushed away by the opposite pole of a magnet.

This first one only looked at the body once. Even then, I got the impression that he didn't avoid looking at the body because it made him feel ill, but because he was more interested in looking at—or maybe *for*—something else. That was pretty weird, because I'd already seen at least six cops lose their breakfast.

What was weirder, though, was what he *was* interested in. And by that, I mean he was looking at my house. Not even just my house—my window specifically. Which was stupid, because no one could see through shutters, even if they weren't as fake as they pretended to be.

He strolled away from the body in the same way he'd strolled down the street, eyes down, lashes lowered. I watched his back as it crossed the road opposite my house. He turned.

Wait, was he calculating the angle of the corpse's eyes? If so, he was looking the wrong way; its eyes were facing the other house. Maybe he wasn't, though; he looked back at my house, my window, his head tilted to the side.

"What you lookin' at?" I said against the window glass. He disappeared in the fog from my breath and appeared again. Now he was walking toward my house again. "Go away."

He didn't stop; he disappeared somewhere out of my sightline, somewhere near the patio stairs. Great. Now I had a creepy weirdo sitting on my patio, and the cops weren't doing a blind thing about it. If I was old enough to legally rent this place, or buy it, stuff like this wouldn't happen. No way I'd let weirdos sit on *my* patio.

The same thing happened when the second one showed up. This one was a tall, broad-shouldered bloke in jeans, leather jacket, and leather boots—different from the first in almost every way. But that same circle of empty space followed him all the way from the top of the street to the corpse.

He was a lot bigger than the first man, too, his skin almost translucently white without tending to the sort of ruddy cheeks I usually see with that colouring. His hair was so white that it was almost silver.

Tree bark, I thought—silver bark, with that thread of silver running through the paleness. He was younger than the first man, maybe mid-thirties. He prowled around below the body, too; his eyes flickering across to my house in the same way that the first man's had.

I saw him stiffen. Oh. Creepy bloke was still hanging out on my patio, was he?

The second man's voice, muffled by the glass and the distance, said fuzzily, "Are you following me?"

That was rich. The other weirdo was here first.

"You seem to have an odd idea of what constitutes following," said the first man mildly, echoing me. He wandered back into sight in a leisurely sort of way. "I was here first, if you recall. Now, if we're speaking of *following*, perhaps you'd care to glance up the street."

The second man and I both looked to the top of the street at the same time, and there was another one there. I say *another one*, because whatever the first two were, he was obviously one of them.

He was a little bit different from the other two, though. There was still that same ring of empty space following him down the street, but this time the cops looked at him instead of a smidge to the side or a smidge beyond. Some of them were staring as if they'd seen the most beautiful thing they'd ever encountered in their lives; others looked once, then away, as if they'd seen something terrifying—then looked again because they couldn't seem to help themselves. None of them approached him, either, no matter how adoringly they gazed at him.

This one looked around boldly; smiled at a few of the female officers and winked at one. Unlike the first man, who had a sort of crème-matte look to him, and the second, who was almost blindingly white-skinned, this one was the colour of milky coffee.

He must have known the others had seen him, but that didn't seem to bother him at all; or make him move any quicker. His eyes were on the leather-clad bloke, and now they were dark and angry, though his lips still smiled. He raised his brow at the oldest man, cocking his head toward him as if asking the leather-clad one exactly what the older man was doing here. I saw those leather shoulders go up and then down again.

For a wonder, it was almost entirely silent outside my window; the babble of police and chattering cameras gone. In that silence, I heard the third man say: "*Hyung? Mwoh haeyo?*"

Great. Now they were talking in—what was that? Chinese? Japanese?

But Leather Coat said, in English, "Aren't you speaking English yet?"

The third shrugged one shoulder and glanced up at the body. "*Waeyo?*"

"Because *everybody* speaks it."

"He doesn't want to speak it until he's perfect," said the oldest man, with a small smile that went right to his eyes. "Until then, he will continue to understand English but speak Korean."

Oh. Korean. Well, I only learned a bit of Japanese from Mum in my homeschool classes, so what do I know? I wanted to learn Russian. But with no Mum, school hadn't been a thing since I was thirteen. Now that I'm seventeen, it's probably too late to think about going back to school, even if I didn't have to work.

"*Yogi waeyo?*"

"Why do you think I'm here?" Leather Coat's voice wasn't impatient, but it was brief. It suggested that they were all here for a reason, and that they each knew what the others' reasons were. So Leather Coat wasn't a fan of small talk, was he? "It's another one. I've got a good chance of catching him now that he's not Behind or Between. He won't be able to hide as well, and there's still another four to come if he holds true to form."

"It's the first time he's severed the head, though," said the oldest man. He was still smiling faintly, and that expression on his face while looking up at the body was something of an odd juxtaposition. "Are you sure it's the same killer, Sero?"

"That's not my name," said Leather Coat, even more briefly. "Athelas, if you're going to—"

"I beg your pardon: Zero."

How was being called Zero better than being called Sero?

The third man must have agreed, because he did a small, hissing noise between his teeth that might have been a laugh.

The older man's eyes flicked curiously over to him. "And if I might turn your own question back on you, JinYeong—why exactly are *you* here?"

JinYeong shrugged that one shoulder again, his hand insolently in his pocket. "*Hyungie yogiayo.*"

This time it was Zero who laughed, a surprised sound that didn't show at all in his face and seemed to startle the other two as well. "Why? Are you still trying to kill me?"

JinYeong shrugged for the third time, and turned a circle around the crime scene, both hands in his pockets now. There was still that impression of barely concealed, molten fury that bled through in the predatory way he walked and the dark liquidity of his eyes, but since he didn't attack either of the other two, I came to the conclusion that Zero had been joking. Weird, but okay.

JinYeong said something I couldn't understand and jerked his head at me. Well, it was at the house, but it was still hard to believe that they couldn't see me.

Have you ever played that night-game where you all hide around the yard and someone has to find you and say, "You're under arrest!" before you jump out and murder-tag them? You're flat on your stomach in the dirt because every good spot is already taken, and when the policeman player comes around the corner of the house he's looking *right at you*. You'd swear he can see you and you feel a right idiot, so you're about to get up with a stupid laugh and give yourself up. Only then you decide to chance it, scrabble to your feet, and murder tag him. It turns out that he couldn't see you at all, but you still felt like you should come out.

That's how it felt. Lucky for me, I've learnt to be a much better bluffer since then. I sat still and listened, ignoring the itch to come out and give myself up.

The one called Zero said shortly, "I don't want your help."

"He could be useful," Athelas said mildly. "Especially if you don't feel like visiting the local police for their forensic help."

"*Hajiman,*" added JinYeong, "*chigeum nemsaereul matcheul su obseo.*"

Zero frowned. "What's wrong with you?"

JinYeong shrugged that one shoulder and said something else in Korean.

Athelas gave a quiet huff of laughter.

"What do you mean, you're sick?" Zero said. "You're a vampire. You don't get sick."

Through a frozen buzzing in my ears, I heard the voice in which JinYeong replied, as eloquent as his shrug, and shivered behind my shuttered covering.

"There's no such thing as vampires," I said against the window glass, in a dry, tight voice. There were no such things as vampires, or monsters, or things that hid under the bed. There were just nightmares and horrible people who did horrible things.

"There's no such thing as a vampire illness," Athelas said. His eyes were still creased at the outer edges. "It's more likely that there's something around this place. Can you really not smell anything?"

"*Nae.*"

"That's a shame."

"If you can't smell anything, you're no use to me," Zero said. "Go away."

"*Aniyo,*" said JinYeong, and followed that by a swift-flowing, caramel stream of Korean.

"I can take samples to the lab."

Another sentence, accompanied by a self-satisfied smile that only turned up one corner of JinYeong's lips and didn't do away with the dangerous liquidity of his eyes.

"You *aren't* better than the lab."

JinYeong spoke again, this time for a longer time, and Zero hesitated visibly. At last he said, "All right. It could be the house causing the trouble. The local police said there were always problems around it; people disappearing and appearing, that sort of thing. There could be something from Behind or Between affecting the house."

"Not to mention JinYeong's nose," murmured Athelas.

That was the second time Zero had said something about Behind and Between—as if they were capitalised. What were they? Companies? Vampire conglomerates?

I didn't get the chance to find out, because by then the three men—vampires?—were walking away from the crime scene again.

I wasn't sure if it was because of the same effect that made the road clear around them as they walked, but a definite sense of relief grew in me the further away they got.

I PROBABLY SHOULD HAVE BEEN MORE CAREFUL WHEN I LEFT the house to go to work the next morning. I mean; I say that, but it's not like I *wasn't* careful; it's what you say after something happens, right? Because something has happened, and if you pretend that something you did or didn't do could have made a difference, somehow you feel safer.

Maybe that's just me.

Whichever way you slice it, the day started out bad and plunged into a free fall of awful.

I got out of bed and had something for breakfast—can't remember what, so it must have been flamin' exciting. I even remembered to brush my teeth, which was a triumph; I don't always. It's not like you can threaten to tell my Mum, so what are you going to do about it?

The cops were mostly gone from the scene downstairs, and so were the cleaners, which meant the street was almost looking normal if you couldn't see the darker patch on the bitumen that they hadn't managed to wash away completely.

Or the missing line between the power poles, I suppose.

Looking at it, it was hard to believe that yesterday's waking had been anything but a bad dream. And those men—vampires, did they say?—ha! Just part of the nightmare.

I shoved my arms through the loops of my backpack, and then my hands into my pockets. It was fine but cold, and my fingers were already a bit pink and numb. My threadbare collar didn't do much to stop the cold chill sneaking down my neck, either, which meant I'd probably get sick again. Not that it mattered; there was no one at home to be annoyed by my perpetual sniffle.

I squinted into the sun as I climbed the slight incline of the street, cautious about any left-behind cops who might be guarding the area. Me and the dead guy were the only ones living right at the bottom of the street anyway, but you never knew.

And it felt like…I dunno, like someone was watching me. Maybe following me. I was probably being paranoid, but it turned out to be a good thing I *was* on the lookout. As I crested the part of the incline that brought me to the other end of the street, there was a cop with his back to me. He wasn't in uniform but I knew he was a cop because of the way he stood. *You* know.

You don't? Oh well, everyone has their talents, I reckon.

From his skin he could have been Aboriginal, but the tight coils of his spongy, black hair said Islander. I hadn't seen him yesterday, I was almost certain. I nipped in between numbers 56 and 58 before he could turn and give me the same kind of once-over I was giving to him.

I was so busy trying not to be seen or heard by the Islander cop that I didn't see the bloke that attacked me until it was too late. One minute I was climbing carefully up through a gap in number 56's fence to get into the park behind, the next, something hefty and leather slammed into me.

Teeth really can rattle.

Mine did; and by the time I could concentrate on anything else, someone had his arm across my throat, threatening to take that concentration away again. I could smell the leather of his jacket, but I would have recognised him anyway—I hadn't seen a bloke this white since I went to school with an albino kid in preschool. Even his hair was white. I mean, I'd seen it yesterday, but that had felt like a dream until just now.

What was his name? Zero?

I made a choking sort of cough at him and he grimaced down at the flecks of spit on his sleeve.

"What?" I croaked. "Got more where—" *cough* "—that came from."

"You shouldn't be playing down there," he said. He sounded nearly reasonable. Well, about as reasonable as he could sound while still casually choking me half to death with one forearm. I wondered if this was what it would have been like to have an older brother; reasonable and kind of murderous. "It's not safe. Someone got killed yesterday."

"Yeah?" And then, because I knew he hadn't, I asked, "Kill him, did you?"

He looked down at me, and I got the idea I'd perplexed him. "No. Why—"

"Cos you're gunna kill me pretty quick if you don't let go."

"This?" he said. "This won't kill you. It's only uncomfortable."

He let me go anyway, and I felt again the same thing I'd felt when I saw him yesterday; the desire to run, to get away, to be safe. To pick up my heels and scarper for it before this person could reach out and grab me and tear me to pieces with his bare hands.

Maybe if I'd had any sense, I would have followed my instincts and run.

But this was just another version of the murder game, and to run away, I'd have to put my back to him. This player didn't really see me; not yet. He definitely would if I ran.

And so for the second time, I stayed still.

CHAPTER TWO

WHILE EVERY INSTINCT IN ME SCREAMED TO GET AWAY WHILE the getting was good, I read his face instead.

I'm pretty good with faces, and his was sort of—I don't know, sad? Resigned? Expectant? Yeah, it was expectant; like he was just waiting for me to run away. And there was tiredness to that expectation, though it was mostly covered up by coolness. It was the kind of expression that made me want to offer him a cuppa, but I didn't think he'd understand the offer.

Anyway, it wasn't like I could actually follow through on the offer—I was living illegally in my house, and there was no money spare to buy him one. Every skerrick of spare money went toward my savings to buy my house.

"You all right?" I asked instead.

This time, he was the one who said, "What?"

I tilted my chin down at where the crime scene would have been if you could see it from there. "You're investigating this, right? Bit messy, was it?"

"I didn't throw up." He said it stiffly. Was he offended?

"Yeah, but the cops said it wasn't pretty. You all right?"

"I'm hungry," he said. Cautious. Like he wasn't sure if it was the answer he should give.

Well, okay then. Corpses don't make me hungry. For example, BBQ isn't the first thing *I'm* gunna be thinking of if I've found a burnt corpse, but the world's a weird place, right?

Maybe he didn't understand the question.

"You shouldn't be playing down there," he repeated.

"I wasn't."

His bright blue eyes narrowed on me. "What did you see?"

"Nothing," I told him. "I gotta go to work."

"Where do you work?"

I grinned. "Why should I tell you?"

"Why shouldn't you?"

"For all I know, you're a serial killer," I told him.

To my surprise, that didn't make him bristle. It didn't make him look sadder, either, but there might have been a slight glitter of laughter in the depths of those cool blue eyes.

"That's true," he agreed. "Where do you work?"

I gave him a look. "Town." And that reminded me. I was going to be late. In case he was thinking about stopping me again, I said, "I'm going now. Don't follow me. I'll call the cops."

"I am the cops."

"Yeah, right," I said, and walked away. This time, he let me.

I SHOULD HAVE KNOWN THAT WOULDN'T BE THE END OF IT. There's another of those useless *should have*s for you. But I went to work anyway because when you need money what else can you do but go to work?

There were only a few places around Hobart that pay cash in hand; my café was one of them. I'd been working there since I was fourteen—hence, cash in hand—and now that I was old enough to be legally working, I still wasn't game enough to make bank and superannuation accounts, let alone accept any payment that wasn't cash. Dad had always taken cash jobs when he was working, and maybe the prejudice stuck with me.

That meant I only had a few options when it came to a job, and none of 'em were much good. There are only two kinds of jobs that pay cash in hand: those that are taking advantage of the Asian students who come to Hobart, and those that are taking advantage of the population that was born here. In the first case, visa requirements meant that bosses could make foreign students work longer hours without those hours being recorded—or, mostly, paid for—and in my case, it meant that my boss couldn't get picked up for employing underaged—and much cheaper— staff. It also meant that if he didn't pay me one week, I had to keep coming back to work the next day to remind him about it.

The first time I walked into his café, thirteen and a half, hungry and desperate, he'd smiled at me, his cheeks moonlike and friendly. I saw straight away that his eyes were harder and colder than pebbles in a creek, but when he said, "You can eat on a tab here, half price," I was sold. There was no other place that was willing to take a chance on someone as young as me, and I needed food.

'Course, if you left it longer than a week to pay off your tab, he started to get short with you, but it was still a cheaper way of eating, even if it wasn't healthier. And it meant the boss could make chalk marks on the tab board and let customers know what a nice bloke he was, looking after his staff. They weren't to know what he was like when they weren't around, and he was pretty careful not to lose his temper in front of them. I always tried to leave before the last customer did, because then I could be pretty sure of getting away without too much trouble, or being asked to stay later when I'd already signed off on the work sheet for the day. We signed off in pen, and there was no pay for any hours that were scribbled over after we'd signed out.

Today looked like being a bad day, but pay day usually was. It was harder to get out before the café closed when the boss was doing the pays, 'cos if he wanted you to stay longer, he just had to pretend he didn't see you waiting for your pay envelope.

I was more glad than usual to finish, because the toilet system had back-flushed again; this time worse than usual, and there was muck up to the ankles in there. It wasn't just a matter of using a plunger this time, either; it would need the plumber.

I shut the door on it hurriedly; the other two girls must have already seen it. I'd wondered why they'd ducked out so quickly after work. They usually hung around with the boss for an hour or two, making him laugh and feel good about himself. It was survival, for them: a way to make sure they could keep working without going mad, being sacked, or having stuff thrown at them.

Hopefully the boss hadn't seen it yet.

I went out to the table where he was stabbing a finger into the worn keys of his calculator, a few pay envelopes sitting in front of him, and waited for him to notice me. If I interrupted him now, he'd only take longer to finish.

"You can clean the toilet while you wait," he said, without looking up.

Heck no. It was a soup of floaters and urine in there: it was a job for the plumber—and probably a hazmat team.

"I've already finished," I said, wriggling my toes nervously. I wanted to be back home and safe, preferably before I met with any more weirdos. "Can't stay back late today. I just need my pay, that's all."

He nodded like he was busy thinking about something else, and my heart sank. It was going to be a fight to get my pay this arvo, was it?

"We didn't make much profit this week," he said, after a few more numbers went into the calculator. "That bloke you made a sandwich for was so angry I had to give it to him for free."

"What bloke?" I asked.

"You put carrot on his salad roll."

"Sorry," I said, though I should have known better. "He was a regular and he wouldn't tell me what his order was. I had to guess it."

"You should have known his order if he's a regular."

"It was my first shift on salad bar—"

"Cost me five dollars to put it right," said the boss. "If I have to pay for a plumber as well, I might as well not come to work. Do you think that's fair?"

I hate it when he asks that. He actually thinks he's in the right, and it's never any use arguing against that much bull-headed certainty.

I sighed.

Oh well. It was already a bad day, and I *had* messed up the customer's order. I didn't think I'd messed it up that badly, but people are weird.

I went and cleaned out the toilet room.

By the time I was done, the boss had gone home. I was relieved to see he'd left my pay envelope on the table he'd been sitting at, but the relief crumbled away when I saw there was a note with it.

'Deductions from this week's pay,' it said. 'Tab: $30, Customer error: $5.00. Mop the floor before you go.'

I grabbed it and went, anyway. It wasn't like I could do anything about it, and if I did try to do something about it, I'd only push the boss into one of his fits a bit earlier than usual.

On the way home, I still had that feeling of being watched; sorta scratchy and uncomfortable between my shoulder blades, like there was a cockroach running down my back. I suppose with what had come out of the toilet at the café, it wasn't too far off being possible, but I was pretty sure the scruffy bearded dude in the holey shirt who was talking loudly to himself on the bank steps was the same scruffy bearded dude I'd seen washing his face at a tap on the street when I started work that morning, too. His shirt should have said *shot* but the hole in it made it *shoot*, so I knew it was the same dude.

Was he following me?

Yeah, paranoid, I know; but I was still feeling jumpy after my encounter with Zero. Anyway, chances are the more paranoid you are, the less likely you are to be dead, so there's that.

I took the long way home, through back gardens and side alleys, just to be sure. By the time I got home I wasn't only wet and smelly; I was sweaty, smelly, and covered with caterpillars. I wasn't supposed to have a shower for another day yet, but flies don't much care about shower day—they don't much care about making sure I don't use too much water to stay hidden, either.

I was probably still paranoid, but I checked out my window when I went up to get clothes. And what do you know, the old bearded bloke was now hanging around the public rubbish bins beside the house across the road!

A sharp stab of panic made me drop my clothes on the floor. How the heck did he find me? How did he know where I live? He was just crouching there, grinning to himself as he picked out coloured stones from the ones on the footpath, and occasionally looking up at my window.

Hang on. I picked up my clothes very slowly, a frown pinching between my brows. I knew this old bearded bloke, didn't I? Maybe without his beard? Maybe not.

I sat on my bed and peered through the shutter slats at him.

I *did*. I knew him. I used to see him when we first came to live in this house. He used to sit near the garbage cans like that, or hang out in the vacant lots further up the streets, where he'd pop up and grin at me every now and then. I hadn't seen him often at first; just once or twice a month. At first he'd only talk to himself and ignore me, but one day I saw him rummaging for food in someone's rubbish bins and gave him my lunch.

After that, I would see him once or twice a week, and the days I saw him were always good days, like he was a lucky charm. If I saw the holey shirt or the gappy grin on any partic-ular day, I could always be sure of seeing something unexpected, or finding a new, hidden place somewhere around Hobart to enjoy.

And him—well, so long as he could pinch my drink from me, he was happy. It didn't matter if I was doing my schoolwork outside with a cup of water, or if it was my drink bottle when I went out riding, he always stole it. I don't know if he even drank what he stole from me, I think it was more the joy of pinching it that made him do it. He always waited until I was looking away, grabbed it, and ran, giggling.

Maybe it was his way of evening out the food he was given; stealing the drink to go with it. He always returned the glasses, anyway, so it didn't matter.

I let out a puff of relieved air. At least I knew he hadn't followed me home—not exactly. He already knew where I lived. Funny that I hadn't seen him for the last four years. Funny that I hadn't remembered him, too; now that I did, I remembered being fond of him.

Maybe the old bloke had lost his mojo: there was nothing good that followed a sight of him today. I went for my shower, feeling less creeped out, but I'd only pulled a fresh t-shirt over my head when I heard the front door open.

I froze. I hadn't even used the fan in the bathroom; there was fog all over the mirror and the air still felt heavy and moist. Worst of all, I couldn't get out of the bathroom and to my bedroom without being seen by anyone passing through the kitchen.

What the heck? No one ever came through the house, not even the agent; nobody wanted to rent a house that had been the scene of a double homicide. I was still surprised they hadn't turned off the power and water ages ago.

I edged the bathroom window open a crack, and softly swung the door inward to let out as much of the damp air as possible. I would have tried to slip out and leave by the back door, through the laundry, but by then they were already halfway across the kitchen and making their way toward the laundry and me.

And when I say *they*, maybe you already know who I mean. Yep. It was those three weirdoes. The sound of their conversation carried ahead of them, Jin Yeong's deep, smooth voice an undercurrent to Zero's crisp tones.

"It's no use whining that you got there first," Zero's voice said.

I climbed into the laundry basket and shut the lid with the hasty and fervent hope that none of them would need to use the toilet while they were in the house.

Do vampires need to use the loo?

Funny, though. I couldn't hear the voice of the agent; just Zero again, saying, "I've paid the deposit and it's in my name."

Wait, what? What deposit? Did he mean bond? I hadn't heard them breaking in, and the agent wasn't with them—they *couldn't* have rented the place! Could they? What about all the rumours? Maybe vampires weren't afraid of supposed ghosts who haunted the house where a double murder had taken place, or of being across the road from a house where even stranger things than the occasional ghost sighting were said to happen.

Jin Yeong spat something dismissive in Korean, and Athelas responded, "Yes, but his skills were enough to break through the vampiric wiles you were winding around the real estate agent. The more interesting question is why you didn't have any trouble getting into the house now that Zero owns it, so to speak."

"I'd like to know that, too," said Zero. I saw him through the gaps in the wicker, wandering past the bathroom doorway to open the linen cupboard. What was he looking for? He didn't strike me as the sort to be checking for mould. "Once the deposit is paid, a house is usually safe enough from vampires."

"It could be the combination of Fae ownership working with the chanciness of only a deposit," suggested Athelas. "Or perhaps this house's original owners are distinctly more powerful in death than they were in life."

What, they weren't all vampires? Some of them were Fae? I mean, it didn't really matter; either they were nutty or *I* was, and

I wouldn't have put my money either way just yet. Not after seeing them arrive, and meeting Zero this morning.

Jin Yeong spoke in some sort of reply, and to my dismay I heard someone take another step toward the bathroom. There was a sick, sudden moment where I was sure I was about to be caught, laundry basket or no laundry basket; then Athelas peered around the doorjamb. Through the wicker I saw a quiet, composed face with grey eyes that smiled as much as the faint lines beside them. Close up, he only looked about forty, but somehow he seemed much older. What was he supposed to be, then? Fae or vampire, or something else?

I saw his eyes roam the room, glancing across the basket where I hid, and his nose wrinkled.

"A little damp," he said, and closed the door. Through the door, I heard his voice say, "I'll air it out tomorrow."

Did that mean they were moving in tomorrow? Maybe I wouldn't have to stay here all night.

"You're not staying here!" But Zero's voice sounded as uncertain as it did annoyed, and I wasn't surprised when Athelas pleasantly replied: "I wouldn't think of leaving you alone."

"Thanks."

So Fae, or vampires, or whatever, could be sarcastic, too? If you assumed that every one of them wasn't crackers and actually *was* what he said he was, that is. They *said* they were vampires—well, the Korean one was—but I had yet to see them do anything vampirish or fae-like. I was hazy on what would count as fae behaviour, but I was pretty sure I'd know it when I saw it.

Actually, if I didn't count the fierce, unreasoning desire to run for it that I'd had the first time I saw Zero face to face, the weirdest thing I'd seen any of them do was when he almost strangled me. And that was really more of a serial killer type of thing than what I'd strictly consider to be a fae thing.

I was almost convinced—*almost*—that I'd imagined the weirdness of their arrival.

. . .

NONE OF THEM VISITED THE TOILET THAT NIGHT. IT DIDN'T have to mean they weren't human, but I heard a percolator going all evening and smelled the coffee, and if they were drinking that much coffee, it should have been going *somewhere*.

Wherever it was going, it wasn't the toilet. I wasn't able to get out of my basket until they all went out briefly well after dark, because they stayed in the living room upstairs, outside my bedroom.

By then, both my legs had gone to sleep and I had to tip the basket over so that I could drag myself out and massage the feeling back into them. I made a bumbling dash for the stairs, muttering, and suddenly heard a voice outside the front door.

I tumbled into my room, heart pounding, and pulled the bookcase door shut securely behind me. Only then did I stop to breathe, and to realise that there was someone knocking at the door downstairs.

Luckily for me, it wasn't *them*; it was the police on the lawn. Well, part of the police force, anyway—it was the islander detective I'd seen yesterday. He was still in civvies, but there was a leather pouch in one hand; probably his badge. He stood back from the patio, looking up at the windows now that no one was answering his knock, but I only caught a brief glance of him before he ducked back out of my sight and onto the patio again. I heard knocking again, then a silence of nearly two minutes before the front door opened and closed.

"Hey!" I said. "You're a cop! You can't do that!"

But he was definitely in the house. I heard him moving around through the entry hall below, and then the kitchen. He wasn't moving very fast, but I had the suspicion he was looking through the things the other men had brought into the house. There wasn't much, so it didn't take long; but I heard rapping on the walls, and that was a bit of a worry—what if he decided to rap on the walls up here? And if he was the type to rap on walls, he was probably the type to pace a room for size, too.

If I was lucky, the other three weirdos would come home before he got too interested in what was upstairs. Stupid of them all to go out at once if they were the sort of people who attracted covert police searches. Not to mention bad timing. They'd only been gone a couple of minutes before the cop arrived.

I was lucky.

The front door downstairs opened and closed with a bang just after the detective got to the second floor with me. I heard the detective swear and grinned a bit. Serve him right. See how he felt, having to scarper right quick through the house because someone was going to be coming up the stairs any minute. I don't know where he went—maybe through one of the windows—but there had been silence in the next room for a couple of minutes before I heard footsteps on the stairs.

I rolled over eagerly on my bed before I knew what I was doing, surprising myself at my zest to hear their voices.

Oh well. I wasn't used to having people in the house. I was bound to be curious about them.

"Pick up your feet!" said Zero's voice impatiently. "If he hasn't gotten away by now, it's a useless cause and we'll have to wipe his memory."

"That would be a waste when we've left the house empty for him to discover a nest of normality," remarked Athelas. "However, I agree; he's a reasonably astute detective, for a human. No doubt he's gone out the window."

There was a brief silence where I could imagine Jin Yeong shrugging, and there were no more obvious footsteps on the stairs. Had they really left the house just so the detective could search it?

I grinned. Sneaky psychos.

Wait a minute, though—why was the detective interested in my three psychos? So interested, in fact, that he took the risk of breaking and entering to satisfy his interest? They were interesting to me because they were in my house, but there shouldn't be a reason for them to interest the local police.

Or even one detective. For a cop around a murder scene, he wasn't very interested in the murder that had happened over the road. He was definitely interested in my three psychos, and there was no reason for that. Unless—unless—did he know about them being vampire and fae?

I knew the answer to that one straight away. Of course he didn't. He wouldn't have broken into their hou—*my* house—if he knew that. Not after the way I'd seen the other cops behave around them. Not after the way I'd felt being face to face with Zero.

Oh. And that was another interesting thing. Since the three psychos had come into my house today, I hadn't felt that same, instinctive, unreasoning fear I'd felt at first with Zero. I hadn't felt the urge to give myself up again, either. Was I getting used to them in so short a time, or was it because I had the wall as a buffer between us?

Maybe it was because no one was actively trying to choke me. Fear was probably a decent response in that situation—which led me right back to the lingering question of whether I'd imagined the whole aura around the three of them when they arrived.

I rolled back over and huffed a breath at the dark ceiling of my bedroom. Whatever they were, all I had to do was keep out of sight until they finished their investigation, or whatever it was they were doing. It wasn't like I kept stuff in the fridge, after all; I always ate at the café during work. Hopefully once they solved their murder, they would leave me and my house in peace. I had a brief flash of memory of that bloody corpse outside my window and shuddered. Maybe three psychos were what you needed to investigate a murder like that.

I fell asleep smiling stupidly at the sound of Jin Yeong's voice murmuring below, and the first thing I heard when I woke the next morning was the same voice.

Oh yeah. I hadn't thought about the fact I'd have to sneak out to get to work. Had JinYeong been talking *all night?* He was making a long, caramel-y complaint that flowed easily through the wall and reminded me that I would have to be *very* careful about moving around in my room from now on. I may not be exactly sure that they were who they said they were, but I was pretty flamin' sure I didn't want them to find me here. How long were they going to be renting, anyway?

"I'm not going to be renting here forever," said Zero, as if in answer to my thoughts. I grinned and got out of bed to hear a bit better; but JinYeong, who had been interrupted, made another, more reproachful plaint. Zero interrupted that without compunction, too. "Don't complain to me about the way the house muffles scents; you're the one who pushed yourself into my investigation. If you want to know why it does what it does, figure it out yourself. This house is in the perfect spot; if everything goes according to pattern, there are still another four murders to take place here."

I stopped grinning.

There's *what?* Four more murders?

"There are often," said Athelas' voice, "Between murders to go along with the human ones. Do you think a human house with significant links to Behind is really the best place to stay?"

"We can get into Between or Behind from here," said Zero. "It's ideal for us. It's also the most susceptible human house I've ever been in; I'm surprised they didn't have things coming through from Between every day."

JinYeong, now alert instead of plaintive, spoke.

"That's true," Athelas agreed. "The reports I read mentioned that strange things were always happening in the house across the street. Perhaps it has a susceptibility, too."

"Now that's something to think about," said Zero, and all sound from the next room ceased completely.

I sat on my beanbag for a long time after the talking stopped, straining to hear. Why had they stopped talking? Did they know I was there? Had they heard me? Were they waiting for me to come out?

But it hadn't sounded like they stopped talking—it had sounded like a window suddenly shut and cut off every noise from the other room. Before that, I had heard the measured tread of someone—Zero, probably—walking up and down the room as he thought aloud, and the soft, thoughtful tap of something against a leather armrest—maybe Athelas tapping a finger against the leather. What sort of thing could make every sound cease so suddenly? Something vampire, or something fae?

Whatever it was, it made the whole house feel empty. It was only when I glanced out the window that I saw the flash of movement from the house across the road.

Hang on. Were they in the house across the road? But that was stupid—how could they be in the house across the road? They hadn't had time to get over there, even if they ran the whole way. Besides, I hadn't heard the front door close, and I should have. It was right below my room.

Was it the same vampire or fae thing that had made the house so suddenly quiet and empty earlier, or—

Nope. Wasn't going to think about that until I'd had some coffee. Maybe it would make sense after that. Might as well not waste the time since they were out of the house.

I pushed open my bookcase door and crept into the living room before I could think too much about what I was doing. They were definitely gone, which didn't surprise me; but it didn't leave me feeling any more comfortable, either. It was ridiculous to think they'd got across the road in three seconds flat, but they must have, because they weren't in the kitchen or any of the bedrooms.

Neither was my coffee.

"Some mongrel's pinched me coffee!" I said aloud in wrathful surprise to the empty kitchen. Coffee was the only thing I kept in the house outside of my bedroom; the only thing worth the risk of detection. I kept it in one of the cupboards above the range-hood, right at the back where it could have been left behind by the previous occupants, if anyone wondered about it.

If anyone had ever come through the house *to* wonder about it.

My little bag wasn't in any of the other cupboards, either, and it wasn't until I peeped carefully out the front door that I saw a familiar, metallic edge of packaging sticking out between the lid and the top of the garbage can. It was split at the side; no coffee left in there now.

I shut the door with an inarticulate growl of rage, glaring around the kitchen. And there—my eyes fell on a deep red cylinder sitting by itself on the island benchtop. *Coffee*, it said on the side, in silver letters. Drawn to it like a moth to the flame, I took off the lid and inhaled, then stopped to appreciate the aroma.

Nice. Someone liked good coffee.

I hesitated before using it; I'm mostly moral. But they were in my house, and they had thrown away *my* coffee, so it seemed fair to drink theirs. Who throws away perfectly good coffee just because its cheap? They even had their own cheap tin of instant coffee on the bench beside the percolator.

I took my coffee cup with me when I left the house for work. There were five of them, after all, and it wasn't likely that three men would notice one missing mug when there were only three of them to *use* mugs. Especially when the mugs had already been in the house to start with.

The muddy remnant in the percolator was scenting the air, too, so it wasn't likely they'd notice the extra smell. Beggared if I know why they wanted the instant stuff when they had the good stuff in the house, but there you go.

I made sure one of the upstairs windows was open before I left. It wasn't like anyone would see me climbing in—there was no one *to* see me climbing in—and so long as the three psychos were in the kitchen making coffee or eating, I was safe.

It worked like a charm. The trick is to leave the window open enough to wriggle a finger or two through the crack and open it properly, but shut enough not to look like it's open. They were all in the kitchen when I got home anyway, probably making coffee. Nice for them, to be able to have it whenever they wanted it, while I had to sneak it like a thief in my own house. Still, it made it easy to sneak in by the window I'd left open in the upper floor at the back.

As I was creeping beneath the kitchen window to avoid being seen, I grinned to hear JinYeong's voice—complaining again, was he?—and Athelas' reasonable voice saying something like, "...and it's an old house that was previously occupied. You have to expect to find hairs in the drain."

Whoops. Guess I'd have to be more careful about clearing out the drain if I ever got the chance for another shower. I couldn't go to work stinking, anyway; but maybe I could use the public showers if I went at a time when the druggies weren't all down there shooting up.

Zero's voice briefly mentioned something about the kitchen floor but I was too far away to hear clearly by then, the comfort of my bed calling to me like siren song. I was careful about climbing over the bathroom window anyway. I mean, even if my shadow had fallen over it, they wouldn't have seen it from the kitchen, but when you've got three psychos in your house it pays to be careful.

Half an hour after I got safely into my room, they all came upstairs again. I swear I could smell coffee, too. I looked down sadly at the empty coffee cup I'd brought back upstairs. JinYeong was muttering to the wall outside, from the sounds of it. The others must have been ignoring him, because he continued to mutter from the time I slid gently onto the carpeted floor until I eased myself onto the squishy beanbag that had been in my room so long it had almost become one with the carpet. I could have listened to music through my earphones, but I couldn't settle myself to it. Not with those three psychos in the house.

And maybe it was nice to hear voices around the house again, I dunno. They were still psychos, but their voices filled the house and danced through the walls, chasing shadows and coldness away. Maybe they even chased away the Nightmare—I hadn't had that since they were in the house, and I usually had it every couple of nights, when I woke screaming and kicking.

Hey, a plus side to having psychos in the house! Who knew they could frighten off night terrors with the sound of their voices?

So instead of listening to music, I listened to Jin Yeong complain and tried to puzzle out what the ringing, metallic scrapings were that sounded at even intervals, like the clashing of sword blades on telly. They couldn't be having a swordfight in there, could they? No, there would have been other noises.

I let that thought settle for later, because Zero was talking again, cutting through Jin Yeong's murmur. "Did you find that coffee cup?"

Whoops. Apparently fae males *do* notice if you borrow one of their cups.

Athelas sounded mildly interested. "What coffee cup?"

"There were five and now there are only four. Weren't you looking for it earlier?"

"There are only four," Athelas said. "I wasn't looking for a fifth."

The metallic scraping stopped. "Are you sure?"

"Reasonably," said Athelas. His voice sounded amused. "They're a set. And they're all in the cupboard."

"You tell him," I muttered, beneath my breath.

"All right," Zero said, and the metallic scraping began again.

Wait. Was he...was he sharpening knives in the living room or something?

"What should we do about the house across the road?" That was Athelas again.

I bet he was. I bet he was sitting there and sharpening knives. Exactly what you expect psychos to be doing in your living room.

"Mark it unsafe for human consumption," said Zero. "Make sure it gets put on the register."

"Should we?"

"*Aniyo,*" Jin Yeong said, a clear negative.

"It's protocol," Zero said.

I heard a short, hissed laugh that might have come from Jin Yeong. He said something in a tone of voice that I found a bit too scornful to be using on someone as big and dangerous as Zero —particularly when that big, dangerous person was sharpening knives.

Was he trying to start a fight? Did that mean he really had been trying to kill Zero like they'd said the first time I saw them? Why was he working with him, then?

"It might well be protocol," Athelas said, "However, I've yet to learn that Enforcers who gave up the gold are expected to hold to protocol."

"I didn't give up the gold." There was a silence from the scraping again. "I put it on the shelf for a few years. I'm still with the Enforcers."

"Did they ask you to do this?" Athelas sounded genuinely curious. "Is this an official investigation?"

"Do you think I'd let you two help if it was?"

"*Mwoh?*"

Zero's voice was emotionless. "I'm not going to fight with you, Jin Yeong. What did the human lab say about the samples?"

"*Amukodo obseoyo*," said the vampire; and this time he sounded sulky.

"He left no trace at all?"

"*Ne.*"

"There's nothing surprising about that," Athelas said. "He's left nothing at any of the previous scenes. Why should he be careless now?"

"I know." The scraping began again. "I was hoping he might slip up in the human world."

"The house is really more Between than human; the murderer must have been pretty comfortable."

"Yes," said Zero briefly. I think he was still annoyed about it, though; the scrapings sounded louder and faster than before.

"Do you think the humans knew about it? The ones who lived in this place were murdered—which, of course, is unsurprising." Athelas' voice held what was almost a shrug. "Living in a susceptible house, it was only a matter of time before something got through and killed them."

I scowled. Well, excuse my parents for being murdered. If it was so unsurprising, why didn't someone stop it?

"Humans usually think susceptible houses are haunted," said Zero. "If they were aware of anything at all, they probably thought the house was haunted."

Superior psychos, weren't they? Humans this and humans that.

But I still leaned forward in my beanbag, eager to hear more.

Athelas, his voice still amused, said, "Then there's no need to be too cautious, is there? Humans will avoid the house anyway, and the Enforcers will only be an annoyance to us if we report the place."

"Us? I thought you were only here to find me. I didn't think you were interested in doing the work of an Enforcer."

"Oh, well! Let us say merely that I find this situation amusing."

"You're in a good mood tonight," Zero said abruptly. "Are

there any bodies I should know about? I don't want to have to leave this place because you've left bodies lying around."

"Nothing of the sort," said Athelas.

I could hear the smile in his voice. It was jarringly at odds with what Zero had so casually suggested of him—with what I knew was a very good reason not to get too attached to the sound of them around the house.

"Perhaps I'm getting maudlin in my old age," he added. "Who knows? I look forward to seeing how this turns out."

CHAPTER THREE

FOR THE NEXT FEW DAYS, EVERYTHING WAS WEIRD AND slightly panicky, and just a little bit nice, too. I wasn't used to having psychos in the house. Actually, I wasn't used to having *anyone* in the house anymore, so maybe normal people would have been just as disturbing as psychos. I don't know.

It was achingly familiar to hear voices around the house again, and that familiarity worried me because my three psychos should definitely have been more off-putting than familiar. They didn't seem to sleep more than an hour or two (and JinYeong not at all), they cooked (and most often burnt) meals at three in the morning, brought home *really weird* smells with them, and talked about murder, their investigation, or both. Out of all those things, I think it was the talk about murder that was the most disturbing. It wasn't so much that they were talking about murder—I mean, they were investigating a murder, after all—it was the way they talked about it.

Zero was matter of fact and entirely unemotional, discussing the most sickening details with a coolness and detachment that was almost as frightening as the things he was discussing. I couldn't understand a word that JinYeong contributed to the conversations, but the relish in his voice was obvious, and as far as I'm concerned, being gleeful *about* murder is only a step or two below gleefully *doing* murder.

Athelas...well, Athelas was probably the most disturbing of the three. When they weren't discussing their own case, Zero would bring up old cases he had already investigated, and present them to the other two. Jin Yeong and his relish were incomprehensible, but Athelas' quiet, well-bred voice was chillingly easy to understand as he said things like, "Ah, yes. He was trying to control the flow of blood—a clumsy way to do the thing. A gentle incline does the same thing and it's less messy. I would not have picked that location."

I didn't seem to be able to stop listening to them, though. Never seemed to be able to settle myself to be able to listen to music when they were in the house, either. Maybe I was just as crooked in the head as them.

After a few days, they mostly talked in the downstairs living room or the kitchen, instead of the upstairs living room. I knew this in the same way that I knew Zero slept in the narrow little study almost below my bedroom, that Jin Yeong liked to shower in the early chill of the morning, leaving the heavy stink of cologne to permeate the whole house, and that Athelas routinely made himself a cup of tea every day at six.

Call it acoustics, or warped design, or whatever you want, but in one corner of my room, you can hear everything that goes on downstairs. I've always thought it's the beam that runs down through my bedroom and into the downstairs area, but I've never been really sure.

When I sit in that corner I can hear everything: footsteps in the kitchen, the click of the kettle being turned on, Zero's huge snores for the hour or two that he actually sleeps, and the changing patter of water hitting the shower tiles as Jin Yeong moves around in the shower.

I couldn't hear anything of Athelas, who occasionally slept in

Mum and Dad's old bedroom upstairs, but everything else? I heard it all. And after those first few days of having psychos in the house, that corner which I'd mostly avoided when Mum and Dad were alive, was where I sat down every day after work.

It was more interesting than TV—more disturbing, too. I mean, you know there's something up when you're so creeped out by the way people talk that you actually forget most of the time that they're supposed to be fae, or vampire. How much weird does it take for a person to forget something as weird as vampires, or fae? That's how weird they were.

When I sat down in my beanbag one afternoon after work, careful not to be too noisy about it, Athelas was saying, "...and it's not the same as the others. If we're to consider it as part of the series, we should wonder why its eyes were looking at that house instead of the one in front of it."

Wait, what? Their murderer made a habit of stringing up corpses for the whole world to look at? So that's what they'd meant when they said there were still another four murders to come!

"He always makes them look at the house he took them out of," Zero's voice said. "It's part of his signature. Behind, in the human world—it makes no difference."

Behind what, exactly? I wondered, pinching a squishy bean from the beanbag between my fingers. Zero or Athelas had said something about that a day or two ago—going behind, things coming through, and that being why weird stuff happened over the road. It was about as comprehensible as Jin Yeong was.

"Yes, but he's never broken a neck before," Athelas said. "And if the head wasn't flopping back like that, the eyes would have been looking right into *this* house."

Jin Yeong, over the sound of the kettle boiling, said something that was as understandable to me as the noise of the kettle.

"Exactly," said Zero. "And there's no one in this house for him to be looking at. The victim wasn't living here, and neither was anyone else."

"Ah," Athelas said. "No doubt you're correct. It was merely a thought that occurred to me."

"Was it," said Zero; and it wasn't a question. It was more of a suspicious *what have I missed?* kind of mutter to himself. "I would like to know why he changed his signature, though."

"Perhaps he's growing tired of his routine."

Routine? This bloke had murdered more people like the man outside my window, and they thought he was getting *bored?* Who thinks like that?

"Still nothing from the human lab?"

"*Ne*," said Jin Yeong; and added something else in a rapid spate of Korean. He didn't seem as angry this morning; more sulky.

"I thought your nose was damaged," Athelas remarked.

Zero said, "I think I heard something about that, too."

I'd heard something about it, too. Jin Yeong had been complaining about his nose for the last three days; enough so that I now knew the Korean word for nose was something that sounded like *ko*. Who knew vampires could be such whingy little pouters?

More talk from Jin Yeong, close and coldly haughty, but still incomprehensible.

"Oh, it's only broken in this house? No, don't start a fight with me; if we make too much noise the police will come by. What did you find out?"

I listened in mounting frustration to Jin Yeong's voice. At this rate, I was going to have to learn Korean if I wanted to really follow anything that was going on in the house.

Zero, sharply, asked, "There was other human trace in the *house?* Not at the hanging site?"

"*Ne.*"

"Blood or something else?"

"*Pi.*"

"Enough of it to mean the human is dead?"

"*Aniyo.*"

"Well, well," said Athelas, his voice amused. "It seems as though we have our first witness. If we can find them."

"Jin Yeong can follow the blood trail," Zero said. Of Jin Yeong, he asked, "You will be able to follow it?"

"*Ne*," agreed Jin Yeong, though he paused significantly before he answered.

"Your nose still isn't working?"

Jin Yeong spoke again, sulkily.

"There's nothing wrong with this house. If you can't follow the blood trail yet, we'll follow the trace of magic I found outside it. It's strong enough to give us a good trail. We'll come back to the blood when you're able to smell it properly again."

They talked until about eleven, then went to bed. I only knew that because when I woke up, stiff and sore and confused to find myself in my beanbag instead of my bed, the LED clock said 11.10 and there was only the sound of Zero moving around in his makeshift bedroom. I could have gone to my own bed, but the sound of him moving around was soothing, so I closed my eyes and went to sleep again, hazily certain that I would be sorry about my late bedtime when it came to getting up at five tomorrow.

I was; but no more than when I stayed up too late reading by the light of my torch. I skipped out of the house in the lull between the beginning of Jin Yeong's shower and Athelas' six o'clock cup of tea, mindful of the faint '*mwoh?*' I heard from the bathroom and glad that I'd thought to leave the upstairs living room window cracked open again in case I needed to climb back in. It was a cool morning, but I didn't dare to make a coffee to take along with me now that I knew about Athelas' early morning tea. If he smelled the coffee or discovered the kettle was a bit too hot...

So it was already a kind of rotten day. I saw the bearded bloke skulking around when I left, but this time I didn't trust his presence to herald anything fun or lucky today; not when the three psychos had arrived at the house after I saw him last.

What's more, I was already sick of having three psychos in my house, so it was pretty rude of them to show up at my work as well. The boss was in a bad mood as well; he was getting close to one of his fits. They were usually a month or two apart, but lately they'd been closer to two weeks apart, which meant he was gearing up to fire one of us.

He threw a whisk at me because I wasn't washing up fast enough for him, then pushed me out of the way and told me to get rid of the rubbish instead. I hate it when he does the washing up himself; all the stuff is done in five minutes, but it's still filthy dirty, and I have to wash it again when he's gone. Either that or give the mucky plates and chocolate-ringed mugs to the horrible customers.

I did as I was told. There are some days when no matter what I do, it's wrong—and then some days when he loves everyone. He's a nut.

It was nice to get out of his sight for a few minutes; it was cool outside, and the alley is always nice to waste a bit of time in. It has some weird architecture left over from when Hobart was first being built; old, bricked up doorways that don't have stairways attached any more, just hanging there in space. And it's quiet, you know?

Usually it's quiet.

Today, as I hefted the garbage bag into the bin and put the lid on, the old bearded bloke dashed past me at a tottery sort of run, giggling to himself, and disappeared onto Liverpool Street.

"Heck!" I said, catching myself against the brick wall before I fell over. "What's got into the mad old coot? Why's he following me again?"

Before I had the chance to catch my breath, something huge and heavy fell from the bricked up doorway in the wall above and beyond me.

I was already ducking when it hit the ground. I took cover behind the rubbish bins as something else hit the ground with a softer thump, and sat down pretty suddenly. It was Zero and Jin Yeong; and they had, impossibly, leapt through the empty brick wall.

Zero scanned the wall and Jin Yeong's teeth showed in a snarl as he darted a look around the alley itself.

Oh man. What *now*? Had Jin Yeong finally goaded Zero into a fight? No; they were both looking back up at the brick wall.

I'd been pretty sure they were capable of melting through walls—or bricked up doorways, in this case—but it was another thing to actually see it. And another thing for them to be doing it out in the open, where anyone else could see. Humans aren't *that* blind, no matter what my three psychos seem to think.

Should I try to sneak away? They weren't looking at me, after all; or even anywhere near me. They were looking at the blank brick wall. The blank, bumpy, porcupiny wa—wait, what? What was wrong with the wall? Were those *sticks* poking out of the bricked up doorway? Or a person?

It struggled through the brickwork inch by inch, much more slowly than Zero or Jin Yeong, until it was free and dangling by one—hand? Stump?—from the doorway.

What was it? A scarecrow? It looked like one, all stick-like and rangy and borderline nightmare. Someone had twisted a bunch of thorns together and made a nightmare thing. Its arms were too long, or its legs were too short, and on the end of each arm were...

What the heck were those?

Were those *claws*?

The scarecrow thing dropped from the doorway, creaking like branches in a high breeze. I ducked further behind my rubbish bin, rubbed my eyes, and popped up again.

Yep. That's what I'd seen. Now there were more of them; scarecrows with claws for hands, and they were still forcing themselves from the brick walls, one by one. Jin Yeong snarled again and dropped into a crouch, but Zero only loosened his sword and drew it out nice and slow. Like he wasn't concerned at all.

Show off.

Well, if I'd really been doubting after all this time that they were fae and vampire, I wasn't wondering any more. Animate scarecrows with claws for hands tend to take your belief to a new level pretty quickly.

One of them leapt across the alley at Zero, long arms scything, and Zero's sword swept up to meet it, far too swift and light for the size of it. Claws and wooden arms swung in a complete circle, snicking low and close by Zero's face. Close enough to give him a haircut if he hadn't ducked.

What. The. Heck. Weren't their arms connected to their backbone?

Zero swung again, this time faster and harder, and a scarecrow arm went flying through the air, a stabby point of wire jabbing the air at its end.

Oh yeah. They were scarecrows. Nothing was connected to anything else except by a dag-end of wire or twine.

JinYeong leaped on the stricken scarecrow, faster even than Zero's sword. I saw a flash of white teeth—which was stupid, because what could a vampire drink from a scarecrow? Sap?— and the thing collapsed, headless. JinYeong tossed the head at Zero, who batted it away and made a savage cut in the general direction of JinYeong's head. JinYeong ducked and rolled forward, and another scarecrow head went tumbling across the pavement.

"More coming!" Zero said sharply. Scarecrows tumbled from the wall, short legs clicking woodenly against the pavement and long arms balancing them. Steel scraped and threw up sparks on the pavement.

JinYeong turned lightly on the balls of his feet and put his back to Zero's. Flaming heck. Couldn't he make up his mind whether he wanted to kill Zero or not? Zero stepped forward one pace, his shoulders aligning with JinYeong's and his knees bending slightly.

He was taking it more seriously now. My fingers closed around the handle of a bin lid, though it probably wouldn't do me too much good as a shield if one of the scarecrows came after me, and inched forward for a better view.

The scarecrows chattered, a wooden rustling of sound, and spread out around Zero and JinYeong, trailing more sparks along the pavement.

Zero didn't give warning; he cut a swathe before him, as quick as thought. Behind him, JinYeong leaped high and fast, his feet kicking against the alley wall. Scarecrows slashed and chattered, shedding chips of wood and straw, and Zero struck between them like lightening, his blade flickering too fast for my eyes to follow. JinYeong darted between both, now high and rolling across Zero's back, now low and skidding between scarecrow legs.

They were fast. They were *so fast*. But there were a lot of scarecrows, and they didn't seem to be exactly *dying*, just missing limbs and swinging drunken arms that were off balance because another had been cut or torn off. I didn't see when it happened, but somehow JinYeong was separated from Zero and driven up the alley toward me. A few of them followed him, but most of them redoubled their attentions on Zero, a thick, unstoppable thicket of wood and metal that mounted up and crawled right over him. There was a groaning of wood, and a sudden yell from Zero, and something bright and shining went flying right over my head.

It hit the pavement with a clang, raising a few sparks of its own.

Oh boy. Zero had lost his sword.

I threw a look at JinYeong, but he was too busy fighting off four of the monsters to have a hand free for the sword, though I was pretty sure he'd seen it flying. The scarecrow monsters ignored it; maybe they thought it was no use now it wasn't attached to Zero's hand.

I looked at it, then at the tangle of wood that was all I could see of Zero.

He'd be fine, right? That big man, all muscle and speed?

But then why was my sneaker edging forward? Why was it doing that?

It's not like I knew how to fight. These psychos had invaded my house and my life; I didn't owe them anything. But...well, it was psychos or monsters, wasn't it? It all came down to whether I wanted the psychos or monsters to win, and now that I'd been living with the psychos for a while, I didn't think I could let them die and go back to the silence of my house with the knowledge I could have helped.

My sneaker edged forward again, and a curve of dented metal grew in my vision. One of my hands, shaking, had put up the garbage can lid like a shield. Ah heck. I was going.

I was going!

One of the scarecrows leapt for Jin Yeong's back as I sprinted past it. Something wooden and clicky swooped over my head, a severed scarecrow arm, and something wicked sharp caught my shirt at the back. I didn't think; I used the pull as a fulcrum and did my best goal-scoring kick at the hilt of the sword.

It connected. Oh *boy* did it connect. I gasped in pain, dragging the scarecrow down with me as I fell, and the sword skittered right into the middle of the scarecrow thicket around Zero. My arm flew up in the fall, rubbish bin lid and all, and clanged very satisfyingly against something wooden.

I scrambled to my feet, still gasping, and hurled the lid into the melee. I think it took off a head, and I saw Jin Yeong rising from the clutches of his attackers. He leapt across their backs, snatching up heads and arms, and tumbled over the broad shoulder of Zero.

As his feet hit the ground, light and sure, Zero said sharply, "Safe, Jin Yeong?"

JinYeong was laughing, his eyes bright; the look he threw Zero was almost...brotherly? "*Ne*," he answered.

Reminded by the exchange that *I* wasn't as safe as I could be, I ducked behind the rubbish bins again. I didn't have time to be dying; I had to live to my eighteenth birthday and try to get my parents' house back.

I could have stayed out in the open. Now that Zero and JinYeong were back together, the fight was short-lived and absorbed them both completely. The scarecrows, once a seemingly endless number, were beginning to dwindle. While JinYeong wrenched off arms, Zero cut off heads; a well-oiled machine. Enemies or not, they'd obviously been very good friends, once.

I left them to it and sneaked back into the café. The boss snarled at me and I was almost glad for it; it was a normal kind of horrible instead of a weird, unworldly kind of horrible I'd just come from.

I finished work early—well, the boss kicked me out—but I still had to sneak through the window when I got home because a shadow moving across the kitchen window told me that one of them was already home. Athelas, probably. Good thing I'd seen that shadow, or I might have been in trouble.

I heard the front door open as I sneaked across the carpet in the upstairs living room. That must be Zero and JinYeong back. I crept to the top of the stairs and got down on my stomach to peek through the triangle wedge of space between the stair frame and floorboards.

They were both still alive, then, I thought, as they stepped up into the kitchen, all bloody and torn as I'd seen them last. Had they been walking around Hobart like that for two hours?

Flaming psychos.

Zero had four gashes of dark blue sticky stuff between belt and shoulder, and if they thought that colour of blood was normal to be strolling around town with, they were off in the head. I mean, wander around Hobart all bloody and you're bound to stand out, but blood *that* colour?

Athelas said, more sharply than I'd heard him before, "What happened?"

Zero stripped off his shirt. "Nothing much. JinYeong and I were following a trace of rogue magic from around the house, and some of the Between denizens objected to it. We lost it after Spiny Men showed up, for some reason, and they've fouled it for us now."

JinYeong muttered and displayed his own injury through the tatters of his shirt. It was bleeding more sluggishly than Zero's claw marks, and the blood was thicker, too. Almost black instead of blue. Seriously. Didn't any of them bleed like normal people?

"I'll get you a new shirt," Zero said. He sat down in one of the kitchen chairs, half in view and half out of view. "It wasn't particularly useful, but it was nice to get a workout. I haven't been exercising as much as I should lately."

"Poison?" Athelas examined the tears on Zero's torso, then looked up at Zero himself, narrowly. "There *is* poison. Not a particularly strong one, but if I don't treat it, it'll be uncomfortable. You should have been more careful."

I hastily gave myself a lookover for broken skin as Zero said, "No need. I knew you'd be able to draw it out. Look after JinYeong first."

"JinYeong can look after himself," said Athelas.

Phew. No cuts. I put my eye up against the space again, and saw that Athelas hadn't moved away from Zero. Not a very obedient steward, was he.

He added, "He's technically dead, anyway."

JinYeong shrugged and sprawled out elegantly on one of the kitchen chairs. He looked like a portrait of a young nobleman, dying young and beautiful.

That's talent. The bloke can even *sit* in an annoying way.

Zero threw a look at him. "You're bleeding on the floor."

"*Hyung.*" There was a reproachful note to Jin Yeong's voice.

"Thank you for getting my sword back to me," said Zero, with as little expression as he'd told Jin Yeong he was bleeding on the floor. "I thought I'd lose an arm."

Jin Yeong's lip lifted slightly. "*Jonun aniaeyo.*"

"Then who was it?" Zero sat up straight, frowning, disturbing Athelas' work—which, to be honest, didn't look like much. He was moving his hands over the four claw-marks on Zero's torso without touching them.

Only, did they look sort of smaller and less bloody than they'd looked a minute ago?

"You should stop moving," Athelas said mildly. "Unless you want an extra layer of skin grown somewhere it shouldn't be."

Yeah, they were *definitely* smaller.

Zero sat back again, but he said, "Someone kicked my sword toward me. I heard the foot connect, and the rattle across the pavement. I doubt one of the Spiny Men did it."

Jin Yeong said a surprised, questioning sentence from his couch.

"Nothing? You didn't smell anything at all?"

"*Ne.*"

"Someone was there."

So the all-knowing fae don't know everything? I felt pretty pleased with myself; I'd heard so much about *humans* this and *humans can't* that, that it was pretty amusing to confound the mighty fae.

That'll teach 'em to talk about humans like they were dogs and cats, I thought happily as I stole away to my room to listen from greater safety. It's not our fault if we can't walk through walls and fight nightmare monsters without dying. Or appear and disappear. It's not like it's something we're born with. Sorta makes you wonder what kind of natural abilities fae are born with—actually, it sorta makes you wonder if they're born at all. Maybe they're hatched. *I* don't know. I'm just a stupid human.

. . .

THE WEEK AFTER JINYEONG'S NOSE BEGAN WORKING WELL
enough to find traces of another human's blood at the house
across the road, I left the window open for myself again. I didn't
really think I'd need it; now that they had a real lead to look into,
they were mostly out doing whatever Enforcers or Investigators—
or whatever they were—did when they found a lead. So I wasn't
surprised to find the house empty when I got back after work,
and I wasn't shy about using the back door instead of the window,
either.

Turns out it wasn't really empty, but I didn't find that out until
I'd wandered into the kitchen for coffee, and a narrow-eyed
vampire came tearing through from the lower living room, coat
flying. I was lucky; I saw his shadow before I saw him, and I was
already ducking behind the kitchen island.

I don't know what the heck he was chasing, or what he
thought he heard, but he skulked around the kitchen for a good
fifteen minutes while I crouched in the cupboard beneath the
island, my arms wrapped around my knees and expecting the
lattice doors to be snatched open at any minute. The worst of it
was that I could see him clearly through the lattice, and despite
the fact that the cupboard was a lot darker than the kitchen, it
felt like I was as easy to see as he was; that he was playing
with me.

JinYeong only stopped prowling around the kitchen when
Athelas arrived. I saw him scowling, so I knew who had arrived
before I heard the faint *tap tap* of Athelas' shiny shoes against the
kitchen floor.

"You seem busy," said Athelas. He said it in his quietly amused
sort of way, and I wasn't surprised to see a dangerous glitter come
to JinYeong's eyes. He obviously felt that he was being laughed at.

He said something sharp and annoyed that made Athelas'
brows go up.

"I shouldn't think so," he said mildly. "Aren't you rather too energetic for this time of day?"

Jin Yeong snarled at him and left the kitchen, though I don't think he went far. Athelas, still smiling faintly, prowled around the kitchen, making himself a cup of tea, and sat down at the kitchen table, crossing one leg over the other. He was very tidy and civilised, and very annoyingly in the way. How was I supposed to get into my bedroom when a slim, dapper fae was sipping tea at the kitchen table, smiling gently at the steam? What did he have to smile about, anyway?

Maybe he liked annoying Jin Yeong. I could understand that.

I sighed, and resigned myself to being stuck in the kitchen until they all went to their own rooms. They didn't sleep as much as humans, but they almost always went into their own rooms after eleven o'clock anyway. They probably got sick of each other. I could understand that, too. Between Zero's everlasting sharpening of knives, Athelas' quiet little digs, and Jin Yeong's whinging, they probably each liked their own space.

Zero arrived not much later; I saw his leather-clad legs approaching the kitchen island before I heard him. Jin Yeong didn't seem to have the same trouble. He darted up into the kitchen again at the same time, speaking rapidly.

Zero listened more closely than Athelas had done, but his reply was nearly as dismissive. "I thought your nose wasn't working here."

"*Ne, keundae*—" Jin Yeong spoke again, as rapidly as before, and stopped expectantly. Through the latticed doors, I could see the alertness to his usually casual shoulders. What had bitten him?

"I haven't noticed anything," Zero said, when he'd finished. "And I would have noticed—Athelas would have noticed. Do you know anything about it, Athelas?"

"I'm inclined to think Jin Yeong is suffering some ill effects from being unable to use his nose as usu—"

An indignant outpouring from Jin Yeong interrupted him.

"I carefully refrained from saying you were imagining it," pointed out Athelas, into the lull that followed.

He had, too. *Very* carefully. I wasn't surprised to see the snarling look Jin Yeong sent him; though I *was* surprised to see the way Athelas responded. Eyes dancing, his lips tilted in the most indulgent of smiles.

Jin Yeong looked away, murder in his eyes.

"Keep an eye on it," said Zero, to Athelas, ignoring that little byplay. "Let me know if you notice anything."

"Very well," Athelas agreed. "Do you have some time at the moment?"

Jin Yeong began to say something else, a distinct pout to his mouth, but Zero talked over him. "Jin Yeong and I are going to try and follow that particular magic again. There was an older trace that might not be so difficult to follow."

Jin Yeong smiled at Athelas, more than a little bit smug. Good grief, how old was he? No wonder Athelas liked needling him.

"Very well," said Athelas again. "I'll try our helpful real estate agent again tomorrow, in that case. Perhaps we can learn more about our victim from him."

"You might ask something about the previous occupants of this place, too," said Zero.

Athelas raised one brow. "Important, is it?"

"Probably not," said Zero. "There are a few things bothering me, that's all. I'd like to clear them up if I can."

"Is there anything you particularly want me to ask about?" Athelas' voice was polite and even faintly interested. Why did it occur to me that he was annoyed? Why would he be annoyed?

"Where they came from, how long they lived here, who actually owns the place, that sort of thing."

"If I may ask—?"

"I don't know that it's important," said Zero. "But things are different this time, and I want to know why. I'd also like to know why this place is so close to Between."

"Very well," said Athelas. "Oh, are you going now?"

JinYeong shrugged and tossed a remark at Athelas over his shoulder as he sauntered toward the front door. I didn't know what it was, but this time Athelas was definitely annoyed. His hand paused in the act of picking up a biscuit, a very faint frown etched between his brows, and although his face cleared a moment later, it had been unmistakable.

"I don't want the trace to fade too much more," said Zero. "If you go to the real estate agent tonight, Athelas, try to bring something back for dinner. You can throw out that saucepan, too."

I *thought* the house had smelled a bit burnt when I got up that morning. Good grief, Zero really was a bad cook—I hadn't ever burned a saucepan, even when I was first learning to cook. Mind you, I like food, so I had an incentive to learn well, but even so...

"Very well," Athelas said again. He sipped his tea tranquilly, with only the slight tapping movement of his foot to show that he'd been annoyed. He didn't seem to notice when the other two left; occupied with his tea. So polite and gentlemanly, and old fashioned. What about Zero's request had annoyed him enough to break him out of that habitual cool politeness?

Whatever it was, it occupied him for long enough to keep him at his tea—and when he finished that, to pour himself another cup—for an hour, his eyes distant and thoughtful. I glared at him through the latticed doors, with his neatly crossed legs and his well-bred sips, and wished that he would go and think elsewhere.

By the time they were all gone and I was able to come out, my left leg had gone to sleep, and I was kind of wishing that my hip had, as well. I must have been sitting on one of the spray clean bottles; there was a red trigger mark etched into my skin above the waistband of my jeans. Great. I've always wanted a tattoo.

I went straight up to my room. I could probably have showered now that they were all out of the house, but I still felt on edge from my close call earlier, and all I wanted to do was pull the covers over my head and pretend I was still in the house by myself. Well, maybe I would go to my listening corner when they got home, but that was as far as it went.

I didn't make it to the listening corner; I lay down in bed and accidently went to sleep instead. That meant I didn't wake up until far too late the next morning—funny how your alarm doesn't wake you up when you don't set it—and *that* meant I had to rush to work. I was late anyway, but the boss is always annoyed with me anyway, so I suppose there might as well be a reason for it.

There wasn't time to open the window for myself as I left that morning, but I was lucky; none of my psychos were at home when I got back. I made myself a cup of coffee and scurried back to my room before that could change.

I'd left my room a bit messier than I'd thought this morning; nothing dreadful, I just hadn't straightened the bedspread like I usually did, and I must have kicked my beanbag on the way out, because it wasn't sitting as plumply as it usually did. I gave it another kick twitched the bedspread straight again.

JinYeong got home first, a few minutes after I shut the door to my room. I didn't hear the front door open, just the sound of his footsteps across the kitchen floor. Funny. The door opening and closing was usually the clearest sound from up here.

"Sneaky vampire," I muttered.

JinYeong was muttering to himself, too; I could hear him pacing up and down in the living room below me. He must have something he wanted to discuss with Zero.

I was halfway through my coffee when I heard him make a sharp, satisfied noise, and stop pacing. Zero and Athelas must be back, too. Good thing I hadn't done more than get a cup of coffee. I peeked out the window, sipping my coffee, and caught sight of Athelas' shoulders and shiny shoes disappearing from my eyeline. Oh, good! They must have been out investigating, which meant there would be something to listen to tonight apart from JinYeong's pacing.

"*Hyung!*" Why did he sound so gleefully bloodthirsty?

Did Zero sound mildly amused? "What is it?" he asked.

I listened to the flow of Jin Yeong's voice and wondered why it was that it had begun to sound so close. Their voices were usually clear, but not as clear as all that. Even the sound of the kettle boiling didn't drown it out. Was he standing right against the wall in the downstairs living room? I put my coffee cup down in anticipation and stood closer to the corner; if one of them was standing up while the others sat down, it meant they were about to discuss interesting things, and the sound had a habit of rising and falling.

I leaned against the wall with one hip and ran my finger over the bubbles in the wall paint. Jin Yeong was still talking, but after a little while he stopped.

Instead, Zero asked, "Athelas, what do you know about this?"

"A little something," Athelas said, with the clink of china against wood. Like me, Athelas liked to have a hot drink in his hands when he sat down. "I wondered how long it might go on. Ah. I got some information for you from the real estate agent, by the way."

"Don't change the subject."

"I wouldn't dream of it."

"It didn't occur to you to tell me about this?" There was the exasperation in Zero's voice again.

"It occurred to me," said Athelas. Oh, he was definitely amused. "But it also occurred to me that I would find this more enjoyable."

"If it comes to that, you deliberately lied to me. I don't know how you've managed to be employed by my family all these years; they value loyalty above nearly everything else."

"I think you know," Athelas demurred. "A person like myself has many uses."

"Not enough," said Zero, and his voice was a threatening rumble. "There were *hairs* on the kitchen floor this morning. Long ones."

Seriously? Who notices *hairs* on the floor! I can't help shedding them, and it's not like they're dog hairs, anyway. At least they were something that could have been from the last tenants, I suppose. It's not like they were talking about me, right?

"It amused me to see coffee disappearing," Athelas said.

I froze. Ah heck. I was in trouble now. They were definitely talking about me.

"I'm surprised JinYeong didn't notice anything sooner," said Zero. "But then, he has been complaining about not being able to smell. And disappearing coffee could be rats or house imps."

"It's an odd imp that takes a shower while we're out," Athelas said. "Or leaves the upstairs windows open a crack so that it can slip in and out. Obviously, we have an interloper."

"Next time," said Zero, and it sounded like he said it through his teeth, "tell me straight away."

"Very well," sighed Athelas.

I suppose at least they didn't know I was actually still *in* the house. That had to count for something, right? They thought I was slipping in and out to steal stuff and have showers, didn't they? Didn't they?

But had my room *really* been this messy when I left it this morning?

"I suppose that's it, then," Athelas said. "JinYeong is taking a while, isn't he?"

"He should be behind it by now," said Zero, sending a shiver down my spine. How did I end up with such creepy men in my house? "We've given him enough time."

Athelas' voice said softly—almost too softly for me to hear without straining—*"He's talking about you, you know."*

CHAPTER FOUR

I WENT COLD TO THE TOP OF MY EARS AND WHIPPED AROUND. Something brushed against the tips of my fingers as I turned, soft fabric and cool skin. I snatched my hands into my chest, stumbling back against the wall.

He was there in the room with me; Jin Yeong.

How? How did he find the door? *How did they know I was in here?*

His hands were in the pockets of his beautifully cut suit and his blue tie matched it to perfection; close up, he was an elegant, aloof thing that made the hair stand up on the back of my neck. When one side of those elegantly pouting lips lifted slightly in a mocking smile, I could see the pointed tip of one incisor.

I'm gunna die, I thought.

"*Ya*," he said. "*Mwoh hae?*"

"I don't know what that means," I said. My voice sounded scratchy.

"*Yogi wae?*"

Why couldn't he speak English? "Still don't know what it means."

"*Nawa*," the vampire said; and there was no mistaking what

that meant, because he grabbed me by the collar and swept me toward the door.

"Don't really want to *nawa*," I panted, unable to resist the strength of that hand on my collar but still trying in spite of that. Squirming and tugging—and, when that didn't work, making myself into a dead weight—I was effortlessly dragged into the living room outside.

Zero and Athelas were already there; they must have hoofed it up the stairs after they did their creepy little dialogue for my benefit. I was scared, so I was probably scowling at them when Jin Yeong chucked me into the middle of the room.

Not that it bothered them. Zero looked me up and down and said, "Is that it? Bring it down to the kitchen. It's shedding more hair on the floor."

"Can't help it," I muttered. My throat had stiffened with fear, and I didn't seem to be able to speak in a proper voice. I'd forgotten how *big* he was when you were right in front of him. "That's what hair does."

"Mine doesn't," Zero said briefly, and led the way downstairs.

"Nor does mine," said Athelas, following.

It was left to Jin Yeong to push me ahead of him at arms-length, as if the few hairs I always shed were likely to house fleas. He said something, too, and it didn't take much imagination to guess that his hair didn't fall out, either.

Was that *really* how they'd figured out I was in the house? I left *hairs* around the place?

They didn't offer me a seat in the kitchen. Well, maybe I wouldn't be offering a seat to someone I'd just found hiding in my house, but they didn't try to call the cops, either. And if you think that's a good sign, you're even madder than they are.

I sat down anyway; jumped myself up on the kitchen counter and crossed my legs under me, still scowling at them. I was probably going to die, so I might as well show them I wasn't scared. I was, but there was no reason for them to know that.

They each stared at me in varying degrees of hostility—and, in Athelas' case, outright amusement.

He looked like being the least dangerous one of the three, so I looked at him when I said, "I was here first."

"What should we do with it?" he asked, and at first I thought he was talking to me even though the question made no sense. "There's precedent for keeping it."

It wasn't until Zero said, "We are *not* keeping it," that I realised I was the *it* Athelas was talking about.

"Oi!" I said. My throat wasn't as tight as it had been, and I found I could still be annoyed by their attitude.

Jin Yeong flicked my knee. When I looked at him, he put one finger over his lips, and there was a dark liquidity to his eyes. I shut my mouth.

"Where are its parents?"

"Maybe they abandoned it?" suggested Athelas.

"Yes, but then how did it crawl in here?"

"I didn't crawl," I said, since it seemed like they were actively looking for information. "I was already here."

Zero's eyes turned on me with a suddenness that made me jump. "You said that before. Is that why you wouldn't tell me anything when I stopped you on the street?"

I'd assumed he didn't remember me. "No," I said. "I wouldn't tell you anything when you stopped me on the street because you're a stranger and you choked me. Why would I tell you where I live and work?"

Athelas smiled faintly. "It's got good instincts. What are we going to do with it, though?"

"We'll give it back to its parents," said Zero shortly.

"My parents are dead."

"We'll find someone else to give it to."

Jin Yeong spoke, a questioning lilt to the end of it. There was still that dark liquidity in his eyes, and I could still see the tips of those very sharp teeth.

My toes curled defensively inside my socks. I edged a little closer to Zero; he was bigger than Jin Yeong and he hadn't actually strangled me to death.

"That's a very good point," Athelas said mildly. "What if it does talk?"

There was the shadow of a line between Zero's white brows. "We *can't* keep it!"

I sat up straighter, my throat unclenching again. I knew that tone of voice. It was the one Mum used when Dad was about to talk her into one of his daft, fun schemes; the disbelieving, protesting tone of voice that knew better but still might be convinced.

Zero was really thinking about me staying there. And I wanted—no, I *needed* to stay. For them it was just a place to stay for a while, while they investigated their murder, but to me it was mine, my home. At least, it would be when I was old enough to legally buy it. All I had to do was wait until they left, putting aside my money as usual.

"I'm quiet," I said, anxiety churning in my stomach. He had to agree to it, because I couldn't leave this place. "You won't know I'm here. Well, you didn't know I was here until now, so—"

Jin Yeong said something indignant, and I glared at him. He mouthed a word at me that I took to mean "what?" by the tilt of his chin.

"I can make really good coffee."

Zero blinked. I wasn't sure if it was because I'd startled him, like the first time we met, or if it was because he was weakening. "You *want* to stay?"

"I can cook, too," I offered.

Jin Yeong's lips made a thoughtful *moue*. He tucked his chin back in and folded his arms. Well. He was ready to listen, too.

"We haven't had a pet in a while," Athelas said. "And if you expect me to continue to put up with your cooking, Zero—"

"Most stewards," remarked Zero, unoffended, "cook for their masters."

"Most of them don't kill for their masters," Athelas responded. "I'm able either to cook or kill. I find it inimical to success to try for both."

Hang on, what?

I coughed, my throat suddenly too bulky and lumpy again to speak.

"I never asked you to kill for me!" Zero said in exasperation. In *exasperation*. Not horror, or disbelief, or disgust. Exasperation.

"If it can cook, we should let it stay and cook."

"What if it gets hurt?"

"What if it does? It's a pet."

I should have cut and run. I should have told them I wouldn't talk—convinced them it was safe to let me go.

But I didn't. It was *my* house, and I should be able to live in it, psychos or no psychos.

I put my chin up and said, "Get me some stuff. I'll cook for you tonight."

I could do with a proper cooked meal after all this time.

"*Coll!*" said JinYeong, and turned on his heel. I thought he was changing his yes vote to a no until I saw him snatch up his overcoat and flip it over his head and onto his back. "*Caja!*"

What a flamin' poser.

"You're a vampire!" Zero complained. "You don't *need* to eat."

"*Ne,*" agreed JinYeong, his eyes glittering. "*Hajiman, johaheyo.*"

"You like killing people and draining their blood, too. It doesn't mean you should be allowed to do it."

JinYeong looked at Zero as reproachfully as if he hadn't just looked at me with liquid murder in his eyes. "*Hyung.*"

Zero's eyes closed for the briefest second and opened again. "It can stay for the night. If I think better overnight, I'll kick it out in the morning."

"And who knows?" said Athelas. "Maybe it will come in useful. It has lived across the road from our scene, after all."

It was a weird experience, shopping with a vampire. Maybe it would have been less weird if he hadn't been a Korean vampire. Maybe it would have been easier if I could communicate with him—or at least if he could communicate with *me*. I was certain he understood everything I said, but I didn't have a clue what he was saying, and he wasn't trying very hard to make sure I did, either. If he particularly wanted something he inexorably steered the shopping trolley in that direction with one finger on the side of it, no matter how hard I tried to go in any other direction.

After a bit, I gave up and let him pull the trolley along wherever he wanted to go. I would have shaken some garlic at him if it wasn't for the fact that he threw a whole punnet in the trolley as we went through the fruit and veg section anyway.

"Sure you're a vampire?" I asked sourly.

"*Ne*," Jin Yeong said, and went for the onion as well.

"And who's gunna peel all that garlic, I'd like to know?" I demanded. Or chop it, if it came to that.

Jin Yeong shrugged and smiled complacently.

"That's what I thought," I said, even more sourly, and steered the trolley down the dog food aisle. I could see the cold section at the end of it, where I would find the bacon I needed to make my bacon and mushroom pasta. It looked bright and cool down there, through the oddly twilit aisle, and it occurred to me that some of the lights in the dog food aisle must be on the blink. I looked up at the fluorescent tubes, but they weren't there— instead, there was the much gentler glow of small lights in straight, fluorescent-tube-length lines dotting a ceiling far higher than it should have been.

"What—?" I said.

Beside me, Jin Yeong made a surprised sound and keeled over.

I didn't so much catch him as I was squashed by him, but I remembered in time that I was supposed to be making myself indispensable to my three psychos. I grabbed the shoulders of his coat to stop him hitting his head on the shelving.

Down the end of the aisle—had it been that far away or that indistinct before?—three men approached us. It must have been my imagination that gave them four arms each, but I knew I wasn't imagining the knives they had in each of their four hands because one exactly the same was sticking out of Jin Yeong's chest, the silver-embossed characters on its hilt glowing softly at me. And now someone's four-armed self only had three knives.

"What?" panted someone's voice again, and it must have been mine, because Jin Yeong didn't speak English and there was nobody else nearby. Well, nobody but the four-armed men who were sprinting at us down the length of the aisle, and if they really did have four arms I was pretty sure they wouldn't be speaking English, either.

I yelped and hauled Jin Yeong's prone body back toward the end of the aisle, careless of the damage to his pants legs, but the edge of the end shelving caught the ankle of my jeans and sent me tumbling backwards with my armful of vampire and cloth before I could clear the aisle. There was a moment of startled comprehension that I was probably going to die, then something swept past us both in a streak of white, cold, fury, meeting the charge of the four-armed men.

I struggled to sit up, my elbows hooked under Jin Yeong's armpits, and there was Zero's broad back and leathery scent, planted directly between us and our attackers.

Over his shoulder, Zero said crisply, "Pull the knife out. He'll be fine."

I pulled it out before I could think about it—at once. At least, I thought it was at once, but between seeing my hand wrapped around the hilt of the knife, and seeing that blade oozing with dark blood, free from Jin Yeong's torso, there was a big, blank moment. There must have been, because when I looked up from the bloody blade Zero's face was right behind it, and there was something black and sticky and wet on his face, too.

"Stay behind me," he said.

I thought he was talking to me, but Jin Yeong coughed up a small spurt of blood and sat up, dragging me with him. He said, slightly hoarsely, "*Ye, Hyung.*"

I'm not sure whether I helped him up or whether he pulled me up with him, but when we were on our feet, Jin Yeong shook me off and straightened his blood-soaked shirt.

"Yeah, that's a lot better," I said, hoping he couldn't see how close I was to chucking up. I gave him a thumbs-up and added, "*Chic.*"

He still wasn't steady on his feet, but he gave me a narrow look with the slightest edge of canine. I'd have been more concerned about that if I hadn't noticed the grocery store had gone...odd. Odder. The bit around Zero's back was still pretty normal, and if I only stared at his back things didn't look too bad.

It was only when I took my eyes off his back that I noticed there was a body at his feet now, and that the air around that body was sort of...swirling. The shelves didn't look quite like shelves anymore—they looked more like steps, or rungs—and the things on the shelves weren't the sort of stuff you find in grocery stores, either.

I reached out a bloody, shaking hand and picked up what had once been a small tin of cat food but was now a stone with a very small tree growing on its dimpled surface, its roots wrapping around the stone. Yeah. You can't pick up stuff like that at your local Woollies.

I put the stone in my pocket to think about later, but I didn't look back up to see if the lights were still different. I wasn't sure if I wanted to know whether we were still in the grocery store, or if we'd come somewhere else during that blank bit of time after I reached out to pull the knife out of Jin Yeong's chest.

Someone threw another knife, and then it didn't matter whether or not we were still in the grocery store, because Jin Yeong was slow on his feet and I had to jerk him down by the sleeve as Zero's bulk moved to intercept another knife and left a sliver of space that was filled with dark figures and glittering knives. Jin Yeong hissed at me and Zero moved again, blocking the sliver. His shoulder jerked backward and I saw the inky blue blot that grew at the back of his shirt around a point that shouldn't be sticking out there.

Jin Yeong snatched his sleeve from my fingers and dived beneath Zero's swinging arm with a snarl, his eyes black and reflective. Someone said, "*Idiot!*" but I couldn't be sure if it was me or Zero, because it was what I was thinking, but my voice *couldn't* be that gruff.

I stayed behind Zero. Now that I wasn't trying to hold up Jin Yeong I could see the full scope of the attack; there were still two men—or were they men? four arms!—attacking Zero, and another two that Jin Yeong was ripping into—literally ripping into, his white shirt soaked in scarlet and his throat slick with the sheen of blood.

My fingers instinctively curled themselves around the leather strap that belted together at the back of Zero's jacket, his momentum pulling me forward, pushing me back. His footwork scuffed across the blood-slicked tiles that were somehow still grocery store tiles even though the rest of the scene wasn't, and I slid after him.

Did he have a sword again? I mean, of course he had a sword; how else could he have been fighting off four-armed men; but where the *flaming heck* had it come from?

Those men, or things, or whatever—they were trying to kill me. Or maybe they were trying to kill Jin Yeong. But Jin Yeong was tearing someone's throat out, and really, should I be more afraid of four-armed men with knives or someone who *tore people's throats out?* I stayed behind Zero anyway, slipping in the blood and clinging to that leather strap for dear life, the buckle grazing my forefinger.

Two more of the four-armed men went down, Jin Yeong looking around in swift hunger for someone else to kill, and Zero ceased dragging me back and forth across the slippery floor.

I took a breather, just glad I was alive, and that all my limbs were attached. Two bloody eyes fastened on me.

Hang on. Was Jin Yeong looking at *me*—

Zero said, "Jin Yeong."

Those eyes flicked away from me and up to Zero's face. "*Hyung?*"

"That's enough for today."

Jin Yeong's tongue ran over one canine, his gaze now on Zero. There was challenge in it, and rebellion, dark and bloody. I gripped Zero's sleeve instead of the leather strap, glaring at Jin Yeong.

"Don't hurt the pet," Zero said. "Who do you think is going to clean the blood out of your clothes if it doesn't?"

Jin Yeong seemed to consider that. He tilted his head to the side for one instant, then very deliberately wiped the blood from his face with the remainder of one formerly white sleeve.

"That's gross," I told him, but he only gave me the smirk that displayed one warning tooth.

Flamin' fantastic. I was sharing a house with three homicidal maniacs, and at least one of them wasn't averse to killing me.

"You'd better do something about the blood before you go back," Zero warned. "You can't walk around in that when there are humans around. They'll get agitated."

"Back where?" I asked. That was sort of stupid; it was obvious we weren't *exactly* in the grocery store anymore. But in my defence, it wasn't as if it was actually possible for us to have left the middle of the grocery store during the fight without moving a heck of a lot more than we had. Or some walls moving, anyway.

Jin Yeong rolled his eyes and stripped off his suit jacket, then his bloody shirt. Zero, as if he'd just remembered I was there, clinging to his sleeve and glaring at Jin Yeong from behind his arm, shook me off and looked down at me in surprise.

"What are you doing here?"

Well, that wasn't good. Had one of the four-armed men clipped him around the head? I said cautiously, "You told me to come here with *him* and get supplies so I could cook tea."

Zero shook his head impatiently. "Not *there*. *Here*. Hobart Between."

"Dunno what you're talking about; I've been with you the whole time. Why do those blokes have four arms? Actually, what I really wanna know is why were they trying to kill us?"

Jin Yeong replied in Korean, and Zero agreed, "That's right; they weren't trying to kill you. They were trying to kill Jin Yeong."

"Oh," I said. "Nah, I understand that."

Oh well. The bloke already wanted to kill me anyway.

Zero's eyes narrowed in amusement despite the line between his brows. "You came with us partway into our land."

Jin Yeong muttered, but to my surprise, there was a dark glitter of amusement to his eyes as well.

"It's yours as well," Zero said. "Maybe not by birth, but birth doesn't really matter much to your kind, does it?"

"*Ne*," said Jin Yeong, and this time he displayed both canines in a cold, deadly smile, "*Kunang—pi.*"

The line vanished from between Zero's brows. "Just blood? I thought you didn't agree with that sort of thinking. Are you finished stripping?"

"What about the bodies?" I asked, as Jin Yeong scrubbed the remainder of blood from his face with his shirt. He didn't try to put it back on; he just put his suit jacket back on, where the darker patches could be taken for water.

Zero was brief. "You ask too many questions."

He'd said we were going *back*, but nothing he'd said about that made sense, and he still wasn't moving. Instead, he gazed, frowning, at the five bodies he and Jin Yeong had made.

Jin Yeong kicked one of the bodies. When he spoke, his voice was curious, but Zero only shrugged in reply and went through the pockets of one of the men closest to himself. I heard him grunt once, an expression of distaste passing momentarily over his pale face, and it occurred to me that apart from when I'd surprised him, it was the only real expression I'd seen on his face.

I crouched beside him. Now that they were dead, they didn't look like people anymore—or maybe it was that they didn't look quite real. I reached out and touched the body with my forefinger, and regretted it straight away. It felt like a real person, not even like a dead person—whatever *that* felt like.

Zero plucked me away by the nape of the neck like the pet they said I was, and said, "Get out of it."

"That one's got something around his neck," I said, wrapping my arms around my knees where he'd dropped me, and pointing with my chin. I wouldn't have touched that thing again, anyway.

Zero didn't reply. He fished something limp and tissue-y out of his pockets, grabbed the hand with which I'd touched the body, and wiped it thoroughly. He wasn't gentle, and if I'd thought it would help, I would have said *ouch*.

Instead, I asked, "What? Is it bad to touch?"

"You're cooking our food later," he said briefly, and grabbed the other hand. "I don't want this filth on our food."

"Oh. Sorry."

I mean, the guy was dead. It probably wasn't a good idea to touch dead guys before making dinner; and now that Zero had wiped down my hands, there was none of Jin Yeong's blood on them, either. That was a plus.

I looked away from Zero, who was taking the necklace from the dead guy I'd touched, and looked at Jin Yeong instead. He didn't seem to be as concerned about the blood being on him as Zero had been about it being on me, and now he looked like a cross between a really drunk guy with a bloody nose and a guy who'd murdered someone.

"You missed a bit," I said, jerking my chin at the smear of blood that ran from his ear to the collar of his suit jacket. The next second, JinYeong's bloody shirt hit me in the face. "Gross," I grumbled into the bloody haze, and pulled it off my face.

JinYeong looked smug.

Zero said, "I *just* cleaned it off! Now you've made it dirty again!"

"*Mianeyo.*"

"I'd believe you were sorry if you weren't so pleased with yourself," said Zero.

JinYeong raised his brows at me and indicated his neck. What a rat. He wanted me to clean him off.

"What are you, two?" I grumbled, but I obeyed anyway. I prefer my blood *inside* my body. It didn't stop me scrubbing much harder at JinYeong's ears than I strictly needed to do, though. Or from saying, "What a sook!" when he made a small, inarticulate protest.

Zero might have been grinning when I finished with JinYeong's neck, but if so, he stopped so quickly I couldn't be sure. He had more of his little tissues, and he wiped my face as thoroughly as I had wiped JinYeong's neck. I didn't make a sound, which made JinYeong's lips purse; and I felt a bit smug about that.

"Time to go," said Zero, when he was done. He didn't throw away the tissues; he put them in a bag and put that bag somewhere, though I wasn't sure where. Wherever it was, JinYeong's shirt went there, too. "Ready?"

I nodded, but it wasn't me he was talking to.

JinYeong said "*Caja!*" and, walking out of the aisle, disappeared for a moment. I blinked, and he was there again, a few feet away but somehow not quite as *there* as he should have been.

"Hold onto my jacket again," said Zero. "Don't let go. I won't come back for you."

I grabbed the strap on his jacket just in time; and as the world dragged around us like molasses, I was tugged back into a world that sat more familiarly around me than it had a few steps ago.

I looked back into the aisle once. There were five bulk packs of dry dogfood strewn across the aisle, their contents spilling out from splits and holes. No bodies, only ruined stock. The aisle was once again the right length, and it had lost that twilight look, but I no longer had any desire to pass through it to get my bacon.

"Bacon," I said, hoarsely, because I didn't want to think about how four-armed bodies could turn into sacks of dog food by leaving an aisle in the grocery store.

Jin Yeong grinned.

Zero said, "What?"

"Can't make bacon and mushroom pasta without the bacon," I said.

"*Jal haesso, Petteu,*" Jin Yeong said, with a bright flash of white teeth.

"I don't know what that means, but you should leave the store," I told him. There were already two cashiers and some sort of manager watching him anxiously; his hair was wild, he was still swaying a bit, and without a shirt beneath his suit jacket he looked, at the best, homeless. "Those blokes think you're gunna steal stuff."

Jin Yeong gave me a look and stalked away. What? I'd hurt his feelings?

I glanced up at Zero, but his pale eyes told me nothing. "Bacon," he said, and grabbed the handle of the trolley.

Zero was much easier to shop with than Jin Yeong. It wasn't so much that he spoke English, it was more the fact that he tended not to speak at all. Well, they do say it's an early sign of an unbalanced mind when you talk to your pet, I s'pose...

At any rate, all I needed to do was announce where we were going and Zero would silently follow me there with the trolley.

When we got out, Jin Yeong was waiting for us, his shoulders propped against the front window of the grocery store and his grin more threatening than welcoming. I wasn't surprised to see people making a wide berth around him, and it wasn't all about the blood, either; Jin Yeong had a dark glitter to his eyes most of the time that was more frightening than blood.

"Don't worry," I told him, wary of it myself. "We got *all* your garlic."

I WAS MAKING DINNER WHEN ATHELAS GOT HOME. I DIDN'T know where he'd been, but they wouldn't have told me if I'd asked, so I didn't bother. Zero, who was sharpening his knives at the dinner table, looked up sharply and said, "Oh, you're back."

Jin Yeong stepped up from the lower lounge room into the kitchen and said languidly, "*Wasso?*"

He must have been there to see strife, because when Zero held up the pendant he'd taken from one of the dead men, his eyes lit up.

"What's this?" Athelas asked calmly.

"You tell me," said Zero, and tossed it to him. He went back to sharpening his knives. "It's one of ours, isn't it?"

Athelas looked up sharply from the pendant. "You were attacked?"

"Jin Yeong was attacked. I stepped in." Zero looked at Athelas down the length of one wickedly shiny blade, and his voice could have chipped ice. "I thought I warned you about sending people after Jin Yeong."

"Dear me," said Athelas.

If Zero's voice could have chipped ice, the entire room now seemed encased in it. I put my head down and chopped garlic fervently. I'd already seen the way Jin Yeong's angry, predatory eyes followed Zero; seen the way they could fight together. What would happen if all three fought each other? Athelas would die, that's for sure. Even JinYeong would probably drop before Zero would, so if there was potential for splitting up, I was best off making myself indispensable to Zero. He was the one who had paid the bond on the house, or the deposit—I still wasn't sure which one. I could be sneaky and conniving, couldn't I? 'Course I could.

"I think," said Zero thoughtfully, putting down the cloth he had been wiping down one last knife with, "that you should begin to talk."

"I had nothing to do with it," Athelas said. He looked pretty unconcerned for a willowy bloke facing off against someone as big as Zero. "It would be a waste of a perfectly good pet."

"Thanks," I said. "Want a cuppa?"

"Be quiet, Pet," said Zero.

I shut up, but I made Athelas a cup of tea anyway.

"What sort were they?"

The four-armed sort, I could have said, but I didn't. I poured boiling water over the tea leaves instead.

JinYeong said something with a sharp edge of canine that was either a smile or a baring of teeth.

"Rank and file?" Athelas took a seat at the kitchen table and leisurely crossed one leg over the other. I don't know how he could do that while Zero sat so still and alert, fairly buzzing with pent up violence. "I wouldn't send rank and file after you, JinYeong. I've no interest in sending you fodder for a day's eating."

To my surprise, one corner of JinYeong's mouth turned up in a real smile. He said something that made Athelas smile back in the first moment of perfect agreement I'd seen between them.

"Exactly," he said. "I would come after you myself."

Yeah, they're definitely psychos.

"If not you, then who?"

"By joining you, I've distanced myself from the Family," said Athelas. "You of all people should know what that means, Zero. I have very little knowledge of what goes on in that side of Behind, and even less say about it."

"I see," said Zero. He went back to his sharpening, and some of the ice in the room melted. "It does seem to push the borders of coincidence to say that they were here for someone else, however."

"Perhaps someone has heard that you're here. It's not beyond possibility, after all."

"*Uri wassoyo*," JinYeong said, shrugging.

"Exactly," agreed Athelas. "If it occurred to both of us that you'd be here, it's no doubt occurred to others as well. And if you're here, it would be a good chance that we're here. The question should then really be, who has JinYeong annoyed most recently?"

That was probably a pretty long list.

"Singularly unhelpful, in other words," said Athelas.

This time, JinYeong grinned outright. Nice to know he had more expressions in his arsenal than a sulky one and an angry one.

"The timing is reasonably coincidental, don't you think?" Zero said slowly.

"Quite," said Athelas, "but we must recall that whoever sent them, sent low level lackeys. Not the sort of thing you expect to take down someone like JinYeong. Or even a normal vampire, if it comes to that."

"I don't know," I said, passing Athelas his cup and saucer. "They took him out pretty quick, if you ask me."

JinYeong gave me a narrow-eyed look that made me shuffle closer to Athelas.

"That was a silver blade embossed with fae magic," Zero said. "Rank and file, maybe; but well-armed. JinYeong would have recovered in time if I wasn't there, but I'd like to know who is outfitting mercenaries with silver, fae-embossed blades."

"Wait," I said, a thought occurring to me. "How did you know we were in trouble? JinYeong got stabbed and then you were there. Like ma—really quick."

"There's a Monitor on you," said Athelas.

At the same time, Zero said, "It's not important."

I looked from an annoyed Zero to an amused Athelas. "What's a Monitor?"

"You don't need to know," said Zero.

Athelas said, "Think of it as a collar. Every good pet has one, after all."

JinYeong asked a question, his voice lilting up at the end.

"No," Athelas replied. "Why would Zero put a Monitor on you?"

JinYeong, outraged, said something swift and sibilant.

"Be quiet," Zero said, with finality, to both of them. To me, he added, "You. Don't think too much of it. I haven't decided you can stay, but I don't like things dying when they're under my protection."

"*Hyung*!" JinYeong sounded reproachful.

I stuck my tongue out at him. "Nobody cares if you die."

"*Ya*!"

"Do you want me to throw you out on the street right now?"

I closed my mouth and JinYeong gave me a smug look.

"I don't have a Monitor on JinYeong because he can look after himself. Monitors are for pets."

I wanted to say that JinYeong obviously *couldn't* look after himself, and to remind everyone who it was who had pulled the knife out of his chest, but Athelas was looking even more amused and it occurred to me in time that everybody already knew that. The only thing I would get out of making that particular remark was thrown out of my house.

I started chopping garlic again. Pity it wouldn't make JinYeong sick. Decent vampires ought to get sick from garlic.

CHAPTER FIVE

THEY DIDN'T FINISH EATING UNTIL AFTER ELEVEN; THEN THEY decamped to the downstairs living room as usual, discussing their investigation. I did the washing up and listened more because it was nice to hear their voices out in the open than because I really wanted to know what they were talking about. It wasn't like I was part of the investigation, anyway, and I had to go to work tomorrow.

But maybe it was nice to feel all the subtle little effects of people living in the house again. A warmth; or maybe it was just the constant flicker of sound and movement in the background.

It wasn't like I was fond of them or anything. I had to live with them until I could get my house back to myself, that's all. But for the meantime, I couldn't help smiling while I washed the dishes.

In the next room, Athelas asked, "What now? This could prove disruptive to the investigation. If they know where you are, it's possibly best to—"

"We're not leaving." Zero's voice was expressionless, but it was expressionless like a brick wall. He wasn't going to change his mind, and it was no good arguing. Then, as if correcting himself, he added, "*I'm* not leaving."

Despite the tone, Athelas said, "I understand that you'd like to continue your investigations, but will that help you if the Family knows where you are? They're not particularly fond of you."

"I'll take it into account," said Zero. "They didn't attack the house, so they obviously don't know exactly where we are. I'll do a working on the house tonight. That is first."

"What's second?" Athelas wasn't stupid enough to argue again; he could tell as well as I could that it was useless. "Your forays Between have yielded more blood than usable information, and if Jin Yeong's nose isn't working well enough to trace the blood inside—"

"*Hal su isseo!*" said Jin Yeong swiftly.

"At some distance from the house, his nose seems to recover," Zero said. "I've got a few thoughts about that."

"Very well; then perhaps that's the second thing we could work on tomorrow," Athelas suggested.

"Yes," agreed Zero. "Jin Yeong is going to try again. The pet can come with me."

"The pet can *what*?" I said to the kitchen tiles, startled into saying it aloud.

"I thought you hadn't decided to keep it?"

"I haven't," Zero said. "But if it's here eating our food, it should be useful."

That was rich! I was in here doing the washing up while they were out there talking, after eating the meal I made them.

Flamin' superior fae.

"I'm already useful," I told the kitchen tiles. At nose-height there was a little cracked one, just like me. I always talked to it while I was doing the washing up; when I was younger, I'd imagined that it talked back. "D'like to see you lot doing the washing up. D'like to see you cooking your own dinner. I'm *flamin'* useful."

I heard the sound of JinYeong's dismissive hiss, then an equally dismissive sentence in Korean.

"It will be useful," Zero said. "There's no need for you to know how—or why, if it comes to that. All you need to do is follow the blood. I'll be right behind you with the pet."

Hang on. Zero and I were going with JinYeong? Flamin' fantastic. It wouldn't surprise me if someone attacked JinYeong again; and even if I didn't care about that, I did care about not being attacked myself.

JinYeong, his voice as indignant as I felt, asked, "*Dweye? Waeyo?*"

"Because I've got a suspicion about why you haven't been able to follow the scent easily, and I want to test it."

Was I part of the test? I looked worriedly at the cracked tile as I pulled the plug out of the sink, and said plaintively, "I don't like tests."

"And I need the pet there to test it," added Zero.

Oh, I *definitely* didn't like tests.

"Do you think it's wise to be taking the child Between with you? She hasn't had any experience, and she's a human. How can she help?"

"It," said Zero. "It said it would be useful. It's not a child, either; it's half grown."

JinYeong said something in a curious voice. I wiped my hands on my jeans and decided that if I was going to have any chance of following conversations around this place, I'd have to start learning Korean.

"My point exactly," Athelas said. He didn't sound annoyed, but I had the feeling he was. "A human child is no use to anyone Between, unless you're offering her—it—up as fodder for safe passage. I don't fancy you need that."

"I don't."

"Then—"

"I don't know yet," Zero said. "Not for sure. I'm going out to put up the wards now. That should stop anyone finding us—or normal humans getting in, if it comes to that."

I heard his footsteps on the stairs and then along the hall, passing through the other side of the kitchen. The front door opened and closed, and the faintest of sighs passed from the other room into the kitchen. Athelas obviously still wasn't happy about Zero taking me into the house across the road. Maybe I'd make him another cuppa.

I swiped my damp hands along my jeans and frowned. Hang on, what was that in my pocket? It was either ovular and cool or cylindrical and cool; and when I took it out of my pocket it looked like it still hadn't decided what it was. It should have been a tin of cat food—wait, had I stolen that?—but it was trying pretty hard to be a stone with a tiny tree growing on it.

"Oh, that's weird," I said.

I put the thing on the kitchen island top and stared at it as if I could make it decide what it was going to be by staring at it; but that didn't do much except make me dizzy. It wasn't even flickering or anything—just looked more like a stone sometimes and more like a tin of cat food at others.

I didn't really want it to be a tin of cat food, since that would mean I'd technically stolen it, so I said to it, "You're a pebble. You have a little tree on your back. Try to remember that."

Maybe it needed to be talked to. It changed back to being a pebble with a tiny tree wrapped around it; and this time, it stayed like that.

"What have you got there, Pet?"

I jumped. I hadn't seen Athelas standing in the cased doorway between living room and kitchen, one shoulder leaning against the frame and one leg crossed in front of the other. He looked pensive. I mean, he pretty much always looks pensive, but this time he looked more pensive.

"It's a little tree on a rock," I said. "I got it from the grocery store."

"I had no idea the local grocery store carried dryads," said Athelas.

"I thought it was a little tree on a rock."

Athelas left the doorway and strolled toward me. "It is. So to speak. Did Zero give it to you?"

"No." Why would Zero give me anything? "I told you. I brought it back."

"From the place where you were attacked?"

"Yes. The grocery store. What's the big deal? Should I show Zero?"

"I wouldn't," said Athelas, shrugging. "But it's entirely up to you, of course. I've got a feeling he'd be rather annoyed if you showed him that."

"Wait, he'd be annoyed? What did I do? Why would—"

"And since you seem determined to stay here—"

My hand closed around the stone, or tin, or dryad, or whatever it was. "Do you want it?"

There was a moment of very silent stillness before Athelas sighed. "Very much! However, I suspect the price is too great."

"I'll give it to you," I said. "I didn't pay for it."

Another silence stretched out, long and incomprehensible. Athelas was wearing that slight smile he most often wore, and I thought he looked regretful.

"Are you determined to put me forever in your debt?" he asked, at last. "I refuse your gift. Don't freely offer such things to the fae—don't offer them to anyone."

"All right, I won't offer it to you!" I said in exasperation. I put the pebble back in my pocket; this time more carefully. "Flaming heck! I only asked if you wanted it!"

"I want it," said Athelas. "Very much."

Strike a light, these psychos were impossible to understand!

"Well, have a cup of tea instead, then," I said crossly, and flicked the button on the kettle.

Athelas looked startled, then laughed. "Very well," he said. "I'll accept a cup of tea. Put that thing in your room, and if Zero asks you about it, you'd be wise to tell him it's always been here, in this house."

"Will he believe that?"

"No," said Athelas. "But he'll believe that you believe it."

"Oh," I said. That didn't make much sense. No, actually, it did make sense; just not *enough* sense. There was something more that Athelas wasn't telling me.

JinYeong, light and elegant, padded into the kitchen, his socks silent against the kitchen floor.

"You," I said to him. "You were already in here when I got home this afternoon, weren't you?"

JinYeong's mouth made the satisfied *moue* I was beginning to dislike as much as his smug look. At least his eyes were glittering with dark humour instead of blood-lust, so I suppose there's that.

"*Moh—bistandae*," he said, and walked past me to the kitchen island.

"Where were you?"

He raised a brow at me and smirked over his shoulder. I didn't think he was going to tell me, but after a moment he sauntered back around the kitchen island, trying to back me up by sheer personality. I would have stared him down if he hadn't touched a finger to my forehead and pushed me backward with that one finger, as if afraid to dirty the rest of them.

"Rude!" I said.

The other brow went up. JinYeong turned elegantly, flicked open the latticed cupboard door, and slid into the cupboard with a liquidity that was disconcerting.

"Oh well," I said. "S'pose that's fair. Did that myself."

It would have been nice to shut the cupboard door on him and make him sit in there for a couple of hours, though. At least he'd only had to wait for a few minutes while I made coffee.

"You were the one who messed up my room, too, weren't you?" I asked, as he coiled back out of the cupboard again.

Jin Yeong shrugged, but he still looked pleased with himself. "*Coppi*," he said, and sat down at the kitchen table opposite Athelas.

"Isn't anyone going to bed tonight?" I complained; but since it was obvious that Jin Yeong was ordering me to make coffee, I put a coffee cup next to Athelas' teacup and fetched the coffee plunger.

"You're very comfortable, Pet," said Athelas, above the rising sound of the jug boiling.

"It's my house," I said. "I'm always comfortable here."

"Yes, there's that, too," Athelas added. "I've been wondering about that. Well, perhaps for some it's no more difficult to deal with Between than it is to deal with Fae."

"Between what?" I asked, jumping myself up on the kitchen bench. "You all keep saying *Between* and *Behind* and I don't understand."

"I mean it in its most basic sense," Athelas said. "This world of yours, where you eat and sleep and go to work—it's only the top layer of—ah, how shall I explain it to a human?"

"Call it an onion," I said, ignoring the casual superiority. "All right, it's the top layer of an onion. What about it?"

"That would suggest more than three layers."

"Oh well, call it a trifle, then," I said, shrugging. I leaned over and snagged the kettle, and poured for them. "I don't care. Trifles can have as many layers as you like. Yours can have three if you like. So *here* is the cream with chocolate sprinkles."

Jin Yeong's eyelashes dropped, then opened again with something of a gleam. This time, I was pretty sure the contemptuous amusement in them wasn't directed at me—it was directed at Athelas.

"The—well, *here* in this house, perhaps not. This is something different. Very well, say that the human world is the cream with the chocolate sprinkles."

"Wait, what do you mean that this house isn't the cream and sprinkles?"

"Pet," said Athelas, the word gentle but ice-edged, "I would really prefer if you didn't keep interrupting."

I pressed my lips together to stop myself asking another question. "Sorry."

"If the human world is the cream with sprinkles, the next layer is the custard—that is Between. Hm, trifle seems to be particularly apt here. From above, the custard receives the impression of the cream. From below, sponge cake and fruit protrude into the custard. And sometimes something from the custard pushes right up into the cream."

I didn't think that was a particularly good comparison, but that was just me. Nobody in their right mind puts stuff in the custard. You put it all in the jelly. Stupid Fae. I nodded anyway, and carefully pushed the plunger down on Jin Yeong's coffee. Probably the only thing I like about Jin Yeong is that his coffee isn't complicated. Plunger coffee, black, no sugar.

"Behind is the very bottom, where all the richness is," Athelas said. He took the cup of tea I passed to him, leaning forward elegantly to do so. "The jelly, the sponge, the fruit. All the reality."

"At least we've got the chocolate sprinkles," I muttered. Superior Fae. As if this wasn't reality!

I was half afraid that Athelas would freeze me again with another of his gentle, ice-edged warnings, but this time his eyes grew brighter with amusement.

"Do you find me disparaging of your world, Pet?" he enquired. "After all, there's nothing wrong with cream. It's a little bland for my tastes, but it's certainly not without its uses."

"Yeah," I said. It was probably the way they talked like that —*not without its uses*—that made it so annoying. I jumped myself back up on the bench and crossed my legs underneath me. "We make good coffee."

"The layers interact with each other, but remain distinct. And once in a while, something from the jelly gets through to the cream."

"Like all of you," I said. I frowned. "Hang on, *that's* what you mean by Between? Stuff from there can get here, but not without going through a middle bit?"

Jin Yeong's brows went up. "*Bisthae, bisthae*," he said.

"Gunna assume that means *got it in one*," I muttered. "Why can't he speak English?"

"Jin Yeong says you're very close," Athelas told me, cupping his teacup in both hands. "Between is indeed the means by which those things in Behind can access the human world."

"Does that mean humans can affect Behind, as well?"

"Would you attempt to push sponge cake into the jelly through the cream and custard?"

He was taking the analogy a bit far, wasn't he?

"Dunno," I said. "Don't usually make trifle; I just eat it."

Athelas looked thoughtful. "It's not that we have laws against it, you understand. It's simply not the natural order of things—I can only imagine the mess it would make. Fortunately, it's said to be impossible for a human to access Between by itself."

I tried very hard not to roll my eyes. "What a surprise."

"It's a matter of seeing things in the right way," Athelas said, shrugging. "And the human who can see things in the right way to access Between would be a very rare human. I can only imagine the mess it might cause, and as a whole, the Fae are only inclined to approve of mess when it's their own doing."

"What do you mean, seeing things in the right way?"

"Don't teach the pet bad habits," said Zero briefly, making me jump. For a bloke as big as he is, he could move as silently as Jin Yeong; he was already in the kitchen. "I haven't decided that we're keeping it, and it'll be a nuisance to wipe its memories."

I looked at him gloomily, but asked, "Want a coffee?" anyway.

It wasn't like Athelas wasn't condescending and dismissive, too, after all. Zero was bigger, so there was more ice to melt.

The offer made him stiffen, but there was no change of expression on his face. After a moment, he said, "Bring a tray into the living room," and went back. Jin Yeong, who had been propped against the partial wall between kitchen and living room, took his coffee and followed Zero, and Athelas rose to his feet languidly.

"Bring biscuits, Pet," he said. "It will be a long night."

IT WAS MORE LIKE AN EARLY MORNING. AT SOME STAGE AFTER I took in Zero's coffee and the biscuits, I fell asleep on the couch, and when I woke in a brief spurt of panic that I was going to be late for work, they were discussing something that must have had to do with me.

"Relax, Pet," said Athelas, his smile faintly mocking. "It's only five in the morning."

Zero, who had abruptly stopped speaking when I woke with a gasp, asked, "Where are you going?"

"Work," I said. "You know. Human stuff."

He didn't reply, but he doesn't, much. I figured if he had something to say, he'd come out with it when he was ready, so I went to get a change of clothes and have my first real, luxurious shower since I'd been living alone in the house.

I shouldn't have done that; it made me late for work. I was only late by five minutes, but the boss was already frothing at the mouth about a drink he'd spilled all over the floor and *bain marie* because one of the girls had left it on the counter as usual and his elbow knocked it off in passing.

It couldn't be his fault, so it had to be hers, and she looked relieved when my lateness called him away from hanging over her to make sure she cleaned it up properly.

"Don't expect to get paid for the first half hour," he said to me. "I don't pay in fifteen minute lots."

"Yeah," I said, because it was too much to expect him to acknowledge the couple of extra hours I'd done when I cleared out the toilet.

He was on my case all day. I'm used to it, but I don't like it. It was a pity that a few of those scarecrow things couldn't seep through the walls again and make a bit of havoc in the café. That'd be nice.

He might have settled down a bit if everything had gone perfectly through the day. Unfortunately, someone lost the scrubber part way through the day—the boss, though no one was going to tell him that—and when I asked for it, the boss spent fifteen minutes howling in my face behind the cook station. Most of it was the usual threats about taking the price of it out of my pay, but some of it was gibbering, too.

I said "Yeah", "Yep", and "Got it", and then went back to washing up. I was probably a bit short, because a few minutes after I did, something grazed my cheek, splattering small wet gobbets of something cold on my neck, and smacked into the splashback. I looked wearily at it—it was the scrubber the boss had just sworn I'd lost—and as wearily wiped the muck from that side of my face with the tea towel.

I should have been more careful. If I'd looked for it myself, he might not have been so angry, but it looked like he was going right off the deep end now. Things were always about to blow when he started chucking stuff.

I didn't have the energy to waste on trying to make him happy again by then, so I went into my second defence—sullen silence. He doesn't like it, but at least that way I don't run the risk of saying anything cheeky to him.

Of course, that only meant that he started muttering to himself, and throwing stuff at the sink.

"Wash this too!"

Bang!

A plastic spatula hit the wall, handle first, and fell into the washing up water. Gravy slid down the wall and probably my hair as well.

"You forgot the milkshake maker!"

Clang! Bang!

Two stainless steel milkshake cups ricocheted between splash-back and sink top before disappearing beneath the soap bubbles. They'd already been washed, but a customer had come in for a milkshake two minutes ago.

I washed them doggedly, then wiped the splashback and went onto the mopping. That was my last job for the day, thank goodness. There were too few customers to stop the boss really going off, and I didn't think I had the energy to deal with his explosions today.

I was halfway down the salad bar when a shout from the boss made me jump.

"You haven't emptied the *bain marie*!" he yelled.

"It's not four o'clock yet!" I called back, wrestling with the mop. "There's still some special of the day left and we usually get the after college rush. You want me to do it now?"

"I want you to do your job!"

I huffed a hair out of my face and mopped out the thin bit behind the counter. If I emptied it and customers came, he would blame me for that, too. Should I do it or not?

Before I could make up my mind, he came barrelling up the narrow channel.

"Out of the way!"

"Just a minute!" I yelped, but the boss snarled and booted the mop bucket into my leg, slopping water over my shoes and the floor. I hissed in pain and cupped one hand over my battered shin, trying not to let the prickle of my eyes overflow.

"Go home if you're just going to get in the way!" he yelled, over his shoulder, and started taking trays out of the warmer, hurling them at the sink and splashing food over the walls I'd just wiped down.

There was a whisper of something behind me, at the counter. I blinked my eyes shut for a second to make the water in my eyes go away, but before I could open them again to deal with the customer, someone grabbed me by the nape of the neck and lifted me bodily over the counter.

I was too surprised to yell, which was just as well, because it was JinYeong. He dropped me on the floor again as if I really had been a pet, and twitched me back and forth to inspect my front and then my back.

Oh. That tracer thing they said Zero had put on me.

"Sorry," I said, waving my battered shin at him. "It was only this. There was a—" I couldn't bring myself to say accident, so I finished lamely, "—thing. It's all right."

One of JinYeong's brows went up. He pointed at me and said to the boss, who was glaring at us over the top of the warmer, "*Nae kkoya. Manjiji ma!*"

The boss glared at him and then at me. "If this is your boyfriend, you'd better get rid of him. I'll fire you if he makes trouble in the shop."

"As if!" I said indignantly.

The boss muttered and went back to lifting out the dishes. Maybe he dropped one, but it looked more like it exploded. There was a dull *pop*, and a very large splash of devilled sausages, the dish of the day, covered the boss from head to toe.

I blinked a bit, but JinYeong only sauntered away through the door, his mouth a self-satisfied *moue*. The boss yelled bloody murder behind the counter, but he'd told me to go home, so I followed the smug vampire out the door without a second thought, leaving the stench of devilled sausages behind.

"You do that?" I asked JinYeong, when we were out in the street.

He made a contemptuous sort of hiss between his teeth and kept walking. I couldn't tell if the contempt was for thinking he would do such a thing, or because my weakly humanness made me unsure of whether or not he'd done it.

I rolled my eyes at him and trailed behind him all the way home. It would be a bad day tomorrow, but for this afternoon it was nice to know that the boss was covered in devilled sausages and would need to clean the whole kitchen again.

Neither Athelas nor Zero asked about my well-being when I shuffled into the kitchen behind Jin Yeong. I didn't mind; it was enough that they'd sent him for me. I mean, it was silly to feel warm and happy about anything my three psychos did—they were psychos, and they wouldn't be around long. It was stupid to get attached to them.

But I still felt warm.

I chucked the shoulder strap of my backpack over one of the hooks in the hallway as I passed, and put the kettle on by way of thanks that was as silent as their care. Maybe that's what they were all waiting for, because Zero and Athelas were already sitting at the kitchen table, Athelas with one leg elegantly crossed as usual, and Zero hulking over something on the table.

Maybe...maybe it was me they'd been waiting for. But that wasn't a safe way to think, either. I only had to be indispensable until I could get my house back to myself. That was the sensible way to act.

I looked over at Zero as I brought out the coffee cups; he had a knife belt tonight, which was about standard for him. He wasn't polishing these knives, though. Perhaps he was putting a spell on them, or something.

"What do you lot want for dinner tonight?" I asked, preparing a teapot for Athelas and the big plunger pot for the rest of us. I would have given them leftovers from last night, but there weren't any. It wasn't like I'd skimped, either; I'd made a double batch.

Jin Yeong looked up straight away, his eyes bright.

Hah. I knew my cooking was that good. I hopped up on the

bench, swinging my legs while I waited for the kettle to boil, and said, "I can cook more stuff like that pasta. You just gotta ask."

Maybe they'd already been talking about it. Athelas said, "She does make a good cup of tea, after all. Let's have her as a pet."

Zero said coolly, "Don't go giving it a name and patting it on the head. Don't get fond of it. It'll die soon enough."

"No, I won't," I said. "I'll stay behind you."

One of Jin Yeong's brows went up and then down. Athelas only smiled faintly, but that was enough to make me look at Zero. There was nothing to see; his face was expressionless.

"Don't make a mess around the house," he said abruptly. "Stay in your room unless you're making coffee or meals, and come when you're called."

"I can stay?"

"For now," he said, and went back to his knives. "Only for now. And if you disobey me even once, I'll kick you out."

"Got it," I said.

CHAPTER SIX

"What do you lot want for dinner, anyway?"

I'd already asked them, but we'd been distracted by tea and coffee, and some little biscuits that I was pretty sure didn't come from any part of the human world. I'll have to learn how to make them: no way they'll kick me out of my house if I can make stuff like that.

"It doesn't matter," said Zero, forestalling both the bright-eyed Jin Yeong and the suddenly interested Athelas. "But make it quickly—we've got somewhere to be."

"What, you and me?" Oh yeah; he'd said earlier that he was taking me somewhere. I felt a bit doubtful about that. "Is it like where we went when we were in the supermarket?"

Athelas stopped smiling abruptly. "You're actually, deliberately taking her—"

"It."

"You're really taking it Between? Zero—"

Jin Yeong spoke, an insistent couple of words.

"You're still coming, too," said Zero to Jin Yeong, ignoring Athelas. "I need you for this."

I curled my lip in JinYeong's direction as I pulled out the frying pan; he was looking far too smug about something so small. Had he been annoyed to think that Zero might be going somewhere without him, and taking me instead?

He saw me; curled his lip right back at me.

I turned my back on him and got out the steak I'd put in the trolley when we went to the grocery store. "Steak and veg," I said. "That's the quickest I can do. 'Bout twenty minutes."

I didn't want to go out again; I had to go to work tomorrow. On the other hand, Zero had the contract on my house, and I was meant to be making myself indispensable until I could get it myself.

Stable income to be able to eventually purchase my parents' house, or keeping sweet with the current owner, who might never move out? At any rate, I could make dinner; and at least for tonight, I could stay out late. The boss was going to be angry tomorrow anyway, so I might as well be sleep-deprived as well.

I put the steak on to cook and a few bits of veg into the microwave ready to hit the button when the steak was almost done. JinYeong sat at the kitchen island as I set the table and watched me unblinkingly with dark, glittering eyes. I wasn't sure if he was hungry enough to consider eating me, or if it was the bloody steak attracting him, but it was off-putting enough to make me sit down at the table after I'd covered the steaks to leave them to rest in their juices.

Since I was supposed to be making myself useful, I sat down and passed Zero a knife when he finished doing whatever he was doing to the one he was working on.

Zero saw the knife hilt; looked up, ice blue eyes pinioning me.

"Steak'll be done in ten minutes," I said, wiggling the knife at him. "They gotta rest."

"The blades are sharp," he said, reaching over to take the point instead of the haft that I offered him.

I couldn't help grinning; I mean, I knew they thought of me like a talking dog or something, but I'd have to be pretty dumb to cut myself on one of these blades. Still, it was kinda nice to have someone around the house who didn't want me to hurt myself. Nice to have *anyone* around the house, actually.

I didn't say anything—just passed him another knife when he was done with that one. Funny. It felt sort of...familiar. Not the knives or anything, just—this. This sitting down and passing things, watching someone work at what they knew well.

Oh boy. I was getting *way* too familiar with my three psychos.

I passed him another knife anyway, and Zero said, narrowly eyeing the edge of it, "You said this was your house first. How long have you lived here?"

"A fair while," I said. "Dunno, since I was ten?"

"The estate agent said the people who lived here last were murdered."

"Yeah."

"Why weren't you?"

"I was in my room."

Zero's eye suddenly focused on me instead of the blade. "That's not the question I asked," he said. "How did you escape?"

"I was hidden," I said, more slowly. Maybe he hadn't understood again. "In my room. They didn't find me."

Those cold blue eyes went back to the knife. "They were your parents?"

"Yeah." Wait. I knew this line of questioning. He was leading up to find out how long I'd been living by myself, and—

"Did you know the dead man?"

Oh yeah. Zero was Behindkind and I was a human pet. There was no reason for him to care about my mental well-being. *And* I was a good source of information.

That would teach me to think he was concerned about me as anything other than an information source.

"Not much," I said gloomily. My coffee didn't taste so good anymore. "He was pretty weird, though."

"How was he weird?"

"Dunno. Never saw him during the day, only at night. And there were always odd smells and lights around the house at night. Actually, maybe it was the house that was weird. Don't reckon I'd wanna stay in it with those lights and smells, either, 'f'I was him."

"What sort of lights and smells?"

I puffed a breath of air out and got up to check on the steaks. "*Weird* ones, I said."

"Think carefully, Pet," said Athelas, looking up from his paper as if he hadn't been sneaking looks at the steak for the last few minutes. "Were they actual lights, or were they pretending to be lights? Were they real smells, or—"

Zero snicked a blade away. "It won't know what that means."

"Hang on," I said, startled to find that Athelas' nonsensical question had struck a chord. "They *weren't* real lights. The smells —yeah, don't reckon they were real, either. You know those phone covers that are clear plastic with little things painted on 'em? It was mostly kinda like that; there was no proper depth to them, so they couldn't have been real."

"What do you mean, there was no depth to them?" Zero's voice might have been a bit sharper, but his face was as emotionless as usual when I glanced up from the veggies I was distributing between four plates. Beside him, Athelas had the faintest of smiles on his lips.

"You couldn't see most of the lights from the side," I said. Now that I was thinking about it, it was ridiculous that I hadn't realised it before. "Even if there was a light bobbing around in one of the rooms when you looked at it from the front, it'd be dead dark when you looked at the window from the side. Same room, but no light. Same with the smells. If you weren't front on to the house, there wasn't any smell."

"A keep-away glamour," remarked Athelas. "Very useful if you're up to something."

"A spell, was it?" I asked, taking away the empty veggie steamer and dropping it in the sink. "Yeah, well, it worked. No one went too near to the place 'cos of it, but none of us called the cops, either. Wish I knew how to do that."

"What about the disappearances?" asked Zero, looking briefly at me.

Ha, I thought sourly. Not such a useless little human, was I?

"Were they real disappearances, or rumour?"

"Real ones," I told him. I snatched my fingers away from Jin Yeong's plate just in time to avoid losing a few, and glared at him. He raised a brow at me and started to eat. I gave Athelas his plate, and said to Zero, "Ask the cops. They were 'round a couple times because people were going missing. They didn't find anything, though; and some of the people turned up again."

Zero slipped the last of his throwing knives into their little belt, and slung it over one shoulder, cross-wise against his chest.

"You wearing that outside?" I asked dubiously. "People are gunna notice if you go around with knives on you."

"I doubt it," Zero said coolly, shrugging himself into his leather jacket and squaring up to the plate of steak and veg I put in front of him.

"I'm going with you somewhere that needs *knives*? Are you gunna give me one?"

"Pets don't carry weapons," Athelas said, in a reminding sort of a way. "If you're behind Zero, no one will hurt you."

"Oh yeah," I said, feeling more cheerful. "I forgot. All right then."

Zero said, "Eat your steak. We leave in ten minutes."

Outside, Zero's knives were harder to see. It wasn't only the summer dusk, either. The knives had been real knives inside the house; sharp at one end and leathery at the other. In the evening sunlight, they looked like tassels of a hybrid cowboy biker shirt, all leathery thongs and studs in a feature slash across the front.

I opened my mouth to ask him about it, but before I could, Zero put his hand over my mouth and shuffled me across the road to the murdered guy's house. Beside us, Jin Yeong strolled along with his hands in the pockets of his perfectly creased trousers, his fluffy jumper glinting in the last embers of the dying sun. He looked amused, and that was annoying.

Okay, so Zero didn't want me to ask questions. That was fine. I remembered the little tree on the rock that had pretended it was a tin of cat food, and I remembered a bit about trifle, too. Things like Zero's knife belt *almost* made sense.

Then it struck me that we were actually going into the house, and that made me want to ask why Zero needed knives if we were only going into part of a crime scene. I made an annoyed puff of air into Zero's palm—and okay, maybe there was some spit in there, too.

Zero took his hand away, grimacing, and wiped it on his trousers.

"This where we're going?"

"Yes," he said shortly. "Give me your hand."

"What?"

"Hand."

I held up my left hand warily.

"The other one."

I raised the other one, and he closed his left around it.

"What?" I protested, trying to pull away.

Zero didn't answer this time; he pulled me forward and shoved the decorative leather strap from his jacket into my hand. "Hold onto it," he said. "If you let go, I won't come back for you."

"Back?" I asked, highly gratified despite his assurance that he wouldn't come back for me if I let go. "Wait, is this the same as the grocery store?"

"Don't talk, either," said Zero. "Be quiet and stay behind me. Don't let go."

I stuck my tongue out at him when he turned away, then yelped as he started forward, pulling me with him. Zero ignored that; just kept walking. Well, I suppose you don't listen too much to a dog's yapping when it's on the leash, do you?

I stuck my tongue out at him again, and maybe he sensed it, because his head turned almost too quickly for me. I might have looked innocent when his eyes met mine, but probably not.

I blinked at him and said, "What?" again.

"Don't let go," he repeated, and tugged me forward again.

We walked through the doorway. Well; Zero walked. I sort of trotted behind him like a kid on a lead, and Jin Yeong definitely sauntered. It was a doorway, so it shouldn't have felt so cold. It shouldn't have been edged in moss and ferns, either. It should have been a door. *You* know; all straight wooden edges and maybe a few bits of paint scratched off it in places. But the more I looked at it as we stepped through, the less it looked like a door, and the more it looked like a cave mouth.

"Oi!" I said indignantly, as something dripped down the back of my neck. "Who did that!"

I looked up at the ceiling, but there wasn't a ceiling there. It wasn't even a ceiling that wasn't sure about itself, like my tin of cat food; it was definitely a cave roof, all wet and slimy and mossy.

"Oh, that's weird," I said, because I could still feel floorboards beneath my feet. When we were in the grocery store, it had mostly looked like grocery store with extra—here it was more like cave that had a bit of root in the human world.

Zero didn't give me a chance to look around. He kept moving, climbing what looked like a steep incline toward the side of the cave but felt like stairs beneath my feet, dragging me along. So we were going upstairs? Was that where the blood was?

When the floor evened out beneath us, Zero snapped his fingers, drawing out a thread of light from the air around us.

"Oh, cool!" I said, staring at it. "I want to do that!"

"*Mwohya!*" complained Jin Yeong incomprehensibly. "*Ddo!*"

"What's bitten him?" I asked Zero, jerking my chin at the vampire. Then I grinned, because it was funny—he was a vampire, so he was the one who should be doing the biting.

Jin Yeong glared at me. "*Noh! Mwoh hanun kkoya?*"

"Ay?" I leaned defensively into Zero's huge, leather-clad side. "What did I do?"

I wasn't sure whether Zero was faintly satisfied, or just more stoic than usual. To Jin Yeong, he said, "You can't smell the blood, can you?"

"*Ne.*" Jin Yeong scowled at me, and said something that sounded like an insult.

I made a face at him just in case.

"It's not the house blocking your sense of smell?"

"*Ne. Uri jib aniaeyo. Ku yoja daemunaeyo.*"

"All right," said Zero. "Can you do something about it, now that you know?"

Jin Yeong narrowed his eyes at me. "*Moh. Manyagae...*"

Hands still in his pockets, he bent at the waist and sniffed at my hair, then my shoulder.

"Oi!" I said again, pressing myself against again Zero in an effort to get away. "Get off!"

"Leave him be," Zero told me. "He needs to differentiate between the blank space and the proper way things should smell."

"'Zat what he's doing?" I asked, scowling at the vampire. "Gross! Don't breathe on my neck!"

Jin Yeong bared a couple of teeth a bit too close for comfort, and drew back. His eyes were glittering with triumph, and he said one deeply satisfied word with a bite to it.

"Good," said Zero. "If you've got the blood scent, lead us where it goes. Between, Behind, it doesn't matter. Follow it as far as you can."

This time Jin Yeong took the lead. I saw him ahead, alert and somehow sharper than usual, despite his soft jumper, and gripped the leather strap tightly as the world changed around us. He led us along a way that instead of *going* anywhere, *became* something. More cavey and less housey. More cold, anyway.

I couldn't feel floorboards beneath my feet anymore; now it was definitely cave floor. Smooth cave floor, but cave floor nevertheless.

"Trippy," I said, but neither Zero nor JinYeong answered. "Where's the light coming from?"

They didn't answer that, either. Of JinYeong, Zero asked, "Do you still have the blood scent?"

"*Ne*," answered JinYeong.

Yay for me. I knew a Korean word. That one was *yes*.

"Rude," I said to myself. It was funny. We were definitely in a cave; I could smell it and see it. There were no lights that I could see, and no windows. But it was light and bright, with soft yellow glowing off the mossy green and gliding in gentle pools of water here and there. So where was the light coming from?

Hoping to touch the moisture there and see if the light came from it, I reached out to the cave wall beside me.

Something small and hairy yelled *"Ahah!"* from inside a hole and tried to stab me with a needle. I yelled, and dragged myself back toward Zero by the leather strap, the buckle digging into my fingers.

"Flaming heck!"

"Don't play with the goblins," said Zero, hurrying me up with one hand on the nape of my neck. "They'll try to drug you and drag you into their warrens."

"Just try it!" I muttered back at the hairy face that was still sticking out of its hole in the wall, snarling at me. "I'll bring some petrol up here and see how you like a flamin' bath!"

It jeered and shook the needle at me as Zero dragged me along in his wake. The sharp feeling of mingled annoyance and fear it had prompted didn't fade so quickly; I was jumpy and inclined to stick closer to Zero after that.

The further we went, the colder it got. I asked a question or two, but Zero didn't answer them, and Jin Yeong never stopped on the scent. I probably should have been more scared, but there was Zero's very broad back in front of me, and even though we were in a cave that had been a house, I still felt as though we might be in a house.

In the grocery store, everything had looked almost right—except for the four-armed blokes, of course—and the oddness was in the smallest details. Here everything looked wrong, but somehow still felt like a house.

"So that's why you call it Between," I said to myself. I almost missed Athelas. He might be as superior as Zero and Jin Yeong, but at least he explained things every now and then.

I wondered whether the little dryad-on-a-rock had come from a place like this, and I couldn't help looking more closely at the cave walls. Those were *pictures* on the cave walls, weren't they? Hallway pictures.

"Hey!" I said. "Someone's grandad is up on the wall here!"

One of the goblins was using it for a door, too.

"I don't think they'd like that," I pointed out. "Goblins using their granDad's photo as a door.

Zero only glanced back at me briefly. "It *is* a door," he said.

"I s'pose someone hung their picture on a door," I muttered to myself. What, so we were *Between*—wherever that was—and something that should have been a picture was a door? Or was it a door that should have been a picture? I wasn't sure. It looked like a door. Only it looked like a picture, too.

It was the sort of thing that made you wonder what else was something that it shouldn't be. Or if anything else was trying to be something it wasn't.

No, that wasn't right. This was nuts.

I tried to grab some other stuff along the way. I mean,

wouldn't you? I wanted to know if it was the stuff it pretended to be, or if it was—hang on. I'm confused again.

The cave was littered with stuff anyway. I stayed away from the walls, too scared of getting on the wrong end of a needle from another goblin to risk it, and scanned the floor instead. It was mostly rocks and stuff, but there were pillows here and there, and stuff like watches and hairbands. They didn't belong in the cave, and they looked like they weren't too sure about *being* watches and hairbands and pillows, either.

I made a grab for a necklace that was spilling over the edge of a glowy, wet, tableaued spar nearby, stretching to the very tips of my fingers to reach it. My fingers closed around the necklace, flipping it up and over the craggy edges of the spar and into my palm in a cool, slithery heap. Got it! I glanced down at it, neglecting to watch my feet, and stumbled over a serration in the ground for my pains.

It was just a necklace.

I made a small sound of disappointment and Zero looked back at me sharply. As I caught his eye, guiltily, something cut my finger open.

"Ow!"

The necklace flew through the softly glowing light and hit the wall opposite it, slithering to a heap on the cave floor, where it was obvious that it was not a necklace, but a small snake. A snake that looked like a necklace; its tail a poniard, glittering with a jewel of my blood.

Zero lunged forward and seized it by the neck, and it wriggled once in his big hands before becoming deathly still. I don't know if he broke its neck or just convinced it that it was very much wiser to be a necklace from now on, but when he threw it at me, it was a necklace again.

I caught it reflexively to stop it hitting me in the face, and shoved it into one of my pockets. The cut on my finger was already welling with blood.

"Ow!" I said again, sadly.

Jin Yeong's eyes brightened, and he took a step toward me, one hand reaching for my wrist. "*Mashiketda!*"

"Get off!" I protested, before he had a chance to take another step toward me. I stuffed my forefinger in my mouth and said around it, "I'll do it myself!"

Lucky I was already half behind Zero, and lucky he'd taken a step forward at the same time as Jin Yeong. I mumbled up at him, "Thought you said he couldn't smell me properly."

"He couldn't," Zero said, brushing past Jin Yeong to continue walking. "But blood is blood. Keep your finger in your mouth until it stops bleeding."

"I flamin' will!" I said, stumbling against Zero in my efforts to both walk and keep an eye on Jin Yeong.

Zero grabbed me around the neck again to straighten me, sweeping my feet away from the ground for an uncomfortable moment. He said over his shoulder, "Jin Yeong, the scent!"

The vampire swept ahead again, his liquid eyes glittering at me too close for comfort in passing. He threw a word or two at Zero, who only said, "As close as you can get without crossing, for now."

"Where are we crossing?" I asked. I didn't think he'd really answer, but he did.

"You're not. Don't touch anything else that you shouldn't."

"What if it's something I should touch?" I argued. "How do I know what's good to touch and what's not good to touch? Yeah, and that thing—is it a necklace or a snake? Because I don't think necklaces should change into snakes just 'cos they want to, and what if it changes into a snake in my pocket?"

"It won't," Zero said briefly. "Mind your step."

Good thing I *was* minding my step, because right as he said it, the hallway or passageway or whatever it was decided that it was definitely going to be a cave passageway, and opened out into a real cave.

It wasn't particularly big, but it smelled fresh and foresty. Beneath my feet were now flagstones of a wide, short courtyard, edged with moss and gleaming with the same glowy moisture as the rest of the cave. They might once have been white with blue veins, but they were now closer to grey with veins of green, merging seamlessly with the greenery around the cave walls. There was less moss to these walls, and more ferns springing delicately from the shadows to fall in a froth of fragrant green.

Across the courtyard was a single, long step that ran the length of the courtyard, and a wooden platform above that. Ferns trailed down toward it from the roof of the cave, almost obscuring the wall and windows that were there, but I saw the glitter of glass, and a shadow of movement within.

There was a *house* in this house that thought it was a cave. It, too, ran the length of the courtyard, and mingling with the moss and ferns were more things that must have originally come from, or maybe still existed in, the house across the road. It took me a while to realise that the wooden frames to the windowed doors I could see were slightly uneven, and looked like they were growing right around the glass and into the ceiling.

"Where's this?" I asked, looking around me. I didn't realise I was smiling until I saw my face reflected in the glass of the windows across from me; a plain, skinny thing in a place that should have been all beautiful. "Why is it here?"

"This is Between," said Zero. "But when I climb that stair and go through the door, it'll be Behind. Stay out here in the courtyard."

"Okay," I said. I was sorry not to see more of the beautiful interior that was glittering at me through those living wooden doors, but it smelled nice out here, even if it was too cold. That cold now felt like it was starting to seep into my bones, so hopefully Zero wasn't going to be long.

"You stay here, too, Jin Yeong," Zero said.

Jin Yeong responded indignantly, which made me grin.

Vampires aren't much above pets, then, are they?

He caught me grinning and narrowed his eyes at me, which made my grin fade pretty quickly.

I mean, he's annoying, but I haven't got a death wish, and Zero was already stepping up onto the living wooden platform. I feel much safer when he's between me and Jin Yeong.

I sat down on the step and shivered as the cool stone met my jean-clad rear. Why was it so flamin' cold? If it was nearly Christmas in Australia, shouldn't Between be warm, too? I peered over my shoulder to see if Zero was just stopping for a minute, or likely to take a while.

He greeted the fae or whatever it was that met him at the door, their voices rumbling together, and sat down in the chair the other offered him.

Flamin' fantastic. He was gunna stay for a while.

I puffed out a sad breath of air and hunched my shoulders, propping my chin on my palms and my elbows on my knees. It's not like I'd actually done anything while we'd been here, so why had he brought me along?

Probably one of those Behindkind Fae things that a mere human wouldn't understand.

Jin Yeong prowled the courtyard in an angry sort of a way, his stride long and quiet, and I shivered a bit; mostly with cold, but partly because my finger still hurt. I turned slightly so I could keep an eye on Zero as well as Jin Yeong, and saw him speaking with another two blokes.

It definitely didn't look like he was in any hurry to leave. He didn't so much as glance at me, shivering out on the step while he was warm and comfortable on his chair inside. I glanced back across at Jin Yeong but he wasn't shivering, even with his light suit pants and jumper.

Stupid vampire. They probably don't feel cold.

I sniffed against the back of my hand and hoped my nose was just cold, not wet. Maybe if I leaned back I'd be able to hear what they were saying in there. It wasn't like they had the long glass doors closed, after all. If I was gunna be cold, at least I could hear what they were talking about.

I leant back a bit, arching my back in a sudden shiver when the small of my back hit the wooden platform, and something heavy dropped over me, all fleecy on the inside and warm with someone else's body heat.

I squeaked and fell over sideways. By the time I'd scrambled out from under the fleece and leather jacket enough to be able to see, Zero was sitting down inside again. He didn't look at me this time either, but this time I knew he saw me, so I smiled and tucked my arms into the jacket.

I'd have to be careful not to lean back while trying to hear, or he'd notice.

Jin Yeong, on the other side of the courtyard, scowled at me.

What was he cranky about *now*? I made a face at him and he turned sharply on the ball of his foot, pacing back towards me with the stride of a hunter.

Oops.

"Don't sit next to me," I hissed, but he dropped down next to me anyway, long legs stretched out elegantly in front of him.

He said something to me that I couldn't understand, leaning too close again.

"Don't sniff my hair!" I told him, in an indignant whisper. "It's weird and gross! What's wrong with you?"

Jin Yeong tapped his nose.

"Yeah, it's not your nose that's flamin' wrong," I said. "It's your personality."

One of his brows went up briefly, but Jin Yeong didn't appear to be offended. I wondered if he'd understood; it'd be a pity to waste a good insult. Casually, he pinched the cuff of Zero's jacket, lifting my hand, and sniffed my wrist for good measure.

"Now you're just messing with me," I said.

He grinned.

What a mongrel. I pulled my arm away and he let me go, leaning back on the palms of his hands with his nose in the air, eyes closed. There was still a faint smile on his face, but I wasn't sure if that was because he enjoyed needling me, or if it was because he seemed to be able to smell again.

"Weirdo," I muttered, and got up. There was enough court-yard to keep us far enough away for comfort, so I didn't see why I had to sit right next to him.

There was enough to see around the courtyard, too; and now that I was warm and happy in Zero's massive jacket, I was content to wander instead of listen—especially if I had to sit next to JinYeong in order to listen. So I wandered and looked, hunching my shoulders to keep my ears warm in the collar of Zero's jacket, my hands stuffed in his pockets.

As I drifted around the courtyard, I saw that even here in the courtyard, there were some elements of the house across the road, even if it was mostly cave and courtyard this far in. The walls were covered with ferns and moss, but between the fresh-scented greenery, in the gaps, there were still pictures hanging on the walls.

And over toward the wall that met with the wooden platform, in a soft green corner with a small waterfall, there were even a couple of umbrellas.

Pretty flamin' typical of the bloke across the road, if you ask me. Who keeps their umbrellas upstairs? I mean, who keeps 'em halfway between what's essentially fairyland and the human world too, I suppose; but at least it was wet here. They could come in useful.

There was even a hall stand to keep the umbrellas in, all over-grown with vines and flowers, with the handles poking out of the greenery. I would have thought they'd been there for a long time if the yellow umbrella hadn't been delicately filigreed with tender vine shoots and newly budding flowers. It caught my eye by the brightness of the tatty yellow fabric showing between the green.

I narrowed my eyes at the hall stand and shuffled forward until the toes of my boots were touching the first step, obeying Zero in the letter if not the spirit, of the law. Everything else there was pretty well covered in old growth, dark green and strong. It was only on the yellow one that the vines looked new.

Was it another Between thing? Or was this umbrella, like so many of the other things around here, not exactly what it was pretending to be?

I reached for it, careful to keep my toes right up against the step and no further, and my fingers touched the plastic yellow handle.

Yeah. That wasn't a plastic handle.

My fingers slid around the grip—did it feel like a sword grip? —and I briefly smelled leather. The umbrella twitched a couple times, like it was trying to decide whether it was an umbrella or a sword, and for a second I saw a sword.

"Yikes!" I said, and nearly fell over.

Something snagged the back of Zero's jacket and hiked me backward in an undignified, arm-flapping bundle, the jacket hoisting me by the armpits.

"Oi!"

Jin Yeong twitched me around to face him, and released the back of Zero's jacket. He grabbed me by the wrist instead, and flapped my own hand in front of my face.

"*Manjiji ma,*" he said.

What, like *don't touch*? Hang on, he said that to the boss today —was he telling the boss not to touch the pet?

I tugged indignantly at my wrist and said, "*Manjiji MA!*" back up at him.

Jin Yeong's eyebrows went up. He dropped my wrist with a fastidious wince, and hooked one finger under the collar of Zero's jacket instead, pulling me back to the centre of the step. When we were there, he pushed down on the top of my head to make me sit down, and dropped back down next to me.

Yeah. He was messing with me now.

Just wait, I thought darkly to myself. He might be a vampire, but my local library had the internet. The internet knows everything, and I was betting there would be something in there about dealing with vampires, too.

A slight sound tickled my eardrums; was that Zero's voice I could hear again?

JinYeong stopped my involuntary turn of the head by grabbing one of my ears, and shook his own head slightly.

Oh. So *he* wanted to listen, too; but he couldn't if he had to stop me getting into trouble or if Zero found out we were listening.

I winked at him and twitched my ear away, wiping it on my shoulder by reflex.

JinYeong looked coldly at me, and then away again.

Looking into the middle distance like a flamin' model.

I hugged my knees instead, without leaning too far forward, and heard Zero say, "It wasn't a normal kind of glamour."

"What does that have to do with the Waystation?"

"Nothing, if the owner of the house wasn't a human. And if he hadn't been murdered. And if there wasn't a trail of human blood leading all the way to this Waystation."

There was a moment of pause. When the other fae spoke, his voice was shocked. "He's *dead?*"

That was a voice blank with surprise. I flicked a look up at JinYeong and saw that he looked disappointed. He knew what I knew—this fae hadn't murdered anyone.

Well, he hadn't murdered the bloke across the road, anyway.

"Murdered," Zero repeated.

"Who would be stupid enough to murder—" the fae cut himself off. "Who did it?"

"Someone I've been looking for. Someone who likes killing a human and then four Behindkind in a row."

"*That* one? But why would he—he wouldn't..."

"Why wouldn't he?" asked Zero, his voice as expressionless as ever. "What makes this human any different from the others?"

I sneaked a peek over my shoulder and saw the fae bite his lips worriedly. "I don't know. I've got to go. You can't stay here, either."

"I have more questions."

"Can't answer 'em; it's a waystation, not a police station."

I kinda expected Zero to bash him one. *I* wanted to bash him one. I mean, it was obvious he wasn't telling the truth—or at least that he knew something he wasn't saying.

To my surprise—and, by the look of it, Jin Yeong's disappointment—Zero didn't either throw blows or put a hand to any of his weaponry.

"*Mwohya?*" I heard Jin Yeong complain, but I was too busy watching Zero.

That must have annoyed the vampire, because he grabbed my ear and twitched my head away again.

"*Haji ma,*" he said.

I would have stuck out my tongue at him, but I heard Zero get up and I didn't want him to see me being that childish. I was mature and level-headed; the perfect pet. The sort of pet who should be kept indefinitely and eventually allowed to rent the house instead of him, preferably.

I got up, leather squeaking, and Jin Yeong rose lithely beside me. Did one of Zero's brows go up at the sight of us waiting together for him?

I wasn't completely sure, but the only thing he said was, "Take it off," flicking a finger at his jacket.

I took it off regretfully, shivering reflexively as the cool air hit my warmed arms, and automatically grabbed Zero's leather strap again.

"Don't let go," Zero said once again, and this time he led the way.

I expected something...I dunno, *more*. But all we did was go home again, back through the cavey house, or the housey cave, until we were descending stairs that looked like stairs again. The house smelled like a real house again, too.

Athelas was waiting for us when we got through the door at home, though I'm pretty sure he wouldn't have admitted it. He had his legs elegantly crossed, as usual, and was pretending to read a book in a careless sort of way.

If he'd *really* been reading it, he would have been in his favourite chair in the living room opposite. They might be three psychos, but in some ways, they're very predictable psychos.

I don't know if Athelas can smell blood as well, but his head came up sharply as I entered the kitchen, his brow suddenly creased.

"What happened to the pet? Pet?"

"*An mogosso*," said Jin Yeong, at once.

"I did gather that you hadn't tried to drain the pet, since I see her standing and alive." Athelas' voice sounded impatient.

He really doesn't like it when I don't answer questions he asks.

"It's a tiny cut," I said. I waved my fingers at him. "Doesn't even hurt anymore."

"Did it bleed Between?"

"I staunched the flow," said Zero.

"He means he strangled the snake," I told Athelas. "Want a cuppa?"

"Thank you, yes. Dear me, a snake?"

"Yeah." I dug the necklace out of my pocket and tossed it on the table.

It made a small tinkle of metal against wood, and slid to a stop halfway across the table from Athelas, who leaned forward to touch it with one long, slender finger and said thoughtfully, "Dear me! He certainly did. Why did you bring it home?"

"He threw it at me and I put it in my pocket," I said, but I didn't think Athelas was talking to me. He was looking at Zero.

Flamin' typical. I think they like being mysterious for the fun of it. So long as everyone *knows* they're being mysterious.

Yeah, my eyes *are* rolling. What about it?

"Best not to leave that sort of thing Between," Zero said shortly, as I poured tea for Athelas. "Coffee for me, Pet."

"I take it that JinYeong managed to catch the scent, this time?"

Zero nodded, shrugging off his jacket. Methodically, he began to remove the weapons I'd seen him strap on earlier.

"How, if one may ask?"

JinYeong jerked his chin at me and made a remark that sounded disparaging.

"Oi!" I complained. "I'm making coffee for you! You should be more polite."

"*Naega wae?*" demanded JinYeong.

"'Cos I'm making your coffee," I said. I bashed the tea strainer against the side of the bin vigorously to get rid of the clinging tea-leaves, and pointed at him with it. "And it's pretty dumb to be rude to the person who's making your coffee. Dunno what could fall in there."

Athelas slid an amused look in our direction, but when he'd taken his cup of tea from me, he asked Zero, "What did you discover of importance?"

"There is certainly a glamour on the house."

"We suspected as much. What, then?"

"I think there a glamour on the dead human, too."

Athelas' hand, teacup poised to drink, paused momentarily. "On the human? Why?"

"I'm not entirely certain," Zero said slowly. "But I think a trip to the morgue is in order."

"*Ne,*" agreed JinYeong. He picked up his coffee from the edge of the kitchen counter where I'd pushed it, eyeing me coldly, and took himself off to the living room. Over his shoulder, he called, "*Ingam aniya.*"

"The victim wasn't human?" Athelas looked as surprised as I'd ever seen him, those soft dove eyes wide and pale and startled above the rim of the teacup. He stood swiftly, following Jin Yeong into the next room, and said, "That can't be so. The one thing we know about the killer is that he *always* kills humans as the main target. Always."

"Then this wasn't the main kill," said Zero, following them both. Unlike Jin Yeong, who had thrown himself elegantly down on one of the sofas, and Athelas, who despite his perturbation had sat down in his favourite leather chair, crossing one leg over the other, he propped himself against one of the brick support pillars, one ankle crossed over the other.

"It has to be!" protested Athelas. "It was hanging in front of the house—it was the first body we found. It was the only body we found here!"

"Then something has changed," said Zero. "I'm certain the real owner of that building hasn't been seen for several months at least. Behindkind took over the house some years ago, I would say."

I couldn't really tell if he was as perturbed as Athelas or not; he's always so expressionless that you can't know.

"Whoever the murdered person was, he was in the field by himself," he said. "They didn't know about the murder at the waystation; they thought I'd come to find the sword."

Jin Yeong made that annoying hiss again, and said something that contained the word *petteu*.

"Oi!" I said, from the stairs. "It's rude to talk about people behind their backs!"

He puffed out another small, dismissive breath and turned his nose back to the ceiling.

I automatically looked at Athelas, who smiled into his tea despite the line that still creased his brow. "He says if the sword had been there you probably would have tried to touch that, too."

"Hang on," I said. "D'you blokes mean that sword that was pretending to be an umbrella?"

"What?" Zero said sharply.

Jin Yeong's sharp chin twitched toward me. "*Mwoh?*"

"Dear me!" said Athelas, replacing his teacup very carefully in the saucer. He set it down on the coffee table beside him and added, "You certainly have a way of drawing attention to yourself, Pet. You saw a sword while you were Between?"

"It was in the courtyard," I said, nodding. I looked from Zero to Jin Yeong. "Didn't you see it? It was yellow. Is it important?"

Jin Yeong, his voice disgusted, demanded, "*Ku akka ko?*"

"I don't speak Korean!"

"He must have seen you touching it or playing with it earlier," Athelas said. "He's annoyed with himself for not recognising it."

"Thought you blokes knew all about this stuff," I said. "Thought you were the ones who could see stuff that isn't what it's pretending to be."

"In general, yes," said Athelas, his light eyes steady with warning. Gently, he added, "Perhaps you should rethink your tone, Pet."

"Sorry," I said, suppressing a yawn. I was so tired that I was letting myself get careless. I knew that, but I was still tired enough to plop down on the sofa beside Jin Yeong, taking up the other cushion. None of the other unoccupied chairs were comfortable enough to curl up on—Jin Yeong knew how to pick the comfiest spot in the room. "But there really was a sword that looked like an umbrella, so if that's the one you're after, I know where it is."

"Pet," Zero said, "how did you see the sword?"

I leaned my head against the sofa arm. "Dunno. There was a lot of stuff there from the house, so I was touching things to see what they really were, and the umbrella was a sword."

"Is it not more important to know why *you* didn't see the

sword?" enquired Athelas. "I hate to encourage our Pet in her cheekiness, but she has a point."

"High level glamour," said Zero, shrugging. "Directed at fae. We've been looking for that sword for years and never seen it; I thought the Family still had it, and it wouldn't have occurred to me that it was at the Waystation if the fae there hadn't thought I was there for it. I'm more interested in knowing how the pet saw it."

"You blokes said humans don't go Between by themselves, or that your Behindkind people don't take humans with 'em," I said, yawning. We hadn't gone further than the house across the road, but I was *dead* tired. "They wouldn't try to stop humans from seeing it because there's no humans *to* see it."

Athelas smiled into his tea once again. "I think Zero's perturbation is more a matter of how a human can see *any*thing Between."

"Oh yeah," I said, yawning again; this time enormously. "'Cos Between's about how you see stuff and if you can see stuff you can make big trouble by affecting stuff, or something."

"Humans can't affect Between," said Zero. "Full blood humans, anyway."

"Oh." I didn't really care. I just wanted to sleep. Everyone had their tea or coffee, and even if the coffee wasn't keeping me awake, it didn't look like any of the three psychos were having trouble staying awake. My duties as pet were done for the night and there was a kind of warmth to the room that made me content in my sleepiness. "I'm gunna go to bed now," I said, but my head didn't want to lift from the sofa arm.

"Not as yet, I think, Pet," said Athelas. "We may have further questions."

"It's not likely," Zero said dampeningly. "If it doesn't have enough knowledge to tell us why it can see something Between, it certainly doesn't have enough knowledge to answer any other questions we might have."

"She might perhaps know more than we think," Athelas replied, as I pushed Jin Yeong's feet onto his own cushion and curled up on mine.

Jin Yeong lifted his head to look quizzically at me, but put his head back down without troubling me and said something that burbled against my half-asleep ears.

I didn't bother trying to interrupt again. They were still talking when I fell asleep.

CHAPTER SEVEN

I woke late, gasping, from a dream that had teeth and claws and a lust for blood.

Funny, that. I woke up to the same thing; Jin Yeong opposite me on the sofa, his eyes dark and liquid again.

"Can't someone get the vampire something to eat?" I muttered, but I don't think any of them heard me.

Maybe they did. Maybe they were ignoring me; they went on talking as if I hadn't spoken.

I wondered how long they'd been talking like this; they weren't taking trouble to lower their voices although I'd been sleeping. It looked as though they were in the last stages of planning something; they were all perfectly relaxed, but still fully dressed. Had they been to bed at all? Probably not; it looked like Zero was still in the same clothes from last night, and even Athelas had only changed his cardigan for a houndstooth jacket.

I sat up and yawned, then pedalled my legs until I could hoist myself up, and trotted up to the kitchen to make tea. A quick look at the kitchen clock said it was already six thirty, so I wouldn't have time to make or eat breakfast. My psychos would have to do without.

I threw a look at them as I passed the cased doorway between rooms, wondering what they had planned for the day. They probably wouldn't tell me, so I didn't ask. I dashed around the kitchen making tea and coffee instead, feeling regretful about life in general and today in particular. It would be interesting to see exactly how bad the boss was going to be when I got to work, after his bath of devilled sausages.

Yeah. *Interesting.*

I put a pot of tea out, and one of coffee, then trudged down the hall to get my backpack.

Zero's voice stopped me, suddenly and impossibly close behind me. "Where are you going?"

"To work," I said, when I'd recovered from my miniature heart attack. I puffed out a breath and turned around properly. "I start at seven every morning."

"No," he said.

"What? But if I don't go, he'll—"

"You can't go to work," he said. "Not anymore; not while we're here. For now you're our pet."

Jin Yeong said something from far too close behind me, making me jump, and smirked as he fetched the milk from the fridge.

"It appears," said Athelas, from the other room, with a faint undercurrent of amusement to his voice, "that they don't want you to slip up and mention anything while you're at work. I feel that it should be said I advocated for trusting you."

I looked up at Zero. "You mean you don't want me talking to anyone or calling the police."

"Yes," said Zero.

"What about money?"

"What about it?"

"I have to earn money if I want to eat."

Was Zero's face as emotionless as usual, or was that the blankness of confusion? Whichever one it was, he didn't answer.

"I don't think you've quite understood your function as pet," said Athelas' voice, carryingly. They had pretty good hearing, these fae. That settled it; they *had* been ignoring me before. "You're fed, watered, and looked after. There's no need for you to earn money. All you need to do is make this place liveable for us and you'll be looked after."

"What about my house?"

"It's not your house," Zero said. "It's mine."

"It's *not*!" I retorted. "It's my house! It's always been my house! And if I can't earn money, I can't save up to buy it when I'm old enough!"

"I've already bought it."

"You—you—" I stared at him, my eyes prickling with tears of rage. "You can't! You weren't supposed to—I was supposed to be able to buy it!"

Those blue eyes gazed at me curiously. "We only need it until we finish our investigation here. You can have it after that."

I caught my breath on a small, angry sob, and saw Athelas smiling into his hand. "Are you blokes having a joke at me?"

Zero blinked. "No. I'll sign it over to you when we finish our investigation. I don't need another house. It was simply convenient."

"You'll—you'll *just sign it over to me?*" I was having trouble breathing now.

"When we finish our investigation. But only if you don't work anywhere else."

"Sorta like payment for being your pet?"

"No," Zero said. "I don't pay pets. Think of it as food and a roof over your head."

"Yes," I said. "*Yes.* I'll do it. No more work. Caput. You promise?"

Zero gave the slightest of nods. "I swear it. On that day I finish my investigation, I'll sign over the house to you in perpetuity. Safe from Behindkind and humans, both."

He looked at me expectantly, and I said, hesitantly, "I won't...*work*, yeah? I won't open my mouth too much around people, either, and I'll make you the best flamin' food you've had"

That must have been what he wanted, because he nodded once more, and took his coffee back into the living room with a full packet of biscuits. Around his leather shoulder I saw Athelas, still smiling, but this time I didn't care.

I hugged my backpack to my chest, dizzy with hope and delight. I was going to have my house.

I was gunna have my house!

Athelas called out, "How would you like to take an outing again today, Pet?"

"So long as I'm on the leash," I called back. I probably shouldn't be cheeky with them, but sometimes it's *really* hard to resist, and I was feeling fine and prancy all of a sudden. My house. If I helped them with this thing, I'd own my house at the end of it. "Wouldn't wanna get lost."

"Stay behind me," Zero said, sipping coffee very loudly. "You'll be safe."

I put my backpack back on the hallstand and skipped down into the living room with the rest of the tea and coffee on a tray. "'S'it matter if I wear the same clothes?" I asked them.

"I don't see why not," Athelas said. "If you've no concern about personal cleanliness, I'm sure there's nothing else to consider."

I wanted to point out that he'd only changed his socks and cardigan since last night, but I'd already been sarcastic once this morning, and I didn't want to chance it.

Instead, I said, "Don't want the rest of my stuff to get mucky if it doesn't have to. These are my work clothes, so they might as well get grubby."

"Do you not have enough clothes, Pet?" asked Athelas.

"What?" Surprised, I stared at him. "I mean, I don't have that many, but I've got enough if I don't go ruining 'em."

"Very well," said Athelas, and that seemed to be that.

"Get breakfast in half an hour, Pet," Zero said. "Something light. We might have to run."

"Run, or fight?" I asked them, but neither Zero nor Athelas answered me, and Jin Yeong only gave a derisive half-smile in the direction of the ceiling.

Probably both, then, I decided, and went away to make breakfast.

"I'M NOT ENTIRELY CERTAIN IT WAS THE BEST IDEA TO dismantle that glamour," said Athelas, some time later.

He hadn't said so earlier, but his lips had pressed together when Zero said he was going to do it. I didn't really know what they were talking about, because I couldn't see what they were doing, but the whole place across the road had felt a bit friendlier when Zero was done with what he was doing.

I wasn't sure if Athelas was afraid that more people would wander into the house now that it wasn't so off-putting, or if he was worried it would warn off the people we were going to see, like some sort of long-distance burglar alarm.

Now, I asked, "Can they tell if you undo their spell?"

"Glamour," Zero corrected me. "It's not exactly a spell; it's a clever use of Between. It changes the way people see things."

"Yeah, okay," I said. "Can they tell if you undo their glamour?"

"Exactly my point," Athelas said. "I really don't see that we should give them more warning than necessary."

"They already know we're aware of the glamour," said Zero, without pausing his stride. I was already panting. "I'd like it best if they think we're here about a dead human—or fae—not the sword."

"I see," said Athelas. He didn't look satisfied, but it looked as though he understood. "Pet, do try not to flick moss on my shoes."

"Sorry," I mumbled, neglecting to pay attention to where I was going and stumbling over a rock. I looked up and said in surprise, "Oi!"

The courtyard was already in front of us, only a few metres away. The day Jin Yeong led us there, following a trace of human blood, it had taken at least twenty minutes. "How'd we get here so quickly?"

"There are longer ways into Between, and there are shorter ways," Athelas said. "Those unused to Between tend to make heavier work of it. We are very well used to it."

"Don't let go of that strap, Pet," Zero said to me. "Long or short, if you get caught Behind, we won't be back for you."

"Got it," I said, renewing my hold on the single piece of leather that stood between me and certain—actually, certain what? "What happens if I get stuck here, anyway?"

"I suppose that depends upon who finds you, or what you wander into," Athelas said. He didn't sound particularly concerned; his voice was as lightly amused as usual.

I wondered if it really did amuse him to think of me wandering Between until I was attacked by a group of goblins or stumbled Behind to be snatched up by the first Behindkind that found me. Yeah, it probably did. It was easy to forget that the outwardly gentle and soft Athelas was just as icily unknowable as Zero on the inside.

"Stop being nice to me," I told him, as my foot found the relative safety of the courtyard flagstones. "It's confusing."

His eyes glowed with laughter, but I had no way of knowing how kindly it was toward me. "Shall I? Will you continue to give me tea if I do?"

"S'pose so," I said. "It doesn't take much longer than just making coffee, anyway."

He gave me information, at least. It wasn't like I was going to get anything sensible out of Jin Yeong if I asked questions, and Zero only answered the questions he wanted to answer.

"There appears to be no one home," Athelas said, looking around the courtyard. He was still smiling, but his eyes were sharp and incisive now.

Zero shook me free and said, "Go find the sword, Pet. JinYeong, with me. Athelas—"

"I'll watch the tunnel," Athelas said, his voice amused. "It's not been so long since we worked together, after all! I'll keep an eye on the pet."

"Thanks," I said, and wandered over toward the bit of the step where I'd seen that yellow umbrella last night.

Zero and JinYeong strode past me and onto the wooden platform, their steps long and fluid. They looked like...I dunno; like they were ready to fight? I wasn't sure what they were *going* to fight—the courtyard was empty, and there wasn't a sound from the beautiful structure in front of me—but at least they were ready?

I trailed along the step, peering into the dark green shadows around the glassy doors. The glass was really mirror-like today. I thought I remembered being able to see right into the room, but today, all it showed was a faint reflection of me and Athelas wandering languidly along the edge of the flagstones in the background.

"Weird," I said, scowling at it.

I kept walking, and saw a warmth of tattered yellow to my left.

"Gotcha!" I said happily to the umbrella. "Thought you could hide from me? Well, you can't!"

I turned around to tell Athelas I'd found the umbrella, or sword, or whatever it was, but he passed me at a quick, smooth lope, clearing the step to the platform without touching it.

"A moment, Pet," he said mildly. He moved soundlessly, gently, out of sight of the long glass windows, and glanced carefully through the closest of them.

I looked back at the umbrella. Should I grab it? Was Athelas telling me he would be back soon, or telling me to wait before I picked it up?

"Dear me," he said. "An ambush!"

"What?" I asked blankly, turning back to an empty wooden platform.

Hang on, where was Athelas? He'd *just* spoken to me!

"Ah heck!" I said. What was there in this place that could ambush people like Zero and JinYeong so silently, or make someone like Athelas disappear?

I should go home.

If I could go home.

Only there was a sword here, even if it looked like an umbrella, and Zero didn't have his sword today, just his knives. Maybe if I could get the sword to him—

"I'm mad," I said. "Flamin' mad."

I reached for the umbrella, bright and yellow in the green shadows, and said to it, "It'd be really helpful if you were a sword, 'cos I don't have much use for an umbrella in here."

Maybe it was plastic I touched first, but when my fingers slid all the way around the handle I could feel the hardness of folded leather again.

"Thanks," I said, and pulled the sword right out of the shadows until it gleamed, all silvery moonlight, in the beautiful courtyard around me.

Flaming *heck*, it was heavy!

I gave a bit of a grunt and let the point down more carelessly than I'd meant to. It made a little metallic sound that shouldn't have sounded as loud as it did in the soft shadows of the court-yard, and left a mark in the flagstone.

I said, "Whoops!" and covered it up with a piece of moss. No one needed to know I'd been the one who did it.

There was no way I was going to be able to *carry* this thing with its point foremost, let alone carry it into a fight.

I looked down at the point of the sword, and up again at the silent, empty windows that should have showed the inside of the room but only mirrored my own face and the courtyard back at me.

Oh well. I'd have to settle for looking menacing.

And if that didn't work, there was always my old fall-back of stark raving troppo.

I hefted the point of the sword again, my arms shaking a bit, and let the flat of it settle against my shoulder with considerably more attention to where the point was than I had shown earlier. It didn't take a chunk out of my shoulder, and I was satisfied with that.

If my menacing look didn't work, and the stark raving troppo went wrong, at least I could get the sword to Zero. He'd been pretty keen to have it, and I knew he could use it. He had to stay alive to sign over the house to me.

I put my foot on the long step, wary and light. Athelas had said *ambush*, I was certain. In this place where things weren't what they pretended to be, probably words could be things they didn't sound like, too, but I was still pretty sure that's what he'd said.

Funny, though.

I lifted the other foot and set it on the wooden platform, all my weight resting on the lower foot that was planted firmly on the marble step.

I should have been able to hear it if it was an actual ambush. Even if I couldn't see it.

I pushed up on my back foot, the balance of weight switching to my front foot; and like a switch, the sound came on.

Screaming. Howling.

An unearthly wail that started as a scream and carved the air with its serrated edge until it died in a sickening bubbling.

"Your side, Athelas!" roared Zero's voice, as my eyes tried to make sense of what I was seeing. "Jin Yeong, the ghouls!"

Ah heck. I wished I hadn't stepped up.

If the windowed doors had been mirror-like one footstep earlier, here they were horribly clear.

A melee of blood and faces and arms—*so many arms*—cut through the pale silk and wood interior. Something screamed again, in a continuous, rage-filled screech that cut through all the other sounds, but it was a sound of hunger and not of pain. A low snarl threaded around and under it, and I recognised Jin Yeong's voice with a feeling of something that could have been relief.

He was alive. If he was alive, Zero must be alive; and if Zero was alive, maybe we would all get out of this alive.

Why the flaming heck had I stepped up into this madness? Why was I still rising from the lower step to the wooden platform, with crimson in my sight and the sound of savage hunger in my ears?

I almost dropped back down without finishing the step, but the sword weighed heavily on my shoulder, pitching me forward, and there was a lack of substance beneath my back foot where there should have been a marble step. I regained my balance with the hollow thud of foot against wooden platform sounding in my ears.

In my peripheral I could see that there was no courtyard behind me, so I didn't even try to look back. If I had been, by stages, in the house and then between the house and some other place, here I was certainly in the Other Place. Was this Behind?

Wherever it was, there was no way back Between for me.

"Ah heck," I said, and went for the glass door.

I opened those doors to a cacophony of battle that reeled and shrieked pandemonium all the way to the walls and ceiling. Four-armed men fought in a whirlwind of arms and knives, dividing a bloody Jin Yeong from Zero, and I could only see the tattered edges of Athelas' houndstooth jacket.

Why was there always a battle going on when they left the house together?

And why did it look like they were losing?

"To the door!" roared Zero.

A massive surge of what looked like oily tentacles rose from the floor around him—or maybe I was seeing things and the battle simply coiled more tightly around him. Either way, it was suddenly a lot harder to see him. I heard Zero roar again, and there were no words to it this time.

I couldn't see his huge silhouette, either. Jin Yeong's snarl rose in the air again, and Athelas panted, "My lord!"

Someone else roared, too; and that must have been me, because my mouth was open and my throat was already raw.

For one frozen second, everyone in that bloody melee seemed to stop and look at me. It occurred to me that since I was howling, I might as well run, too; so I ran, howling, into the mob, with the sword on my shoulder and no strength to lift it from there.

Four-armed men scattered before me, yelling in fear. Ridiculous.

But the others, the ones that didn't look like they had a real body, scattered as well. So I ran, and yelled myself hoarse, gathering a shadow in dark, glistening blood by my right, and another in sparkling silver at my left.

Someone's hand on my forehead stopped my flight with a jerk, the sword bouncing from my shoulder to rest on dark, blood-stained leather.

"Good pet," said Zero, and his other hand easily removed the sword from my hands. "Behind me."

I ducked the blade and his elbow, gripping the familiar leather strap of his jacket; and the shadows that had until then flanked me, flanked Zero instead.

There was a brief moment of utter quiet on my side of that Behindkind wall of fae and vampire.

"Oh, much better!" sighed Athelas, and the world went blood red.

I remember having such a sore arm. I remember the sticky,

itchy feeling of blood between my fingers, and the searing pain of something cutting my arm.

Athelas' houndstooth flickered in my peripheral, and where it flickered there was sudden quiet. In front of me, leather creaked and grew red, though I never saw the sword; and sometimes I saw half of Jin Yeong's face, the other half tarred in blood and unrecognisable.

But my arm ached so much, torn nearly out of its socket, and there was so much noise and disturbance that when I realised my arm was flopping against my side, I was grateful to hobble away and find a quiet corner.

There were no quiet corners. There was a sudden lessening of noise, but it didn't bring any kind of rest with it; just a bloody expanse of fallen bodies that wouldn't stop groaning and keening; bodies that should have been dead but wouldn't stop moving long enough to die.

I heard myself sob, and looked down at the hand that should have been holding onto Zero's leather strap.

It was there, and the leather strap was there, dangling its buckle, but Zero wasn't.

I stared at the torn piece of leather for far too long, trying to understand what it meant, but the only thought that seemed to make sense was that I had been a good pet. I had done as I was told, and they had still left me behind.

A sob caught in my throat again. What was I supposed to do?

"Can't stay here, anyway," I said aloud, to try and drown out the groaning of the dying Behindkind around me. I sniffed. "Flamin' goblins'll try to stab me with a needle."

More than that, there was something about the slickness and the smell of it all that made my stomach roil, my mind going back to a night when I had woken unexpectedly. A night when the floor had glistened and the air had been heavy with a scent I didn't recognise.

A night when my parents—

"Can't stay here!" I said again, this time louder. I didn't remember what happened on the night that my parents were murdered. I'd never remembered.

And now my eyes were watering. I'd never get out of here if I couldn't see properly.

I wiped my eyes and said in a snubby sort of voice, "If they're not coming after me, I'm gunna get out by myself."

I didn't stop to look where I was going because there was nowhere to go that made sense. The long, windowed doors were dark and broken on my way out, so I must have gone the right way there, but there was still no sign of the courtyard or cave when I stood on the wooden platform.

Instead, there was forest. Light, beautiful forest with enough space between the trees to make mysterious shadows and send a cool, scented breeze wafting up toward me.

I looked out at it in despair. The courtyard had vanished as soon as my foot left the marble step; now even that step was no longer visible, a wealth of green, plump grass springing up at the edge of the wooden platform instead.

It wasn't a case of the forest pretending to be something it wasn't—it was definitely forest and grass cover. Just like the human world, where everything was absolutely human and real, and utterly unlike the Between area where things could be one thing or another, depending on how they were feeling or how I saw them.

"Ah heck," I said.

I wiped my bloody hands on my jeans—the stains already would never come out, so why not?—and found that the blood had already dried on them. The strap of leather was stiff with it as well, the stitches dark in blood.

I was probably lucky I hadn't lost a finger or an ear.

"Ah heck," I said again, and hastily felt for my ears and nose. They were still there, and still in one piece, but they were sticky.

There was a pretty big cut on my arm that wouldn't stop bleeding, too.

I was going to have to shower like Jin Yeong did; fully clothed, blood flowing away down the drain, until I could peel the clothes from my body and the caked blood from my face.

That was if I ever got back home. I could almost hear Athelas' calm voice warning against getting caught Behind, and Zero's blunt assurance that they wouldn't come back for me if I let go of him.

"Didn't let go," I said, and sniffed. My fist still ached around the leather strap.

I'm not sure how long I stood staring at the waving grass that edged the wooden platform; or how long it took me to realise that the waving of the grass wasn't from the wind.

"Weird," I muttered. If it wasn't wind, what was it?

I crouched at the edge of the greenery, watching the swell of something through the grass, and came to the conclusion, very slowly, that the grass wasn't moving either. It was a movement of something else that I couldn't see; something above the grass that could have been a heat shimmer but wasn't.

I stared at that for a long time, too. I mean, it could have been a sign that there was something else there, some way back into Between—and from there into the human world—but it could also have been something bad about to happen.

It was quieter out on the platform, and easier to ignore the noises from inside the waystation. Maybe I would have stayed there for much longer, but the same comparative quiet also meant that when the sound of someone calling through the forest threaded between the trees, I could distinctly hear that, too.

There were more of them coming.

For the third time, I said, "Ah heck."

I looked once more at the swaying grass that wasn't really swaying, closed my eyes, and stepped down from the wooden platform with the sick hope that I would feel cool, hard marble beneath my foot and not the softness of grass.

It was further down than I expected. I jerked forward, eyes flying open, and stumbled into a confusion of flagstone and grass that resolved when I hit the flagstones, hard.

I might have rolled, but it felt more like I collapsed like a sack of rocks.

Quite clearly, I heard someone say, "I thought it'd never step off! Think it'll be all right?"

I looked wildly over my aching shoulder, but the wooden platform behind me was empty.

"The goblins'll get it," said another voice, dispassionately. Obviously it didn't know there was no one there, and that it *couldn't* be speaking. "I don't mind, so long as it's Between and we don't have to explain it to the Order Force when they get here. They're tough on displaced humans at Behind waystations. Did you get rid of the other one?"

"It ran for it when the ambush failed," said the first voice. "We'll have to catch it again later; I don't know how it keeps getting away. Wait—doesn't it look like that one can hear us?"

"Don't be stupid," the second voice said. "I had to open Between for it. There's no way it can hear us. Not sure why they brought it with them."

"Yeah? Well how did it get the sword, then?" demanded the first voice belligerently. "There's going to be a price to pay for that. We were told to keep it safe. They said he'd never find it here, and now they'll think we gave it to him."

I turned my eyes back toward the ground very carefully, and pushed myself up from the flagstones, the knuckles on my right fist seeping blood that was my own instead of someone else's. Zero and Athelas had said not to bleed here, but how could I help it? Even my arm kept welling up, though it didn't drip like my knuckles were.

I put my knuckles in my mouth, the leather strap pushing into my cheek, and tried not to look back. There were two vague shadows in the corner of my eye that could have been something on the platform, flickering and getting easier to see by the minute, and I didn't want to see them.

"It probably thought an umbrella was as good of a weapon as it was going to get," the second said. "It's a human. Just a human. If the goblins don't get it, it'll spend the rest of its life thinking it's gone mad. Serve it right, pesky little creature."

My first step upright hurt and so did the second, but I took them anyway. It was very necessary, a small, loud part at the back of my mind told me, to get away from the invisible things that were becoming more visible the longer I stood near them. If I could see them properly, I might not be able to pretend well enough that I couldn't. I was pretty sure they were Behindkind, and I was *very* sure they would kill me if they knew I could see them.

When the pain in my knee and ankle settled into a dull throbbing, I started to trot. It was a bit of a drunken trot, sideways and not quite steady, but it covered ground more quickly and lessened the feeling of panic that clawed on the inside of my chest. My face felt stiff, but I didn't know if that was because of the blood or because of the fear.

It was darker now, too. Did time pass differently Behind and Between? I didn't know that, either.

It felt like a long time before I began to see knick-knacks on the cave floor and regular pictures on the walls around me, but it can't have been that long; I only had time for about ten trotting strides. I know that because I was counting them. I don't know why I was counting, but it made sense at the time.

And soon, like I'd done earlier beside the wooden platform Behind, I heard voices though I couldn't see anyone.

Athelas' voice asked, "Where's the pet?"

Oh, that was weird. Hadn't it been hours since I lost Zero? Had they only just noticed?

Jin Yeong's voice asked a question, too; and gave a small, derisive laugh. I would have liked to have been able to see his smug little face, so I could stick out my tongue at him.

But I couldn't help feeling glad—they were alive!—and hopeful. Even if I couldn't see my three psychos, I could feel the smooth give of wooden floorboards beneath my feet instead of the rough stone of the cave floor. It didn't look right, but it *felt* right.

I took several more steps forward, but I didn't start to see bits of the house as I should have by now. I stopped, bouncing on the balls of my feet to test the feeling of wooden boards.

It was definitely wood. So why couldn't I see the house this time?

I looked around for something—anything—that might give me a clue of how I was supposed to keep going, and something sharp and icy-edged bit my left foot.

I gasped and looked down.

A goblin laughed gleefully, its small fist gripped around a needle that protruded from the general area of my big toe. I kicked it away by reflex, gasping again as the needle tore out of my foot, and a sensation of lethargy seized me by the toes, spreading swiftly upward.

No time to be stuck Between, or I wouldn't make it home. I looked at the piece of leather in my fist and said to it, "Home, Lassie."

I knew home was there. I knew exactly what it should look like, too; a dark, narrow room with the blinds drawn and the smell of mildew lingering on the air. A door in the centre of the wall ahead that should be edged in softer grey than the walls around it; beyond that, the landing and the stairs, carpeted to muffle my clumsy steps.

I saw it in my mind as I took the first, dragging step forward. Then, as I took another, and another, I saw it properly. It was soft around the edges, too; like a frosty dawn smudged into condensation on my window, but as I kept walking it grew certain of itself. More and more certain until I was walking in the human world and not Between, the real world as solid around me as Behind had been not so long ago.

I fell against the bannisters as I came to the top of the stairs, my legs briefly giving way beneath me. I couldn't stop, though. Not if I didn't want the goblins to drag me back into the coldness of Between, far away from the sunlight of the human world.

So I kept moving forward and down, my feet clumsy against the carpeted stairs; and an age later I found myself without stairs to descend. But that was all right, because Zero was there instead, all silver-bark and bloody in the half-light of the house over the road.

I felt a warmth grow in my stomach, the sight of him familiar and welcome.

"Shall we go back?" Athelas asked.

Oh yeah. Athelas was there, too. I liked Athelas. Where Zero was silver and crimson in my fading eyesight, bright against the maroon living room wall, Athelas was only silver.

Zero, harshly, said, "Didn't we agree? We said we wouldn't get fond of her—"

"It." Was that Jin Yeong? The mongrel!

"Yes, it—shut up, Jin Yeong!"

Athelas reminded him mildly, "You were the one who said no names, no humanising pronouns."

"It was my fault, anyway," Zero said shortly. "We'll go back, for all the good it will do. The goblins will have it by now."

The last, little piece of ice that had been in my stomach, sharp and cold, melted. He was going to come for me, after all. Would have come for me, only I was already out.

"I'm all for going back," said Athelas, "but I fail to see how it was your fault. The pet came to us."

"I told it not to let go of the strap."

"*Kurom—*"

"It didn't. Look." Zero showed them the torn piece of his jacket that had once had a strap attached.

Their voices sounded very far away now, and when Athelas gave his soft chuckle, Jin Yeong behind him silently laughing into his collar, that was very far away, too. My legs had finally lost the ability to move, and—oh, no; there they went again, one foot after the other.

Jin Yeong saw me first, and I had the dim satisfaction of seeing the laugh utterly wiped from his face; then Athelas saw me, and his eyes widened for a brief moment. Zero turned last of all, his face unreadable.

"Oi," I said to him. "Got a bit of your jacket." Then the floor hit me, or maybe I hit it. There was a garble of voices above my head, but I didn't really expect them to do anything else but leave me there on the carpet until Zero's voice said, quite clearly, "Take her, Jin Yeong. I've got the sword."

There were cool, strong fingers around my wrists, then I was being piggy-backed by someone whose back was disconcertingly slender, for all its muscle. There was expensive, blood-sticky fabric beneath my cheek, which meant Jin Yeong must actually be carrying me.

"Too skinny," I mumbled in his ear, and passed out.

I segued seamlessly from unconsciousness to sleeping, and woke to the sensation of warm weight supplemented by the pleasant, childish feeling of hugging a favoured toy to myself. That feeling very quickly resolved itself into the realisation that my arms were still wrapped around Jin Yeong's neck; myself prone on the couch in all my gore, him clasped against me like a slender, well-dressed teddy bear. He didn't weigh much more than that, either. His eyes were closed and he was lying perfectly still, as if pained to find himself captive but unwilling to do anything so undignified as struggle.

I snatched my arms away from his neck like I was scalded and he sat up at once, opening his eyes. "*Kkaene?*"

"I don't know what that means," I said, but I didn't expect him to reply, and he didn't.

He stood and padded away across the living room carpet, leaving dark footprints behind. A moment later, I heard the shower start.

"So you're awake," said Athelas' voice, and I turned my head to see him sitting on the chair that was at right angles with mine.

"Yeah," I said. Ah man; now I smelled like JinYeong. What a *pong*. Why did he have to wear so much body spray?

Athelas looked away from his book for one moment, his eyes resting thoughtfully on me. "It's what JinYeong said."

"Oh. JinYeong—"

"He carried you over the road. By the time we got back you had a death grip around his neck."

I sat up carefully, wriggling the toe that had been stabbed by a goblin needle. It still felt a bit numb. Flamin' goblins. Next one I met was gunna get a good punch in the nose.

"He's a vampire," I said. I felt vaguely hard done by. It was bad enough to wake up on one of Mum and Dad's old sofas all over blood and gore; it was worse to find myself cuddling a teddy-bear like JinYeong. "Why didn't he pull my arms apart? I'm not *that* strong."

"You'd have to ask JinYeong about that," said Athelas, turning a page with one elegant finger. "If you'll excuse my curiosity, Pet, why were you clinging around his neck?"

I blinked and looked down at my hands. Zero's leather strap was still gripped between my fingers, my fist clenched so tightly that it was aching—so tightly that now it seemed I'd forgotten how to release it. "Don't know. Maybe for the same reason I've still got a bit of Zero's jacket."

I opened and closed my mouth a couple of times. Ugh. Woolly.

"Want a cuppa?" I asked Athelas. If he didn't, I did.

And after that, I wanted a shower.

CHAPTER EIGHT

I DIDN'T SEE ZERO AGAIN THAT DAY—NOT THAT THERE WAS much of it left by the time I came to. I would have taken him a cup of coffee when I made some for myself and Jin Yeong, but he'd already left the house by then, and he didn't come back until late the next day.

Jin Yeong had used nearly all the hot water, so I had to have a lukewarm shower that quickly became icy cold; but even a cold shower was better than sitting around in all that blood. I came out feeling damp and more than slightly wrung out, but it was surprising how warm it made me feel when Athelas trailed a touch of magic along my cut arm as I passed him his dinner, and followed it up by saying carelessly, "You're a good little pet."

Jin Yeong only scowled at me, scowled at his stew, and ate it anyway.

"What's wrong with him?" I demanded of Athelas. I was pretty sure there was still blood in my hair and I was annoyed enough to talk about Jin Yeong as if he wasn't there. "He's been stroppy since yesterday. You can't tell me it's because I'm the pet, either, because he's happy enough to eat what I make for dinner even if he does look at me like I might have poisoned it."

"Dinner is perhaps the issue."

JinYeong made a disgusted noise, picked up his plate and utensils, and left the room. I heard him stomping up the stairs, too, and since he usually walks as silently as Zero, he must have meant for me to hear it.

Were Athelas' eyes dancing? Yeah, I was pretty sure he was laughing.

"I'm not certain JinYeong knows what to do with a human who doesn't smell like dinner," he said. "Or, to put it in another way, like necessary sustenance."

"He looked pretty flamin' hungry when he finished killing those four-armed blokes in the grocery store," I said. "Zero had to tell him to leave me alone."

Athelas' head tilted; a slight sign of disagreement. "You could be confusing hunger with blood lust. JinYeong finds it hard to stop killing when once he's begun. It's one of the things that makes him so dangerous."

"Well, yeah, that makes it *much* better."

There was a decent amount of sarcasm in my voice, but Athelas replied in all seriousness, "Yes, I believe so. It will certainly cut down on the chances of an accident around the house."

I giggled at that a bit, because it was pretty normal for a pet to be having accidents around the house, even if those accidents were caused by the pet themselves and not a blood-crazed vampire. Athelas gazed at me curiously but didn't ask what I was laughing about.

"Wait!" I said suddenly. "I thought it was the house that stopped JinYeong being able to smell me. We weren't in the house, so he should have been able to smell me, right? I mean, it's gotta be the house, because I'm just a human."

"Perhaps it is," said Athelas, "but I find myself doubting it. It is certainly why Zero took you with him when he went Between the first time yesterday. He wanted to test if JinYeong would be able to use his nose properly once they were out of the house, or if you were the problem."

"Ohhhh!" I said slowly. Then Jin Yeong's behaviour yesterday made a heck of a lot more sense. He had been sniffing me not to weird me out, but to try and differentiate between the lack of smell that was me, and the other smells. So *that* was what Zero had been talking about. "Did Jin Yeong say something to you?"

Athelas went back to his tea. "No. It's more what he isn't saying. I'm not sure Jin Yeong knows quite what to make of you."

"Hopefully not dinner, anyway," I said, and that made me giggle again. Obviously I'd been living with psychos for too long. I wasn't sure, but I thought that the curve of Athelas' teacup was hiding a smile. "Is Zero coming home soon?"

"Zero comes home when he's ready."

"Yeah," I said, "but you always seem to know when he's nearly here. Is that because you're his steward? How does that work?"

"It works in a way that a human couldn't possibly understand," Athelas said. "Go to bed, Pet. I've a feeling that Zero will have some questions for you tomorrow."

I swallowed a bit. "Yeah?"

"And it is perhaps best to warn you against being as...er, delightfully honest as you usually are."

"Stroppy, is he?"

"Perhaps if I understood what you meant by the vernacular, Pet...?"

"He's gunna be angry at me? Why? What did I do?"

"Humans aren't supposed to be able to move through Between by themselves. Nor are they meant to be able to pull things that are Behind out into Between. They are not, Pet, supposed to be able to see them at all."

"Yeah, but that's not my fault!" I protested. "I don't make the rules! And if you didn't want me seeing stuff I shouldn't see, you shouldn't've taken me there in the first place!"

"Exactly so!" agreed Athelas.

Oh yeah. He hadn't wanted Zero to take me Between the day before, either.

I looked at him suspiciously. "You know this was gunna happen?"

"As I may have already mentioned, Pet, it is supposed to be impossible. Who would expect the impossible?"

"Reckon if anyone did, it'd be you," I said.

"Pet," Athelas said, shifting his weight very slightly, "do go to bed."

I went to bed.

ZERO CAME BACK LATE THE NEXT DAY, AND I COULD SEE RIGHT away that he'd been back to some *Between* place—probably the house over the road. He didn't look like he was right here and now like he should have. Maybe it was because he had a slightly exultant look to him, like he'd blown off steam by killing some Behindkind.

"Want a coffee?" I asked him. Was there a sort of band across his forehead, like a crown-type thing? Or was that just my imagination?

"Yes," he said. "But I want food more. Athelas!"

Athelas came from the living room, and surprised me by making the slightest sign of a bow. Maybe he got the same sense of a crown as I did. Maybe he was being polite because he'd been gone all day, too, and was expecting Zero to be angry about leaving me to the less-than-tender care of JinYeong, who was looking *really* hungry today.

"Tea for me, Pet," he said. His eyes said, *Don't mention my absence, or you won't live to regret it.*

I blinked at him, and reached over to set the kettle boiling.

"*Coppi*," said JinYeong, through his teeth. You'd think he'd've had enough blood in the ambush last night, but he had that red look to his eyes that made me certain he was hungry for blood, not food or coffee.

"Dinner's already on," I told Zero. "You can have coffee while you wait for it."

He nodded briefly. Again to Athelas, he said, "The waystation is running again today. No sign that they've lost the sword, and no sign of the ambush. I suspect they've been cleaning up."

Jin Yeong spoke, his deep voice impatient.

"Yes, the glamour is back," agreed Zero. "I saw it on my way here."

"They certainly didn't waste any time!" Athelas said. I wondered if that was dark amusement or respect in his voice. "They must be working on something very lucrative, if they're willing to start up their operation again the day after the Behind-kind Order Force visits!"

"The Order Force only did a routine inspection," said Zero. "Or they would have found the clear indications of human incarceration."

"Hang on!" I said sharply. "Incarceration? You mean they were keeping humans prisoner there?"

"It happens," Athelas said, nodding.

"What for?"

Zero looked surprised at my indignation—well, he had a human pet, so I suppose it must have been a bit weird for him to think that human people might not want to be pets, or prisoners, or whatever.

He said, "If a human has seen too much, Behindkind have three options: Kill, imprison, or remove memories."

"What's wrong with removing memories, then?" I demanded. "Who said it was okay for you lot to start kidnapping people?"

"No one said it was all right," Zero said. His voice wasn't icy, but that was probably only because it lacked any emotion whatso-ever. "But it happens. Behindkind laws forbid the imprisonment or exploitation of humans except under agreed-upon situations."

"Who do they ask for agreement, though?" I asked grumpily. "Bet it's not the humans! And if there are still Behindkind doing it, they mustn't be policing it too well!"

"Not for some time," agreed Athelas. "There was once an irregular unit of Behindkind Fae who policed such matters—"

"*Han myong; han myongiya,*" JinYeong interrupted.

"Very well, it was an irregular unit of one—and for a time, two —who policed such matters. His end wasn't a particularly happy one, and it left a sour taste in the mouths of more than a few Behindkind and humans."

"Let's not discuss ancient history," Zero said abruptly. "Whatever the waystation is doing, it's none of our business. I couldn't find any sign of humans there, damaged or otherwise, and they let me look properly this time. I have my sword now, so there's no need for us to visit them again. We have a murderer to catch."

I made spaghetti that night. All three of my psychos were still in the kitchen with me, hanging out at the kitchen table. I think they were all pretty hungry, though at least Zero and Athelas were making a pretence of doing something else.

Zero didn't show any signs of hunger; he was studying something out of an ancient book instead of his usual sharpening. Athelas was a little more alert than usual, and glanced over at me once or twice more than usual, but at least he tried to be cool and look like he was busy reading, too.

JinYeong didn't even pretend to be doing anything else; he watched me like a particularly suspicious hawk, his mouth pursed, following every move I made.

It made me nervous, so I said to him, "It's no use glaring at me because your sniffer doesn't work properly around me."

JinYeong's head jerked back. "*Wae?*" he demanded, sounding surprised.

"Don't talk to me in Korean," I said. "It's rude. I don't understand it."

JinYeong made an annoyed noise that sounded like "*Aight!*", spinning away on his chair, and stalked elegantly out of the room.

I hissed a dismissive puff of air after him, and my eyes chanced on Zero just in time to see the grin that he hid behind his book. For some reason, that cheered me up. Zero didn't smile much, and I didn't like that. If it was clever to have a favourite psycho, he would have been my favourite, and I would have liked to see him smile more.

I mean, he didn't display much of *any* emotion. With JinYeong, you could count on being able to see at least arrogance, self-satisfaction, and a few instances of pouting; and even Athelas displayed some evidences of emotions other than his usual, faint amusement. Zero, on the other hand, so rarely showed emotions that it would have been easy to think of him as being as cold and white as his skin and hair.

S'pose you get that way if people react to you in fear and loathing like they seem to with Zero, but it still bothered me like it didn't with JinYeong and Athelas. I didn't know why that was, either, unless it was because of that faint, intangible feeling that Zero, in spite of his lacking emotions, was somehow more human than JinYeong or Athelas.

The idea worked away quietly in my mind as I cooked, and after the three psychos were served, I looked at the spaghetti coiled around my own fork and asked idly, "Zero, are you part human?"

Athelas choked on his spaghetti, an indication of surprise that startled me a heck of a lot more than the question should have startled him, and JinYeong's eyes narrowed on me.

Zero stared at me for a few moments, silent and unreadable, before he asked, "Who told you that?"

"You, just now," I said. "You actually are human?"

"Half," he said. "What made you think so?"

I shrugged. "Dunno. Want me to pat Athelas on the back?"

"He's fine. There must have been something that made you think of it."

"Maybe it's the vibe you give off."

"The—what do you mean, vibe?"

"I believe," said Athelas, dabbing with his napkin at his mouth and then, lightly, at his eyes, "that Pet is referring to your aura."

"'Zat what it's called? The feeling that you should run as quick as you can in another direction?"

"Yes," said Zero. "I'm surprised you noticed it."

"Couldn't help noticing it," I said. "It's a flaming strong feeling!"

"I believe Zero is more concerned with the fact that you analysed and catalogued the feeling. Most humans simply run."

"I've been meaning to ask you about that," said Zero. His eyes were particularly steely, which was a bit worrying. "Amongst other things. You were evasive when we met, but you didn't run. Why?"

"'S'not like you wouldn't have caught me anyway," I said matter-of-factly. "And Athelas gives off the same feeling; that's not the vibe I mean."

Jin Yeong's brows rose. He said something to Zero that sounded sarcastic, and this time Zero put down his fork.

Uh oh.

"Pet," he said. "Listen very carefully. I am going to ask you two questions, and I'd like a very carefully considered answer to both. And don't—" he added, as I opened my mouth to ask another question, "try to distract me by asking another question. I think you'll regret it if you do."

I gave him an uneasy grin. "What are the questions?"

"When we first met, why didn't you run?"

"Dunno," I said. "It's that vibe you give off. Sorta sad, or lost. I could feel the *run-like-mad*—what is it? Aura?—shoving at me, but the other vibe was there, too."

Athelas and Zero exchanged a look, but Jin Yeong gave a short hiss of laughter.

I stuck my tongue out at him.

"That aura thing, though; Athelas gives off the same feeling," I said. "Is it a fae thing, or a Behindkind thing?"

"Fae," said Zero shortly. "What did I say about questions?"

I blinked at him and did the *zip-the-lip* thing that every kid learns at some stage.

Zero must not have learned it, because he stared at me and then asked, "How long exactly has it been since you stopped feeling the urge to run at the sight of us?"

"Dunno," I said again. "I was pretty safe in my room, so it wasn't too hard for me. It's not like the feeling can get through walls, is it?"

"It gets through anything," Athelas said. "It's meant to encourage people under cover to give up their cover and make a break for safety."

"Ah," I said. I had definitely felt that impulse; good thing I was used to resisting it.

We ate in silence until Zero had emptied his plate twice, and I'd refilled it twice.

Then he asked, "Pet, do you remember what I asked you to do when we went to the courtyard yesterday?"

Uh oh. Was this the time when I was supposed to be not-so-honest, or what?

"Um," I said. "Something about finding the sword."

"That's right. Why did you pick it up?"

"Well, I couldn't see you two, and Athelas said something about ambush and disappeared, so I thought you might need it."

"How did you pick it up?"

"What?" Was that a trick question? How do you usually pick up an umbrella? "I grabbed the handle."

"The hilt."

"Yeah, that. Just picked it up."

Zero looked at me for a very long time, swirling spaghetti around his fork and inhaling it again and again.

I sank my chin in my hand and stared back at him. If he was trying to intimidate me into giving something else away, the joke was on him. That was all I'd done; I'd picked up the sword. There was nothing more to tell.

"Who taught you how to see Behind?" asked Athelas.

I tried not to shiver, and glanced over at him. His eyes said *lightly amused*, and so did his tone, so why did I feel so flamin' cold? And why was he asking me questions when he'd warned me against being too honest with Zero?

"Didn't know what Behind was until I met you blokes," I said. I was still a bit hazy myself on what Behind *was* exactly, and that was after seeing it for myself. "Who's had *time* to teach me? And who's gunna teach a human anything, anyway?"

"That's a reasonably good point," said Athelas; and now he sounded like his usual aloof, slightly patronising, self. "I should certainly not try to teach a human anything; there's so little point. They can't understand."

I made a face at my empty plate.

Zero slurped up one last forkful of spaghetti, and pointed at the corner of the dining room.

"Pick it up again," he said.

"Oi!" I said, in surprise. The yellow umbrella was there again; how hadn't I seen it? "When did that get there?"

Athelas' eyes flickered over to meet Zero's. "It's been there since Zero got home," he said.

"How come I didn't see it?" I demanded.

"Who knows, Pet?" sighed Athelas. "Thus the point of contention: You're an anomaly."

"Oh," I said. I hoped my voice didn't sound as unimpressed as I felt. I caught the look in Zero's light blue eyes and hastily got up.

Better if I don't get kicked out right now.

Now that I could see it again, it was easy to see it. A yellow umbrella, propped up in the corner next to the china cabinet. It didn't look as shabby as it had looked yesterday, but it didn't look like it was a sword pretending to be an umbrella, either.

That made me feel uneasy, because if it wasn't inclined to be a sword, who was I to tell it any different?

I wrapped my fingers around the plastic handle, hoping for the feel of folded leather, but all I felt was plastic; smooth and a bit grubby. I picked it up anyway, and it made that little flutter of cloth that umbrellas always make.

"Maybe it doesn't want to be a sword today," I suggested, turning around to face my psychos.

"*Kugae aniya*," said Jin Yeong impatiently, rising. He padded over to me, socks soft against the tiles, and took the umbrella away from me.

"Rude," I said.

Jin Yeong ignored that. He set the umbrella against the wall again, and waved one slender finger in my face. "*Jal bwa*."

Oh great. One more annoying thing to add to his other fun personality traits. Seriously, who waves their fingers in people's faces anymore?

He raised one eyebrow at me; jerked his head at the umbrella.

"All right, all right, I'm looking!"

Maybe his hand made a colour in the air as he went to pick up the sword. Maybe it passed *through* a colour. Whatever it was, I could see the effect of it; and in the relief of that effect, I saw the sword instead of the umbrella.

"Oh, *cool!*" I said.

Jin Yeong smirked at me, and let it go. It was an umbrella again, but despite the smugness of Jin Yeong's back as he padded away to the table again, I could see that the umbrella could almost be—might perhaps agree to be—a sword again.

I stuck out my tongue at Jin Yeong; he obviously thought I couldn't do it, and was baiting me. Still, he'd shown me enough to make me think I could—yep! There it was under my fingers, folded leather.

Zero said something under his breath, and so did Jin Yeong, but I was too busy trying to persuade the sword to be a sword to pay any attention to what it was they said. It was there beneath my fingers, but for some reason it didn't seem to want to come out properly.

I glared at the yellow brightness of it. "How come I can't do it again?"

"We're more interested to know why and how you could do it at all," remarked Athelas. He was back to being entertained. "Perhaps you're not motivated enough, Pet? Perhaps we should recreate the circumstances again? Jin Yeong is certainly hungry for blood again."

"Dunno," I said; and for some reason my voice sounded sulky. Was I actually annoyed that a sword didn't want to play with me? "Maybe it really wanted to be found yesterday."

"I sincerely hope not," Athelas said, his eyes bright with rueful laugher. "The ramifications, Zero; the ramifications!"

"It's ridiculous to think about," said Zero abruptly. "Find your amusement somewhere else. This is nonsense."

"Certainly," Athelas said, and there was that suggestion of a bow again. "Pet, stop playing with the umbrella and clear away. We've time for a cup of tea before we take ourselves off to the morgue."

"They let people into the morgue at this time of day?" I asked, but I put the umbrella back down and cleared the table anyway.

"Certainly not," said Athelas. "But we're not really people, now, are we?"

"Got *that* right," I muttered, tapping the *on* button on the kettle. "Was the murdered bloke really one of your lot? He looked like the bloke across the road."

Zero flicked a look at me but didn't answer.

It was Athelas who said thoughtfully, "Seeing that our pet inexplicably can see Behind and a number of things Between, perhaps it's not a bad idea to take her word for it that our victim was, in fact, a human."

"I'd rather make sure," said Zero shortly.

I found myself exchanging a glance with Athelas; neither of us bothered to argue about it, and later, when they'd finished their tea and coffee and got up to go out, Athelas seemed content to go out.

Jin Yeong might threaten and snarl, and Athelas might turn the room to ice with his voice, but when Zero made up his mind, both of them stopped arguing.

They all left together while I was filling the sink and gathering dishes; Zero and Athelas to the morgue and Jin Yeong to the hospital. Since he didn't look hurt, I guess he was going there to pinch some blood. Neither Zero nor Athelas asked if I wanted to visit the morgue; and I mean, okay, I didn't want to, but they could have asked, you know?

I was only half way through the washing up when I heard one of them at the front door again. I knew they could travel Between and get places quicker than if they walked, but that was pretty quick, even for them.

"That was flamin' fast!" I said, impressed. I came around the corner as I said it, wiping my hands on my jeans, and stopped in my tracks.

It was the islander detective. I stared at him for a bit because it was so unexpected, and he stared at me like I was just as unexpected to him.

"What are you doing here?"

I blinked at him. "I live here. What are you doing here?"

More surprise. Whatever he'd been expecting, it wasn't that.

"You *live* here? You live with them?"

"Dunno about you," I said, "but I reckon this is the part where I call the police, not answer questions."

"I am the police," he said, and showed his badge.

I made a big show of looking it over, which annoyed him

because he'd only meant to flash it at me. "Reckon you still shouldn't be in here," I said, peering at the badge even more closely. Detective Tuatu, was it?

He snapped the badge shut.

I said, "Wasn't done looking."

Strike a light. *That* was a look.

"Yes, you were. I came in," he said, licking his lips and hesitating, "because I thought I heard someone calling for help."

"Good grief," I said. "Thought they only said that in the movies."

The detective's jaw tightened.

"Hey, don't blame me if you broke in because you thought the house was empty and it wasn't."

Actually, I'd forgotten to turn the lights on again after Zero and the others left; they didn't seem to need the lights, and I'd gotten so used to living in the dark while I was squatting that it was hard to remember I could have them on now.

Flamin' fantastic. I'd only been living in the same house as Zero and JinYeong for a month, and I was already getting as creepy as them. Athelas wasn't as bad, but still.

He said defensively, "I wasn't breaking—"

"Yeah, you were."

He fished out a card and said stiffly, "You can make a complaint to this number if you—"

"Coffee?"

"What?"

"Want a coffee? I was just gunna make some." Besides, JinYeong would probably be home from the hospital soon, and it would annoy him if I had someone in the kitchen. There aren't that many things I really enjoy these days, but annoying JinYeong is high on that short list.

"Do I— I don't drink coffee."

"Tea?" With Athelas' fondness for tea, there was enough in the house. Zero and Jin Yeong might only drink coffee if it was made for them, but Athelas would take the trouble to make his own tea if there was no one to make it for him. It hadn't taken long for me to discover that the gorgeous coffee in the red tin must have been particularly for me—some kind of amusing joke for Athelas, knowing I was there, knowing he knew it, but I didn't know he knew...

Actually, Athelas is kind of creepy, too.

"I—" the detective stopped. "Yes, please."

"You like earl grey?"

"Yes."

He didn't say anything else to me until we were in the kitchen. Mind you, I didn't say anything, either; and I think he was still confused. But I figure if he's there, why not ask him some questions?

After the kettle boiled I poured him a cup of tea and asked, "So what are you doing sneaking back in here, anyway, Detective Tuatu?"

For the second time, the detective froze. "Sneaking *back?*"

"Sugar?"

"No."

I pushed the cup toward him, handle-first. "Yeah, I saw you the first time, too. You do a lot of breaking and entering for a cop."

"Actually, it's only entering," he said. "That's the idea of the picks."

Rude. He was getting comfortable pretty quick.

"You said you live here," he added, before I could open my mouth. "But I haven't seen you."

"Been watching the house, have you?"

His eyes flickered down to his teacup. "If you've been around those three, I should have seen you. Who are you?"

"Nunya," I said.

Nunya business, for you blokes that don't know.

Hoping to change the subject, I asked, "What's so interesting about this place?"

"Nothing," he said. "But *they*'re interesting."

I snorted, and made coffee for myself. "Yeah, well; that's one way to put it."

"Are you going to tell them about this?"

I thought about that. As a loyal pet, I should definitely tell them all about it. I could feel the instinct to tell Zero; to feel the warmth of approval for doing it. Problem was, I was a pet that could think, and this thinking pet was pretty sure it was more useful to get information than to give away the source of that information.

"Not if you answer my questions," I said, taking a moment to savour the scent and warmth of my coffee before I took the first sip. "No need to tell 'em you've been letting yourself in. What are you looking for?"

He grinned. It took me by surprise, because mostly he'd done a lot of thoughtful looks and scowls, and I wasn't prepared for how much younger it made him look. His teeth were very white against his skin.

"I don't know," he said. "And that's the truth."

It probably was, too. I might have been stymied if I hadn't been living with my three psychos for a while now, but they had a way of asking questions from the right angles, and if there's anything I'm good at, it's learning.

"What made you want to look for something enough to break in?" I asked. "Especially if you don't know what you're looking for. It's a whole lotta risk for you, and not much to gain."

"That." The detective looked rueful. I think he'd been hoping not to have to say; he was pretty honest. "That was something... weird. Actually, there were two weird things. The first thing is the way they keep getting information out of my lab."

"*Your* lab?"

He sighed. "The police department's lab. They seem to get the results before I do—I've seen that skinny one in the suit walk right through the doors without being stopped by a single person. I followed him the other day; all the way to the lab. He left with some paperwork that should never leave the building without signing in, signing out, or signing anything to say he was taking the papers. And the officers looked—they looked—"

I grinned. That was going to be a tough one for him. I was pretty sure that was an extension of Jin Yeong's personality—or maybe it was a vampire thing—a kind of opposite to the aura Athelas had told me about. What had he called it? Manipulation? That thing where people just did what my three psychos told them to do.

"Yeah," I said. "I understand that."

"And then, there's the way they got this house."

I looked up from my tea, startled. "What? What do you mean, the way they got this house?"

"It's been under observation, and the real estate agents were strongly encouraged not to rent it again without telling me. They *sold* it. Not a word to me, either."

"There was a murder here—actually, two—several years ago. The case was never closed but we had a good idea it was part of a serial case where another incident usually takes place after a certain amount of years. We strongly encouraged the real estate agents not to rent it again or sell it until that period was up."

"Strongly encouraged?"

"And I've been dropping by every month or so for a quick look."

"Oh," I said. So that's what he meant by observation. He must have been pretty flamin' good, because I'd never seen him.

"Then *they* moved in. No trouble, no fuss, no mention from the agent to us; and yesterday they sold the place to those three. I want to know what their connection is to this house—and this case, for that matter."

"You think they're connected to the murder?"

"I'm certain of it."

Oh well, good for him. It wouldn't help him, but he was a clever cookie. I might actually have to warn Zero about the detective, if it came to that.

"Do you know what the most interesting thing is, though?"

Was he pausing for effect? "Go on, tell me," I said, pinching a biscuit before he could finish them all.

"Those three—I don't know much about them, and they're annoyingly hard to pin down to anything, but I've at least got names for 'em. You, now: I can't find a name, a photo; not a single trace to tell me who you are."

"That is interesting," I said. He must not have got to the café where I used to work, then. That was probably just as well. There was still about half a year before I turned eighteen, and I didn't want to run the chance of being sent off to the group home or anywhere else. I only had to keep my head down for another six months. "Fancy that."

"What is your name?"

"Don't have one," I said. It was sort of true—in this house, at this time, at least. I was a pet who wasn't allowed to have a name. Funny thing is, we'd once had a pet I wasn't allowed to name. He was the Christmas turkey, and he'd been killed just before Christmas.

I winced. I wished I hadn't remembered that.

"Everyone has a name."

"Christmas turkeys don't," I muttered.

"What?"

"I don't."

"You *must* have!"

"Well, I don't, and that's all there is to it," I said. "If you're going to sit there and complain at me, I won't give you any more biscuits."

"All right, if you don't want to give me your name, what about these men—why are you with them? You're a bit too young to be boarding with three grown men, aren't you?"

"Only two of them are grown up," I said. The other was a sulky vampire who'd probably spent the last fifty odd years at exactly the same mental age. And speaking of the sulky vampire, that was a pretty familiar step outside the door.

JinYeong in the house with the detective; this was going to be interesting.

"Don't panic," I said to the detective, who looked far too comfortable and relaxed to have heard the sound of JinYeong at the door, "but one of 'em is about to come home."

He might have jumped up and sworn if there had been time. There wasn't. JinYeong came into the kitchen at a predatory prowl, his eyes narrow and his teeth showing. He saw us and stopped short, astonishment taking the place of blind instinct to hunt the warm-blooded human who wasn't supposed to be in the house.

The detective stared at JinYeong, and JinYeong stared at the detective.

"*Petteu*," said JinYeong, showing the slightest edge of canine, "*Mwoh hanun kkoya?*"

Oh, I knew that one. He was asking me what on earth I was doing. "The detective came to see us," I said. "He saw you at the police station before."

The detective's brows rose. "You understand him?"

"Not really," I said. "But he can understand me, so mostly it works out."

JinYeong gave me a warning look, his lips pressed together, and I grinned at him. If he wanted to say anything that needed understanding, he'd have to say it in English.

"Want a cuppa?"

He blinked. Considered. "*Ne*," he said, as if conferring a favour. I might not know much about vampires in general, but you can distract Jin Yeong from practically anything by offering him food or drink.

I boiled the jug again, and turned around to see Jin Yeong gazing narrowly at the detective. I might have been worried if his eyes weren't back to normal instead of narrow and hungry as they had been earlier. Jin Yeong had definitely had a bit of blood since I saw him last.

The detective didn't stare back this time; he was trying to sip his tea nonchalantly. I know from experience that it's not easy to be nonchalant in the face of Jin Yeong's disturbingly non-human gaze, so I gave him full marks for the attempt. It was pretty nearly successful.

When he'd finished his tea, he put the cup down very precisely, and said, "I'd better be going, then."

I grinned, and I don't know if it was that or the detective which annoyed Jin Yeong, but he said, silkily, "*Aniyo.*"

That meant *no.* I knew that one.

Detective Tuatu didn't; he still got up. Jin Yeong was on his feet in a moment, edging in front of the detective before he had a chance to take a step, and said a single, short sentence, the pointed tips of his teeth showing through grimly smiling lips.

Detective Tuatu cleared his throat and said, "Yeah, sure," then edged away with the pretence of picking up his teacup.

Jin Yeong looked at me, astonished. I don't know what he'd discovered to make him need to share his astonishment with the pet, but I only shrugged at him. He said something at me in Korean, making shooing motions at the detective and then at the door, and for a brief moment I thought about pretending I didn't understand.

The detective had more sense than me. He came around the kitchen island to put his teacup in the sink, and said, "I'm off."

"Coward," I said, but he didn't crack a smile.

"I'll see you around," he said, and headed back down through the hall and out the front door.

"Not if I see you first," I muttered. He wasn't as creepy as my three psychos, but he was definitely threatening. If I make a cuppa for a bloke in my kitchen—all right, *their* kitchen—he shouldn't turn around and make threats at me. It's flamin' rude.

"*Petteu—*"

"Don't start with me," I said to Jin Yeong. "I'm just a pet. I can't stop people coming through the door, can I?"

Jin Yeong narrowed his eyes at me.

I said, "*Woof!*" at him and turned my back to wash the coffee things.

CHAPTER NINE

ZERO AND ATHELAS CAME BACK FAIRLY *HUMMING* WITH something—energy, or magic; or maybe it was sheer enjoyment, I don't know. Zero was bigger and brighter, and Athelas was more moonlike than usual, all quiet beauty and terrible eyes. Whatever they'd been doing at the morgue, it had agreed with them.

I would have asked them if they wanted tea and coffee as a way of leading in to find out what they'd discovered, but Jin Yeong got in first.

He said, "*Hyung!*" and gave vent to a brief spate of Korean.

I gave up on asking and started to boil the kettle anyway. They were all obviously caught up in the news Jin Yeong had shared. I may not have been able to understand his astonishment, but Zero's brows went right up, pale and surprised, and Athelas' mouth rounded momentarily.

Athelas was the first to find his tongue. "Not at all? He didn't respond to you at *all?*"

"*Ne.*"

"It's unusual," Zero said, more slowly, "but not unknown. There are some humans who aren't susceptible to vampiric manipulation."

Oh. So that's what it was. Jin Yeong had been at the police lab successfully wriggling his way in with his sneaky vampire wiles, and the detective wasn't susceptible to them.

No wonder Jin Yeong was so astonished to find someone not doing exactly as he asked them to do. I grinned and poured boiling water happily.

"Perhaps we should try a little persuasion of the fae kind," suggested Athelas. "A thrall should do the trick, should it not?"

He took the cup of tea I offered him and gave me a dreamy smile. I don't know about other fae, but I've come to the conclusion that this is his way of keeping things even. He doesn't like to be in debt to anyone; if I give him a cup of tea, he gives me a smile. If I make dinner, he compliments me. And sometimes he gives me things for free. I still don't know whether to be worried about that or not, so I try to make sure the scales are balanced as much as possible, too.

"Maybe you're getting old," I said to Jin Yeong.

That made him look as offended as I'd ever seen him look, and say something to Zero that must have concerned me, because he jerked his chin at me.

"A very good question," said Athelas, the traitor. "Perhaps you'd care to explain why you were entertaining the detective in our kitchen, Pet?"

"Reckon I'll have to get used to looking through the peephole before I open the door again," I said, hoping I sounded suitably pet-like and apologetic. Just a stupid pet. Don't know better.

"That would be wise," Zero said. His eyes were still on me, and he looked thoughtful.

I tried hard not to let myself swallow; Athelas was right, I gave away everything I was thinking with my face.

"*Choshimhae, Petteu,*" said Jin Yeong mockingly, and left the kitchen.

"He says," Athelas said helpfully, "be careful, Pet."

"Yeah," I said, getting out the biscuits. I'd make them a pie later. That'd make 'em happy again. "Got that idea."

THERE WERE A LOT OF STORIES ABOUT VAMPIRES WHEN I WENT to look them up on the library computer the next day. Stuff like them not being able to go out in the sunlight—false, since JinYeong was more comfortable in the sun than I was—not being able to eat garlic—ha! Garlic was a staple of any food he wanted me to make—stakes; number obsessive; bloodragey when hungry...it went on and on.

I already knew the sun and garlic myths were just that, myths; but there wasn't much else that I did know. And since I preferred not to anger JinYeong by something as potentially deadly as stakes, and already knew he tended to be bloodragey when starved for blood, I began my Vampire Experiments with something simpler.

I mean, I say *experiments*, but mostly I wanted to annoy him a bit. Sorta payback. And there wasn't anything really scientific about it, either; I went around the house and took away a piece of every ornament that had more than one bit to it.

If there was a bowl of decorative fruit, I took away one of the apples; if there were ten miniatures in the hallway, I took away one. I went through the house like a particularly beady-eyed bower bird, picking out this and that, and when I'd gathered a collection that was too big to conveniently hide, I put it all in a cardboard box under JinYeong's bed. He didn't sleep there, so if he noticed the missing things, it should take him a bit of effort to find them in order to put things right.

I considered raiding his sock draw for every second sock, but that seemed like it was going too far, and I was going for something subtler, anyway. The missing items weren't noticeable if you weren't the kind of person who noticed, counted, and catalogued every last thing in your mind. Time to see if my pouty little vampire was as obsessive-compulsive as the older stories said vampires were.

That done, I went happily down to the kitchen again and made an apple pie. Apple pie tastes better with payback.

I was reading a book in my usual spot on the couch that evening when Jin Yeong came stalking down the stairs, his back as straight as the crease in his trousers, and dumped the cardboard box on my lap.

"*Haji ma*," he said, and stalked away again.

Athelas, who was also reading, looked at me over the top of his book, and one of his brows rose very slightly. Over at his desk, surrounded by open files and reference books, Zero's eyes narrowed—heck yes! A Zero grin! Score!

Mark two for vampire myths, then. No aversion to sunlight or garlic, but inclined to notice if someone had been in their room, and *definitely* inclined to obsessive-compulsive tendencies.

And score one for the pet, I thought, hugging my cardboard box of odd items. Since my reading was already interrupted, I asked Athelas, "The murdered bloke—was he human after all?"

"It's too early to tell," said Zero, closing one book and opening another.

"Or perhaps we should say it's too late?" Athelas suggested. "There was very little left of him by the time we got there, after all."

"There was a trace of magic," Zero corrected him. "Maybe enough to run an event reconstitution spell."

I looked from Zero to Athelas, and back again. "What, someone did something to the body?"

Athelas put his book down. "You could say that. By the time we got there, it had completely melted away under the influence of as pretty a piece of spell-work as I've ever seen."

"It's not as if he wasn't already in pieces," I said disapprovingly. "Who went and did that to the poor bloke as well?"

"That is exactly the issue," Athelas replied. "And springing from that issue is another: How did whoever disposed of him know to dispose of him before we got there? Or were we simply unlucky?"

"If I start a Reconstruction spell going, we should have a good idea of what games he was playing—or at least, who he was playing with."

"The bloke got murdered," I pointed out. "So it prob'ly wasn't him playing the games, if you get what I mean."

"Zero," said Athelas, with gentle humour, "is still more than half convinced that he wasn't human, and that he had a very powerful glamour on him to prevent both fae and human from recognising as such."

I poked at the plastic pear in my cardboard box. "Why would anyone want to do that?"

"I'd like to know that, myself," Zero said. "If I'm correct, this murder looks less like a killing of the sort we thought it was, and more like something else entirely."

"A waystation does seem like an odd place for a murder to randomly occur," agreed Athelas. "But then, it also seems an odd place for Behindkind to be making mischief."

"Does it?" asked Zero mildly. "I find it a very good place to be getting up to mischief. They're Between, so they have one foot Behind and one foot in the human world. It's very easy to play Behind against the humans if you've got an eye to both."

Athelas inclined his head. "Perhaps so. However, if the victim was fae and not human, and if he wasn't murdered by our murderer, why was he killed? If there's a glamour on him, he was more than likely part of whatever was going on at the waystation. Fae killing fae is...unusual. And in this particular way, too—no, I'm more inclined to think he was certainly human, and that it's certainly our murderer."

"What if your murderer thought he was human, too?" I asked. "Sorta didn't notice he wasn't, and killed him? Then it's still your murderer, even with something weird going on Between."

Zero's eyes rose from his books and rested, curiously, on me.

"Oh, I think not," said Athelas. "He couldn't have made such a mistake!"

"Neither of us noticed," Zero said. "Perhaps we'll get some clarity now that JinYeong is able to properly scent the blood samples he collected from the lab."

"Now that his nose is working again," I remarked. "But didn't he already follow the blood trace from the house?"

"Ah yes," Athelas said thoughtfully, "JinYeong still has blood samples. Did we not already establish that they led us only to the waystation?"

"JinYeong followed the blood trace we found in the house," Zero said. "It was human, and there was quite a lot of it. We thought it was a witness, but perhaps it was the real owner of the house. There are other samples from the victim; JinYeong took them two days ago."

A dawning apprehension lit Athelas' eyes. "I see. However, it still leaves me with a few questions. Pet, I believe you said the odd happenings have been occurring for some years now."

"Since we moved here," I said, nodding. "That's when I was about ten."

"Then my first question would be—"

"Why the secondary blood loss at the scene was from the day of the murder," agreed Zero. "I was wondering the same thing."

"'Cos if there was a fae going around with his face for seven years, where's the actual bloke been, and why did he only start bleeding that day?"

"Exactly so," Athelas said. "Your reasoning isn't dreadful, Pet. Perhaps if we work on it, we can make a decent Investigator out of you."

Zero was short. "Don't encourage the pet."

"Yeah," I said. "Can't tell what us pet's'll do if you teach us too much."

Those blue eyes rested on me for a moment. I shut my mouth.

"Shall we pay a visit to the waystation once again?" asked Athelas. "Is that the plan?"

"Not just yet," Zero said. "They won't tell us anything, and if the Order Force isn't making proper checks we can't lean on the Waystation by threatening to tell, either. I think we should find out more about what they're up to before we try to find our witness."

"Ah," said Athelas, smiling. "We might be able to make an informational trade if it's juicy enough?"

"Oi," I said.

Athelas looked indulgently at me. "Yes, Pet?"

"Reckon a clever human could escape from fae?"

Athelas smiled slightly again and said, "I think not."

"If there was a distraction big enough, yes," said Zero, surprising me. "It's not unheard of. What exactly makes you ask that?"

"Well, when I came after you blokes—"

There was an almost inaudible murmur from Athelas that might have said something like *My lord. He's my lord and she refers to him in the colloquial!* but I ignored it.

"—when I came after you blokes, there were a couple of fae who watched me go."

"They *watched* you go?"

"More like, they opened Between for me," I corrected myself. "That's what they said, anyway. And I couldn't see how to get out until it went wafty, so they were probably telling the truth."

I didn't expect Zero to look so relieved.

Athelas said, "Now didn't I say there must have been more to it than the pet finding its own way out? A human, able to make its way Between at will? Nonsense."

"It's still able take things from Between," Zero reminded him, but he still looked relieved—or maybe just less tight-faced.

"*Anyway*," I said, slightly pointedly, "they kept talking 'cos neither of 'em knew I could hear them, and they said *another one* had escaped from them thanks to the ambush and all the fighting. They sounded a bit annoyed—reckon the bloke must have given 'em a lot of trouble before this."

"*Another one*," murmured Athelas. "Well, it certainly does seem to suggest that there was another human there, but we've yet to establish that our original victim wasn't the owner of the house. And even if it *is* a human, and it *was* there, it is there no longer."

"Unless they caught him again since then," I pointed out.

"My thoughts exactly," said Zero, and went back to his books. "Make dinner, Pet. Don't bring it in here; I'll need space to lay out a few things when I begin my spell. We'll eat at the table."

So I made dinner while Zero and Athelas went out to find ingredients—or maybe they went for a walk, who knows? Jin Yeong went out for a while, too; I saw him skulking through the bushes beside the house, then further down the street. Goodness knows what he was up to: Sniffing stuff, probably.

It wasn't until I finished making dinner that I found someone had pinched the apple pie I'd made and left out to cool.

"Flaming rude!" I said, indignantly.

Was that why Jin Yeong had gone out? Because he was eating the pie? I didn't even get a piece! Next time I was gunna make myself a small one of my own, and the three psychos could do what they wanted with theirs.

I set the table, still muttering, but none of them seemed to notice when they came back in. They sat down to eat, then went back to what they'd been doing before they went out; Zero to working on his spell, Athelas to watching him, and Jin Yeong to being moody upstairs.

THE SPELL ZERO WANTED TO DO MUSTN'T HAVE WORKED REALLY well for him, because he was still working on it when I went to sleep on the couch that night, and he was polishing stuff again when I woke the next morning.

Athelas was waiting for tea over on his chair, looking faintly amused at something as usual, so I went and made us all a cuppa. JinYeong wasn't in the house, but that was no loss. He must have gone out again last night after I went to sleep, because this morning the faint scent of his far-too-strong cologne still permeated from the bathroom. It stunk, but it was still better than JinYeong in the house with the cologne clinging to him and following him wherever he goes.

I'd given Athelas his tea and biscuits and settled Zero's coffee next to him when the front door opened and closed, wafting in the scent of JinYeong once again.

I made a *pft* of disgust sat down in my chair with my own coffee. What a pong.

Zero looked up sharply, a knife-edged crease between his brows, just as JinYeong led a human woman by one hand through the kitchen and toward the stairs, a challenge in the tilt of his chin.

"JinYeong!" said Zero, and it felt like the whole house shook.

"Ah heck," I said quietly to myself. Whatever JinYeong was doing with a human woman, Zero wasn't happy about it.

JinYeong turned his head, one brow up as if surprised, and changed direction. The woman followed him down the two stairs into the living room with us, her face blank and her eyes wide and starry.

Ohhhh. So that's what a person looked like when they were under vampiric manipulation. It must have really freaked out the detective, because I'd been around JinYeong for a while now, and it still freaked me out.

"Don't bring humans back here," Zero said, his voice icy. "There's blood in the fridge for you."

There's *what* in my fridge?

I mean, I know it isn't really my fridge, and it's not like I'm paying the power bill, but...but why the flaming heck are they keeping blood in my fridge? Couldn't Jin Yeong go to the hospital again?

Also, where were they keeping it that I hadn't seen—oh. Yeah. There was an esky at the back that Zero had told me not to touch.

Gross.

Jin Yeong pouted and said something I couldn't understand.

I froze where I was, wishing I could run for it. If he was pouting, his eyes should be soft and soulful like they quite often were with that expression.

They weren't. They were dark and liquid and ragingly angry.

"If you feed on that human in here, I'll tear the teeth out of your mouth," Zero said, his voice dropping an octave and growing very soft.

Jin Yeong spat an angry sentence, leaving the woman to sink down on the sofa, and stalked toward Zero with long, predatory strides.

In his leather chair, Athelas put down his teacup, smiling.

Zero's shoulders might have settled into a straighter line, but that was the only sign of aggression he gave. He didn't even put a hand to the knives I knew he had beneath his leather jacket.

"There's blood in the fridge," he said, again.

I got up very quietly, my feet silent against the carpet, and crossed the room behind Jin Yeong, who had neither ceased to make incomprehensible, sibilant remarks in Zero's direction, nor his advance toward him.

Athelas saw me. He didn't try to stop me, only smiled again and went back to watching Zero and Jin Yeong as they squared up across the living room.

So I kept walking until I could grab the woman by the wrist and pull her to her feet. She got up in a docile kind of way, and she didn't resist when I led her across the room; just followed me as if I was Jin Yeong.

There was a snarl behind us that set the hairs up on the back of my neck, and a shadow, big and icy cold, that passed between us and the snarl. I didn't stop walking, and she didn't, either.

Then we were out the door, and it was shut behind us.

"What's going on?" said a suspicious voice.

"Flaming heck!" I gasped, reeling back against the door. The detective was there in front of us, his eyes narrow and suspicious. "Don't *do* that to me!"

"Who's this?" he asked, ignoring that. He scanned the woman up and down, and I knew he could see the dazed look in her eyes. "Did they do something to her?"

"Nope!" I said, squinting against the morning sunlight. "She came over to visit JinYeong. She's going now. Wanna give her a lift home?"

"I need to see those three."

"You can't," I said. An un-dazeable detective in that room at the moment would probably get killed. "Not unless you've got a warrant. Bet you haven't."

He went to say something, but cut it off angrily and said instead, "Then I want to talk to you!"

"Okay," I said. I didn't really want to go back in the living room right now, anyway. "But we've gotta take this woman across to Elizabeth Street first."

"Can't she find her own way there?"

I shrugged. "Dunno."

She looked brighter than she'd looked around JinYeong; like maybe she could see the difference between the sun and a lightbulb by now. There was a tiny bit of a frown between her manicured brows.

"Does she live on Elizabeth Street?"

"Dunno," I said again. "But she can catch a bus from down there if she needs to."

"I thought you said she was a friend of yours."

"Nope. Said she was visiting JinYeong. I don't know his friends. C'mmon if you're coming."

The detective followed me, and if his eyes were still narrow and hard with suspicion, at least he came away from the house.

I took him through the shortcut behind the next house, brushing past foliage and ducking through the hole in the fence with the woman following me obediently. I could understand Jin Yeong thinking of humans as less than people if this was how he usually saw them.

Pity I couldn't do something that'd remove his ability to daze people. Bet the internet wouldn't have much to say about that.

By the time we got to the main street, she'd woken up a bit more. I let go of her wrist and walked beside her for a few more steps, and after a while she looked across at me in a puzzled sort of a way, shook her head, and walked on more quickly.

"How did I get all the way up here?" I heard her mutter.

I grinned and slowed down, shoving my hands in my pockets.

"What the heck was that?" asked the detective, stepping in front of me.

I skipped around him and kept going. "Don't ask me. I'm just out for a walk. You coming or going?"

"Coming," he said, grimly. "Let's stop for a coffee."

"There's coffee at home," I said, but when he ducked into the closest café as we passed it, I followed him anyway.

Better than him going back home and knocking on the door.

"Want a drink?" he asked, at the counter. "I'm buying."

I shook my head. "No thanks."

I sat at one of the tables outside. There was coffee at home, and I could wait that long: if there was anything I knew after living with Behindkind and travelling through Between and Behind, it was not to accept food and drink from people. Detective Tuatu might not be a goblin, and his food and drink might not put me out like a light, but there were other kinds of compulsion. Like the compulsion of being helpful to someone who has been kind to you. The compulsion to talk to someone who's buying. That sort of thing.

For someone who says he's not into teaching humans because they can't understand, Athelas has taught me a lot in a short time.

The detective came and sat down a minute later. "Still don't have a name for you," he said.

I grinned again. "'S'that why you asked if I wanted a drink? So they'd ask what name to call?"

"They don't call names, here," he said, resting one booted foot on the next chair. "They bring the drinks to your table."

"What'd you want to talk to the boys about, anyway?" I asked, shifting my chair so I could still get around his legs if I needed to. Somewhere out there in the street, I'd glimpsed the bristly bush of beard that ducked into a shop; and lately, whenever I'd seen the old bearded bloke, there had been trouble.

Detective Tuatu said angrily, remembering his wrongs, "They've been in my station again! And this time they've melted the body!"

"Nah," I told him. "They were annoyed about that, too. They didn't do it."

"Why should I believe that?"

I shrugged. "Dunno. You're the one who wanted to talk to me."

"Who else would melt a body—*how* did they melt the body?"

"Yeah, that's what they want to know as well. They're trying to find out, but I don't think it's working."

Detective Tuatu opened his mouth to speak and then closed it again as a tiny Chinese girl in an apron put his tea on the table between us. When she was gone, he said, "All right, if they didn't do it, who did?"

"Beggared if I know. What I want to know is why your lot wasn't looking after it better."

"You've—they've—we can't even stop them coming in and getting information out of us! How could we look after a body if someone like them came in?"

"Oh, that's a good point," I said. "So whoever we're after, they're Behindkind."

"They're what?"

"Nothing you need to worry about," I told him. It was nice to be cheeky without worrying about losing a limb or a few litres of blood. "Don't you have security cameras in there?"

The detective looked at me with dislike. "Funnily enough, they weren't working."

"Yeah," I said. I wasn't surprised. Sympathetically, I added, "Annoying, isn't it?"

"Annoying? It's f—it's suspicious."

"Oi."

"You—what?"

"Seen an old bearded bloke hanging around here?"

"Don't change the subject!"

I grinned at him. "Free country, isn't it? You have, haven't you?"

Detective Tuatu said exasperatedly, "He's as bad as you—no name, no identification, just sheer oddness."

"Thought I wasn't imagining things," I said, in satisfaction. "He keeps turning up in weird places, and I don't know whether to tell the ps—whether to tell *them* about him or not. He doesn't seem to do much, just hangs around and cackles to himself a bit."

"Don't tell them," the detective said.

"Yeah, that's what I thought," I said, and I saw the relief in his face. He really thought my psychos might do the old bloke a mischief. Well, if it came to that, I wasn't sure myself that they wouldn't consider him a risk if they knew about him. He was lucky they hadn't caught sight of him yet.

"Oi," I said again.

"What?"

"You see anyone there before that corpse got melted?"

"Why am I the only one answering questions?"

I shrugged. "You don't have to answer 'em if you don't want to."

"There's nothing on the CCTV."

"Yeah, I know. They were annoyed about that, too. Think they're trying to run a sp—ah, something that'll tell 'em who was there before them, but if you *saw* something—"

"I didn't," said Detective Tuatu, but I had the impression he was uneasy about something.

So what, he saw something, but didn't want to admit to what he'd seen? Might have been something Behindkind.

"What do you mean, they're running something to find out who was there before them? If the CCTV doesn't work, how on earth are they going to—" His eyes went very wide. "Have they got *surveillance* equipment in the station?"

"Nah." Only magic, and spells, and fae voodoo.

"Then how does it work?"

"Dunno about that stuff," I told him. "Dunno how it works, dunno what it is."

He sat back in frustration. "You're not going to tell me anything, are you?"

"You don't ask the right questions," I told him, grinning again. "You need to fix that. I've gotta get back. See you next time."

"Wait!" he protested, but I skipped past his legs anyway, and left him trying to decide whether to come after me or finish his tea.

He must have decided to finish his tea, because when I got back to my street there was no one following me—well, no one except the old guy with the beard, and I still wasn't exactly sure he *was* following me. Me specifically, I mean. If he followed me while the three psychos were around, I might be sure of it, but it's a bit silly for someone to be following just me around.

When I got back inside the house, the walls weren't splattered with blood, and neither Zero nor Jin Yeong was dead. Athelas had picked up a book instead of his empty teacup, so I went and took the teacup away.

"We'll take an early lunch," Zero said to me. "Jin Yeong is hungry."

Jin Yeong, his sulky mouth pursed around a blood bag and his eyes back to normal, released the bag momentarily. "*An chuget-daeyo*," he said to Zero, his voice thick and reproachful.

"Accidents happen," said Zero briefly. "Even if you didn't mean to kill her, it's possible. We've already been noticed by a few humans who shouldn't have noticed us. If we have bodies to clean up, we can't stay here."

This time, Jin Yeong's eyes flicked over to me.

"What?" I demanded.

His mouth quirked sideways in an unamused, tooth-displaying smile. "*Kidaehae*," he said.

"Don't hurt the pet," said Zero, and left the room.

There's no understanding him. One day he makes sure I've got a jacket because I'm shivering; the next, he leaves the room when Jin Yeong is making threatening remarks at me.

That's flamin' cold.

I'm stuck between an icy human-fae hybrid and a loco-as-all-heck vampire who doesn't seem to care who he drains.

It was funny, though. Jin Yeong had looked ready to murder Zero; it had looked, actually, like he was *trying* to cause a fight. I'd seen the liquid anger in his eyes, his willingness to fight and kill; and I had seen Zero's shoulders square, ready to fight. The funny thing was, though, that it wasn't either of them in all their deadliness that had made the biggest impression on me.

The thing that stuck in my mind the most—the thing I didn't think I'd forget—it was Athelas, putting down his teacup and crossing one leg over the other, smiling faintly in enjoyment. Like he would have enjoyed watching them fight to the death for the interest of seeing who would win.

CHAPTER TEN

BY THE NEXT DAY, ZERO STILL HADN'T BEEN ABLE TO GET HIS spell working, and Athelas was padding around the house with the saintly air of someone who is very conscientiously *not* saying "I told you so".

Zero had brought himself to be faintly approachable again when he came to breakfast, and Athelas was looking less saintly. Maybe it helped that I gave them boston beans on toast for breakfast—it's pretty hard to be icy or saintly while you're eating glorified beans-on-toast.

Athelas helped himself to a second slice of toast and suggested, "If you're so sure it's got to do with the Waystation, why don't we go back and have a proper look around this time? Below the surface, so to speak."

Zero shook his head. "They've got a habit of knowing when we're coming and it's too easy to hide things."

Jin Yeong, eschewing the beans and raiding the jam instead, suggested something in an indolent sort of way, shrugging one shoulder up and then down.

"I suppose that's a possibility," Athelas conceded. "If they're expecting to be bothered every so often, it would be wise to have a second location in which to store incriminating evidence."

"Even the Order Force would occasionally do an audit, and they wouldn't always be able to avoid someone not on their payroll," agreed Zero, his eyes a little keener. "It would have to be somewhere connected but not on Behind land; Between would be ideal. Even if one of the Order Force did find something, they'd be unlikely to report it if it wasn't happening on Behind territory."

"Somewhere like the house across the road," I said, serving the tea and coffee. "Only in a different wing, sorta."

Those bobbing lights hadn't all been fake ones, a glamour to keep people out. There had been a real bobbing light or two, and they hadn't been on the side that held the way Between the human world and Behind, either.

That mad old bloke, I thought. He'd been busy for years. Funny that I didn't start to remember him until recently. Maybe I thought I'd dreamed him.

"Exactly," said Zero. There was a sharpness to his icy blue eyes; if Zero was a dog, his ears would be pricked up, his snout quivering, and his tail straight out. "I did a routine inspection of the house when we first arrived, but that was when we expected it to be a normal human house with a few weak spots. Now that we know it's a front for the Waystation fae, and that they're most likely keeping human prisoners and playing a game of tag with the Order Force, I can look more thoroughly."

"We'll need to be more careful this time," Athelas warned. "We've set off enough security magic lately that I'm beginning to wonder if we need to go back to basic training."

Zero opened his mouth, and I could almost see him thinking better of what he'd been about to say. There was a brief beat of silence before he said instead, "We'll be more careful. Our timing doesn't seem to have been very good lately, and I would *very* much like to know why."

"I was wondering if you'd noticed the coincidental way in which several events have occurred," agreed Athelas. "One feels as though one is being watched."

"One does," Zero said dryly. "If we're unfortunate enough to have trouble again today, I'll have to look into it."

He said that pretty suggestively, I thought. Did he suspect *Athelas* of telling someone about their movements? Suspicious psychos.

Athelas looked amused; Jin Yeong maliciously smug.

Of Zero, Jin Yeong asked, "*Chigeum?*"

"We might as well go now," Zero said, rising. "Our answers are all in that house, one way or another, and we can't know which direction to move until we have a few more of them."

"I've yet to find that stops you," Athelas said, making me grin. He got up too, buttoning his soft, plaid blazer, and said to Jin Yeong, "Shall we, Jin Yeong?"

Jin Yeong was already halfway to the front door without waiting for the other two, his stride long and loose. What was he so excited about? They were trying to *avoid* fights this time, weren't they?

Athelas, still looking highly amused, followed him.

"Stay here, Pet," said Zero. "Don't go out. Don't cause trouble."

He shut the door behind him before I could agree, and I said with relish, "Heck yes!"

I could take a long shower and use all the hot water before Jin Yeong got back to use it.

Gleefully, I charged upstairs to my bedroom, grabbed a few clothes to change into, and dashed back down to the bathroom before any of them changed their minds and came back to demand tea or coffee.

I emerged from the bathroom half an hour later, my hair damp around the edges and my face very pink, and went back upstairs to get my socks. I could feel the grit of stuff under my feet in the kitchen—crumbs, and dirt, and tiny pebbles—and *that* meant I should vacuum; but since I didn't have a vacuum cleaner, I would have to make do by wearing socks so I didn't feel the grit.

What a shame.

I pulled my socks on, leaning against the wall to stop myself falling over, and caught a flutter of something across the road.

The public garbage cans were moving.

Nope, not the garbage cans; something shabby and dark *near* the garbage cans.

I looked closer; grinned.

It was the bearded bloke again. What was he doing, hanging around on the nature strip near the house across the street?

And had he popped *out* of the garbage cans, or was that my imagination?

He wasn't any better dressed today—he was wearing a different shirt, but this one had a hole in it that was as big as the hole in his other shirt. He was still barefoot, too, which struck me as dangerous if he was going to keep nosing around the house across the street.

I mean, *everything* was dangerous about the house across the street, but the old guy was probably potty enough not to notice anything beyond something stuck in his foot, anyway.

Still, better if Zero and the others didn't find him wandering around the place. He'd probably go away if I gave him a bit of food like I used to. I pulled my boots on over my socks before I grabbed a banana and one of the leftovers containers full of stew, and went to look for the batty old bloke.

I kept an eye out for the detective as I crossed the road. He'd showed up enough lately that I didn't want to risk getting caught by him, sneaking around the house across the road—especially since it would lead him right to my three psychos.

The street was empty, but I still kept to the green, leafy edges of the footpath once I was off the bitumen. From this side of the road, I could hear the bearded old dude humming something to himself. That wasn't good. Zero would hear it, too, if it was much louder.

I sneaked around the hedge, looking cautiously left and right, and saw the bearded man poking at a mushroom with a stick.

"Oi!" I called, in a loud whisper.

He snapped around like a tiger snake, beady little eyes dark and deadly, one fist raised. Nope, it wasn't a fist; he was just kind of making an emu beak with his fingers that looked like it might dart out and peck me.

Ah heck, I thought; but I didn't say anything. This bloke wasn't only batty—he was *dangerous* batty.

"Oh, it's you," he said, and suddenly the deadly gleam to his eye was gone. "You should be more careful. Might have bitten you."

I looked at his stiff fingers and tilted my head at them. "What, with that?"

"Of course not," he said, his arm dropping. "Fingers don't have teeth. Well. Mine don't. Someone else's could, but not mine."

"Yeah, mine don't, either," I said cautiously. I showed him the banana and the leftovers, careful to move slowly. "You hungry?"

"Is it real food?" he asked, a shade of suspicion darkening his eyes again.

"Yeah. Made it myself. Well, not the banana. That came off a tree."

"They don't, always," the bearded bloke said, his eyes darting back and forth.

I looked at him sideways. "Don't they? Well, this one did."

He grabbed it straight away, making me jump, and bowed at me. "Million thanks, lady!" he said, and grabbed for the leftovers as well. "Good tuck, good tuck!"

"Yeah, that's what everyone reckons," I said. "Oi."

"Oi," he said back, with a mouth full of banana.

"You're the one that ate that pie I left out, aren't you?"

His eyes gleamed at me. "How'd I get inside the house? Huh? Can't prove it, can you?"

"Yeah, that's what I wanted to know as well," I said. Zero had said he'd done wards around the house to stop humans getting in, so how had the old bloke got in? "How *did* you get inside the house? And how'd you know *when* to come in? If my three—"

He shook his head violently, flicking banana chunks in every direction. "Nope, nope, nope. Don't go in the house when they're there."

"That's a good idea," I said. "Oi."

"Oi."

"You've been following me as well, haven't you?"

This time his eyes were sly. "Can't prove that, either."

"Nope," I agreed.

"A lady shouldn't go into that house," he said, nodding at the wall of the house across the road. He took the lid off the leftovers container and tipped it up to slurp up the stew, ignoring the plastic spoon I offered him. He gulped down a mouthful and said in a potatoey sort of way, "It's not safe."

"I know," I said. "But there's someone who keeps me safe, so I'll be all right. You should keep away, too."

"No one can keep someone else safe," he said seriously. "Even with an umbrella."

I had to stop myself from saying *yeah, but an umbrella can keep off the rain really well*, as if we were talking to each other in code. The bearded bloke sent me another surprisingly sharp look and grinned a bit, then gulped the rest of the stew in a few noisy mouthfuls.

I waited until he'd swallowed a few times before I asked, "You know anything about funny noises around this place? People coming and going?"

"I'm coming and going. *So much* coming and going!"

"Yeah, but other people. They might not look like people."

He tilted his head, eyes bright. "What do they look like, if they don't look like people?"

"Maybe *I'm* the one going mad," I muttered to myself. To him, I said, "Just people. But maybe they were taking other people who didn't want to go with them."

"No one comes in and out here," he said, licking out the plastic container. "Only me. It's warmer sleeping out here, anyway."

"Reckon it would be," I said, thinking of the cold draught that came from Between. "Want me to get you a blanket?"

He looked at me for a long time, his eyes fixed and bright above that dirty birds nest of a beard. At last, he said, unexpectedly, "That was a good pie. Threw the dish away in the bins over there. If you want it back."

I followed his pointing finger, and wasn't surprised to see the two public bins he'd been climbing out of earlier.

"Thanks," I said, turning back to him.

He was already gone.

"Sneaky beggar," I added, with respect. No wonder he'd been able to sneak in and out of the house without me seeing or hearing him. I'd probably need to figure out how he managed to get in the house, if I wasn't going to tell my three psychos about him. Not telling them was one thing, but them being injured by what I didn't tell them was another.

I'd also have to find a way to smuggle a blanket out to him without my three psychos finding out.

I wandered over toward the fence that was nearest the bins, my curiosity roused. He was definitely hinting at me, crazy old coot; what was in the bins, then? He'd been messing about in them when I saw him from the window, so there must be something there. With my luck, it was probably his earthly hoard. Maybe that's where he kept his other holey shirt.

Still, I thought, gazing at the bins, if you thought about it—if you thought about the fae and their superior attitude to humans, and if you thought about the way Between depended so much on how people thought, a rubbish bin was probably exactly where they'd put the entrance to a group of stolen humans.

Flamin' superior fae.

I narrowed my eyes at the bins, and it seemed to me that they didn't sit exactly *right* in morning sunlight. I tried to think of the cans as a door, but that made it harder to see instead of easier, so I stopped.

"Just wait," I muttered at them. "I'll get Zero; he'll set you straight!"

I tilted my chin at them to make sure they knew I meant business, and waded back through the long grass to the house over the road. Zero had told me to stay at home, but I'd discovered new information, after all.

He'd be pleased to see me, right?

I grinned and opened the door anyway. Even if he wasn't, he'd be glad for the info.

Maybe it was because I'd seen a bit of Between on the garbage cans, but the hallway seemed more Betweeny than they had last time I was here.

Quiet, I told it mentally, stepping lightly across the floorboards. I didn't want to come across anyone except my three psychos; and if I did, I wanted to be able to run before they heard me. *Nice and quiet. Socks on feet. Gluggy air. No sound. Nice and quiet.*

I don't know if it worked, but I could see a little puff of something that could be dust every time one of my feet touched the ground in a step. Dust, but more sparkle to it.

I was concentrating on my dusty steps so completely that I almost didn't see my three psychos in the master bedroom when I came upon them. They were all looking at the window, Zero expressionlessly, Athelas with a faint frown, and Jin Yeong with a slight pout.

I grinned. They hadn't seen me.

"Still looking for some Between storage?" I asked.

JinYeong didn't jump, exactly, but his eyes flashed up at me, and I grinned to know that I'd startled him. I didn't know if my experiment had worked, or if I'd just walked quietly enough not to be noticed until the last minute, but it was satisfying to startle him.

"Still," Athelas agreed.

"Yeah," I said. "I don't reckon you're gunna find it inside."

"I told you to stay at home," Zero said, his eyes hard. "I won't come looking for you if you get into trouble by yourself."

"Yeah," I said again, "but I reckon I figured out something."

Zero paused a moment; probably trying to decide whether to listen to the pet or send it home with its tail between its legs.

"All right," he said. "What was so important to tell me?"

"You said you're looking for another place, right? Somewhere the Waystation Behindkind can store stuff or people?"

JinYeong muttered something, and Athelas said, "Something big enough for several prisoners at least."

"Definitely human prisoners, though? Like the people that went missing around here?"

"What exactly are you getting at?" Zero asked, his tone briefer than before.

"Well, they're fae, aren't they?" I said, a bit more quickly. "Where else would they make a place to get to human prisoners Between than in the garbage? There's a couple cans outside the yard, and it looks to me like they're not really sitting right today."

Athelas blinked. "Good heavens. Perhaps I'm getting old, but that wouldn't have occurred to me. What a good little pet you are, sniffing that out by yourself!"

"I know a few fae," I said, and if my voice sounded dry, well that was understandable, wasn't it? "Seemed like a good bet."

Zero's eyes narrowed in his version of a grin. "We would have looked at the perimeter eventually," he said. "Don't be too proud of yourself, Pet."

"Wouldn't think of it," I said. "Just a human, me. Nothing important. I'll go sit in the garbage, shall I?"

Jin Yeong grinned.

"Since I found it," I added, while they were all still in a good mood, "does that mean I get to come along and see what you find?"

"*If* it's what we're looking for, and *if* there are no traps, you can come along," said Zero. "I'm not looking after you if there are traps to dismantle as well."

"Okay," I said cheerfully. I was pretty sure he'd look after me anyway; call it instinct, or maybe the suspicion of fellow feeling from someone almost human toward someone human, but I knew Zero wouldn't leave me to get hurt, even if he threatened to do it.

I would have led the way out, but Jin Yeong grabbed me by the ear and hauled me backward, tossing me in Zero's direction. I saw the malicious grin on his face as I attached myself to the hem of Zero's jacket, and hoped that the bearded bloke was long gone by now. I felt a bit protective of him; he'd been around so long, and no one seemed to look after him. It wouldn't be fair to sic the three psychos on him.

He wasn't around the yard when we got out, though; and he wasn't hanging around the garbage cans, either. I hoped he'd had sense enough not to go back inside them, and when Zero, with a brief nod at Athelas, lifted the first can's lid, I breathed a sigh of relief.

The can was empty.

Really, really empty. There was scum around the top to make it look real, and a tatter of black plastic bag showing when the lid was on, but there was nothing actually inside.

Except maybe a twinkle of starry sky.

I blinked at it, and the stars shifted.

"Who the heck thought it was a good idea to put stars down there?" I demanded.

"Those aren't stars," said Athelas, and his smile was all moonlight, even if it was still sunshine around us. "Well done, Pet. This isn't the door in—it's someone's back door out."

"That mean there won't be traps?" I asked, hopefully.

"There could be traps," Zero said, "but it's not likely they'll be from this side. I think we know how that human escaped the fae at the Waystation."

"He got out here?"

Zero put a hand on either side of the bin and stuck his head right in. When he pulled it out again, his white hair was slightly ruffled. "It looks like it," he said.

The poor bearded bloke! No wonder he was a bit mad. He must have seen someone climbing out of the garbage can; maybe he even caught a sight of the night sky in there. He probably hadn't been too sound in the mind already, and that would have been enough to send him over the edge completely.

Or was it possible that he *was* the escapee the fae were looking for? Zero and Athelas had said it was almost impossible for a human to wander Between without being taken or lured there, but he would have been escaping, not going in.

Yeah, he was definitely the escapee the fae were looking for.

In that case, he was almost definitely the witness Zero was looking for, too.

Oh boy. Good pets should definitely tell their owners when they knew about a witness to their murder investigation.

"Pet?" Athelas said curiously, his voice quiet. "Is there something else you would care to share?"

"Just curious about something," I said. "What are we gunna do when we find that witness?"

"I see that it's occurred to you that our witness and their escapee are one and the same," said Athelas.

His congratulatory tone felt like a pat on the head, and I was a bit annoyed to find that I felt pleased about that.

"Question him and then turn him over to the Order Force," Zero answered. "They'll want to question him, too. Humans shouldn't be able to wander Between as easily as this one seems to be able to."

That settled it; I was never going to tell my three psychos about him. He'd had a hard enough life already. If they couldn't solve a fae murder without him, they should give up their badges. There should be some protection for humans, even if I was all that protection was.

"Reckon they haven't got him back again, yet," I said. "Otherwise they would have found this door, wouldn't they?"

"More than likely," agreed Athelas. "Now I'm no expert in matters of magic—"

Zero coughed suddenly.

"—but it does seem to me that if we were *very* careful, we could use this back door to our advantage when it comes to visiting the Waystation again."

Zero looked at him. "You're no expert in matters of magic?"

JinYeong, his eyes glittering with amusement, asked a question that lilted up at the end.

"My expertise lies...elsewhere," Athelas said, with a small smile. "I shouldn't like to claim expertise in magic. Shall we?"

"Shall we what?" I asked.

Athelas began, "If you'll look on the inside rim of the garbage can, Pet—"

"*Don't* teach the pet how to see Between. It doesn't need to know."

But it was too late; I'd already seen what Athelas meant. On the inside rim of the garbage can there were chalk marks, a whole series of them that looked like piano keys or maybe just...stairs. If those stairs were flat and a bit cylindrical, that is.

"Cool!" I said. "How far down does it go?"

Zero's light blue eyes rested on me for a moment or two. "Far enough to see the stars when you look up," he said. "I'll go first. Pet, behind me. Put your hand in my pocket this time."

I grabbed his pocket where the inner lining joined the thick outer leather, my fingers catching fast to the seam; and, following Zero, I stepped into the garbage can and onto the first stair.

I wish I could have said whether the garbage can got bigger, or if we got smaller. It could have been both or either, and none of them made any sense to be actually happening. But I could see the stairs, and from my last outing Between I knew that if I could see them, I could walk down them; so I did.

I heard Athelas walking behind me, humming beneath his breath in a way that set off whispering echoes all around the cylinder we were descending, but it grew so dark so quickly that I couldn't even see more than Zero's hulking outline in front of my nose.

When there were no more stairs to descend and the floor grew hard and cold beneath us, I looked up. Zero was right; I could see all the stars as clearly as if it was night. I could also see the fog of my breath rising against the stars. *So* cold. Why was it so cold in summer?

"Pretty," I said, and I heard Athelas laugh softly.

Well, that couldn't be good.

I narrowed my eyes at the darkness all around, trying to see through the gloom. It wasn't really big—well, it was the inside of a garbage can, so I suppose the space had to stop *somewhere*—but it was insanely cold. Piles of something lumpy made shadows against the faintest edge of starlight, and I squinted at them. The whole floor looked lumpy. What was it, rags? Tyres? No, it was too sharp and bumpy to be tyres.

"Perhaps some light?" suggested Athelas.

A soft, cool blue light wafted from Zero's fingers, spreading out over the bumpy ground, and all of a sudden I knew exactly why it was so cold.

It wasn't tyres. It was bodies. The entire place was a Behind-kind morgue with human bodies stacked on top of each other around the circular space, mostly clean and entirely devoid of colour.

"I thought you said they were abducted," I said, shivering. There were so many of them; twenty, maybe even thirty bodies, men and women. "I thought you said it was disappearances!"

Zero tugged my hand out of his pocket effortlessly, and tossed me by my wrist in Athelas' direction. "Take the pet home," he said. "It's no use to us here."

"Hang on," I said, swallowing. I felt sick, but at least there were no entrails on show here. Just coldness and lack of life. "That bloke—that one with the blue jumper. I know that bloke."

"A friend of yours, Pet?" asked Athelas, in mild interest.

"No, just someone who goes to the café I worked at."

Zero prodded the body gently. "Jin Yeong. How long have they been here? Any of them. All of them."

Jin Yeong pursed his lips and turned his head to one side. Was he sniffing?

Yeah, he was sniffing. He leaned in close to the body, eyes closed, and drew in a deep breath through his nose once again.

Oh well, so long as he didn't—

Yep. There he went. He stroked one finger across the small, dark trail of blood on the guy's hairline and touched it to his tongue. I mean, it wasn't even still *wet*, for pity's sake.

"That's so flamin' gross," I muttered.

One brow went up at me; Jin Yeong spoke, his voice certain.

"As long as that?" Zero's brows went up as well. "What about the rest of them?"

"As long as what?" I asked sharply. "It can't be *that* long—I saw him last week. He comes in for a bacon, egg, and cheese muffin every coupla days when he's in Hobart."

"How very talented of him," said Athelas, crouching briefly by the body, "considering he's been dead a good four weeks, according to Jin Yeong."

"He *can't* have been," I protested. "I saw him last week! He didn't have his usual muffin, but he was drinking coffee and he can't have been dead if he was drinking coffee!"

Jin Yeong narrowed his eyes at me.

"Not much good glaring at me," I told him, feeling sharp and cold and off-balance. "Your sniffer is probably wrong again."

He only made a *pft* sort of noise at me and looked smug, which was worrying. One of the most annoying things about Jin Yeong's smugness is the fact that it's usually pretty merited.

"I don't think so," said Zero. "Pet, take pictures of all the dead people."

"What?"

"Photographs. Take photographs of them."

"Yeah, but what with? I don't have a camera."

"Modern—" Zero stopped, and started again, "You can take pictures with your mobile phone, can't you?"

"I think our pet is trying to say that she doesn't *have* a phone," said Athelas gently. "Is it so, Pet?"

"I didn't have money for a phone!" I said. "I had to buy food and stuff."

Unsaid was the fact that *and stuff* was my parents' house, that I had planned one day to put down a deposit on with the cash I had hidden around the house, even if that money was now no longer needed.

Jin Yeong looked alert. "*Ah, ku don nemsae? Utkida!*"

"Pet," said Athelas, a slight gleam to his eyes, "have you been depositing small amounts of cash around the house in odd spots?"

The vampire can smell *money*?

Who the heck can smell *money*?

I glared at Jin Yeong again. "Mostly around my own room—which you wouldn't know if you hadn't invaded my privacy in the first place!"

"I believe we've gotten off the subject," Athelas said. Now it was more than a gleam in his eyes; it was a definite laugh.

I didn't think he should be laughing when we were in a room full of bodies, so I said a bit snarkily, "Even if I had a phone, why would I want to take photos of dead guys?"

"Perhaps I spoke too soon about the investigative skills of our pet," mourned Athelas.

"They've kept the bodies," Zero said, as if neither Athelas or I had spoken. "Fae don't tend to keep bodies once they've killed them. Not unless there's a specific reason."

"Nobody does!" I muttered. "Not unless they're psychopaths or something. It's not just a fae thing: Humans don't keep bodies for the heck of it, either!"

Zero's eyes flicked over to me and then back to the bodies. "The point being—"

"Yeah, that we gotta figure out why. But I still haven't got a camera, so what are we gunna do?"

"I have a phone," said Athelas.

He must have surprised Zero as much as it surprised me, because Zero looked up at him sharply and suddenly. "When did you get a phone?"

"If one lives in the modern world, one should avail oneself of all the conveniences."

"A mobile phone is only a convenience if one lives in the modern *human* world," Zero said. "We don't live in the human world for long enough to make it necessary."

"I beg to differ," said Athelas, slipping a thin, white smartphone from his back pocket. "Since it is certainly necessary in this situation."

Did Zero roll his eyes? He looked away, anyway; and he didn't answer Athelas. Unconcerned, Athelas took picture after composed picture, directing JinYeong to turn bodies and position faces. JinYeong looked annoyed to be told what to do, but he didn't seem to mind touching the bodies, so I was glad Athelas hadn't told me to do it. I didn't think I could have.

"What are we taking photos for, anyway?" I asked Zero. "That's the sort of thing the cops do."

"We are cops," said Zero. "Their equivalent, at any rate."

"Yeah, that's right; you're investigators or something."

"Enforcers."

"What's the difference?" From what Athelas had said, I'd thought they were the fae version of police.

"Investigators only investigate," Zero told me. "Enforcers investigate, weigh evidence, and apply the law."

I frowned. "What do you mean, apply it?"

"It would be more correct to say that he applies judgement," Athelas said, standing up again at last. "A rather more active version of a hangman. I should mention that I am not an Enforcer. I am merely an onlooker."

"Good," I said, still feeling a bit snarky at them all. There was no way Athelas should be dispensing justice if it came to the human world.

Athelas only smiled a little and put his phone away. "Shall we proceed to the police station?"

"I don't think we'll need the police station," Zero said. "We'll only need a computer and internet access. I've got the feeling that what we're looking for won't be hard to find."

Half an hour later, at my usual computer at the library, I grumbled, "We need a computer at home if we're gunna be doing stuff like this."

Athelas had plugged his phone into one of the computers—something I was pretty sure the librarians usually objected to, and Zero's sword was *really* easy to see in the shadows against the bookcases.

"People will look at us weird if they see us comparing dead people's faces with photos on the internet at the library."

"People will see what they expect to see," said Athelas. "Nothing more, nothing less."

"'S'pose Zero did a spell," I muttered. "It prob'ly hasn't got anything to do with people not seeing stuff cos they only see what they expect to see."

"Hush, Pet," said Athelas, uploading his photographs with a

swiftness and surety that I wouldn't have expected from someone non-human. "JinYeong, who was longest dead?"

"*Ku saram*," JinYeong said, pointing to one of the fair-haired victims.

"Dear me," said Athelas, as the screen populated with much healthier looking pictures of the dead guy. "How interesting! It appears that this man is a very famous Tasmanian singer who is currently supposed to be on tour in Canada. He's very influential in politics and is expected to make the switch from music to politics in the next few years."

"They mustn't have noticed him missing yet," I said. "How come he's here, though? How'd he get from Canada to here?"

"The others," Zero said, ignoring me. "Who are they? That one specifically—who is he?"

Athelas clicked, and scrolled a little. His brows went up. "More and more interesting. This one is the chairman for a company who is currently buying up land in and around Hobart for redevelopment. And *that* one—yes, I thought as much. He's in local government, and until a few months ago he was opposing plans to redevelop empty lots into apartment housing."

"Hang on," I interrupted. "I remember when that one went missing. There was a really big fuss about it, but they found him again. How come he's dead now?"

Athelas smiled curiously. "Well, Pet; according to this article, he isn't dead. He is well and alive, and giving a speech at this very moment in a city planning meeting."

"I give up," I complained, leaning around Zero again to get a better look at the computer screen. "I don't know what's happening any more. D'you mean the fae at the waystation are trying to make sure Hobart gets more developed? Why? And how are they getting these guys to change their minds—and how come they're dead but alive?"

"Who was the other one?" Zero asked, turning abruptly to

face me and disturbing my precarious balance. "You said he came to the café to eat muffins."

I caught myself by grabbing the hem of his leather jacket, and let it go again just as quickly. "Sorry. Um. Well, not just to eat muffins, but he liked the food, yeah."

"He's an ordinary person?"

"He's human, yeah. The boss said he was one of the people who owns half of Hobart, though."

"He owns half of Hobart and he goes to a small, dingy café to eat his breakfast?" Athelas sounded sceptical, but interested.

"Yeah. The food's good there. And he's not the sort of bloke who worries about expensive food, so long as it's warm and good. He's pretty nice, for a rich bloke."

Zero and Athelas exchanged a look.

"Pet," said Athelas, "*which* half of Hobart did this muffin-eater own?"

"The parking half," I said. "He owns at least three of the parking lots, the boss said. And a house in about two other countries, as well."

"Ah!" Athelas purred. "*Now* things begin to be very clear!"

"Do they?" I looked glumly at him. I was still confused about who was dead and who was alive, and I'd seen the bodies. "Well, if it's all about redevelopment, there's a couple people round Hobart who are gunna be against it."

"I very much doubt it's about redevelopment," said Athelas. "As such. When you saw him last, was your friend behaving as he usually did?"

"Yep. Same food, same drink; same smile. That sorta thing. You think something was after him then?"

"I think not," said Athelas. "No, I think not. He was well and truly dead by then. Changelings, wouldn't you say, Zero?"

Zero was brief. "Yes."

"And if I'm not very much mistaken, anti-Family changelings."

"Yes."

"What's Family? Whose family?" I had definitely heard them talking about a *Family* before.

JinYeong shot me a narrow look and said something that sounded annoyed.

"JinYeong feels that you're becoming noisy," Athelas told me helpfully.

"Thanks," I said sourly. "Thanks for telling me. Think I prefer not knowing what he's saying."

"One feels that one should pat them on the back and give them leave to continue," Athelas continued, without regarding me. "If it's all the same to you, Zero. They've got some nice, key players ensconced, and the enemy of my enemy..."

"Yeah, and what do you mean when you say *changelings*?" I demanded, reminded of my other, pressing question. "I know that word, and in the stories it's always a bad thing."

Athelas shrugged, a faint smile etched delicately on his lips. "In this case, I shouldn't think so."

"Changelings," said Zero, surprising me by answering directly, "are fae versions of particular humans. It's one of the most logical reasons for bodies to be kept: If they're needed to maintain a fae's changeling appearance and personality. If they don't have the body, they don't have the memories and personality."

I really shouldn't have had breakfast. I looked back up at Zero's expressionless face and asked a bit thickly, "So they're really dead, but someone else is going around with their faces?"

"Not only their faces," he said. "Their faces, their tastes, their personalities and their memories."

"Those people were killed so someone else could take over their lives?"

JinYeong muttered something dismissive, but I ignored him, my eyes on Zero. I got the impression that he wasn't enjoying the conversation, but he didn't look away, either.

"It's a necessary part of the process," Athelas said, disconnecting his phone from the computer again. "If a changeling takes over, the human has to die."

"Death isn't necessary," said Zero, his eyes leaving me for a fraction of a moment to rest on Athelas instead. "Merely convenient. It ensures that your real human can't escape or come back to disturb the changeling."

"If we—if we burned the bodies," I said, conscious of a cold, dizzying anger, "would the changelings go back to what they really look like?"

"Yes."

"What about that glamour you said about? Wouldn't they glamour themselves?"

"Glamour affects perception, not the actual appearance. Changelings need to interact with family, friends, and fans; perception shifts, and if only one thing is wrong, the whole appearance is ruined. It would only be a temporary solution. Changelings aren't only the appearance of their host; they're the very thing. Once the original body is gone, there are no memories and personality to draw from."

"All right," I said. "Then what are you going to do about it?"

CHAPTER ELEVEN

ATHELAS BLINKED A LITTLE. "PET," HE BEGAN, GENTLY. "THERE are operations like this all over the human world."

"You mean it's just humans so it doesn't matter?"

"More that it's impossible to stop all of them," Athelas said.

"You don't *have* to stop all of them," I told him. "Just this one. This one that's under your nose. Show 'em they can't go using humans like—like monopoly pieces."

"That's the sort of action that starts a dangerous precedent," replied Athelas. To my surprise, he didn't object to my tone. There was a soft sort of amusement in his eyes—at me or at the world, who knows which.

"There's legal precedent for it already," said Zero.

That startled Athelas a lot more than I had. After a pause that was slightly too long, he asked, "Do you mean to say that you're going to do something about it?"

"The pet found my sword. There's some form of payment due."

"There is," agreed Athelas. His grey eyes were light as the sky, bright with interest. "This human side of you is fascinating to see, Zero!"

"It's not the human side of me," Zero retorted. "There's law and order concerning humans even Behind, and as an Enforcer, I'm pledged to uphold it. Here or there, it doesn't matter. We'll deal with this ourselves."

"*Koll*!" said Jin Yeong, his eyes glittering. "*Calaeyo, hyung?*"

"Should we really be interfering in someone else's no doubt er, *anti-Family* endeavours?"

I opened my mouth to demand to know again what something *anti-Family* was, and why it was more important than human lives, but Zero fixed me with an icy look.

I shut it again.

"We might as well clean it up," he said. "If it gets too messy the Order Force will clean it up anyway; and we're on the scene already, so to speak."

He *said* "we might as well", and there wasn't much interest in his voice, but his fingers were pretty tight around the hilt of his sword. I looked from his whitened fingers to his expressionless face and kept my mouth shut this time, too; because Zero never answered my questions, and this time he had, even if he didn't have to. And because, no matter what reason he was doing it, Zero was going to make sure that humans didn't keep disappearing and dying around Hobart.

"The changelings?" Athelas sounded resigned.

"We'll clean them up bit by bit," said Zero. "While they're trying to figure out what happened and uphold a constant glamour. First, we'll need to go back to the waystation. That's their headquarters, and that's what we need to clean up."

"Very well," Athelas agreed. "Perhaps it will be enjoyable, after all. We've the sword now, so we're fighting with our best foot forward, so to speak. Shall we go at once?"

"No," said Zero. "We'll go better prepared this time. We know what's going on and who is to blame; we'll finish it properly."

· · ·

I DON'T THINK THEY REALLY MEANT TO TAKE ME WITH THEM, but when we were a few houses away from home, JinYeong scented the air and said a sharp something to Zero.

"That detective," said Zero, "has very good instincts, and is very good at his job."

That's what he said, but I was pretty sure what he really meant was that the detective was starting to be a moderate annoyance, which cheered me up a bit. Score one for the humans—especially ones that couldn't be thralled or manipulated!

"The pet will have to come with us," Athelas said, shrugging.

"That isn't a good idea," said Zero tightly.

JinYeong made a *pft* sort of noise, and must have said what I was about to say—that I'd been Between and Behind before, anyway—because Athelas nodded.

"The pet seems to be relatively good at looking after itself," he said. "And it hardly seems likely that the detective will follow us into a rubbish bin. He *will* follow the pet."

Zero's pale blue eyes closed and flicked open again. "Hold onto my pocket," he said. "And stay behind me."

"Gotcha," I said at once. I didn't want to give him a chance to take it back, so I grabbed the join of stitched leather where his pocket met the outside of the jacket. There was no way I wanted to leave fae by themselves to deal with humans. Not when they looked on us like pets, or chess pieces. There should be a human to watch out for other humans. "Let's go."

JinYeong grinned, but I wasn't sure if it was because my enthusiasm amused him, or if it amused him to think that I could come to mischief Between. I stuck my tongue out at him anyway, which made him purse his lips and narrow his eyes, and gave my attention to following Zero without pulling too much at his pocket.

I'm not sure why I noticed it, or even how I noticed it. Maybe it felt like someone was following me; I looked behind when we got through the bodies, my stomach still unsettled at the feel of the stickiness beneath my feet.

"Ah heck!" I said.

Athelas' eyes glowed softly in the half light of Between. "I see you've noticed our follower, Pet."

"How'd he get in here?" I said in disgust. If he'd seen us climbing into a rubbish bin, why the heck would he follow us? If he hadn't, how had he found us?

The pull of Zero's jacket didn't lessen, and Zero didn't stop. "He came through the house," he tossed over his shoulder. "It's more open than they're aware—or maybe they're trying to catch him next. He'll turn back when things begin to feel wrong around him, if his instincts are good."

"At least he won't set off the warning spells," Athelas said. "They wouldn't have conditioned them to recognise humans."

"What if his instincts aren't good?" I asked. It wasn't so much that I didn't think the detective's instincts weren't good; it was more that I thought his instinct to catch my three psychos, no matter what it was they were up to, was stronger than his instinct to avoid danger. "Think he's seen us; he keeps looking in our direction."

"He's not quite in the same part of Between as we are," Athelas said, easily. "We came through the back door; he's come through the front. We should manage to avoid a meeting. If not, I suppose we'll have to do something about it."

I saw the tip of Jin Yeong's tongue run lightly along the inside of his upper lip, his eyes gleaming and hungry.

"Not like that!" I protested. I stumbled as I walked, my attention dangerously divided among Jin Yeong, Athelas, and the detective.

"Don't drain the detective," said Zero, without looking at any of us. "And don't kill him, either."

Jin Yeong looked sulky but not too angry; he was probably looking forward to a fight ahead. Athelas looked mildly regretful, especially when the detective kept coming, a vague shadow in the darkness that had wide, white eyes and white, grimacing teeth.

He was already regretting following us, I could tell. But he was also determined to catch my three psychos, and even if he couldn't see us, he kept coming. His head swung left and right, eyes staring at the walls and the shadowy representation of a hand resting on the gun holstered on his belt. If he was anything like me, he'd started seeing movement in the walls by now.

I opened my mouth to tell Zero that Detective Tuatu hadn't given up, but something Between twisted and snapped, and I accidentally said, "Ow!" aggrievedly, instead.

"They know!" said Athelas swiftly. "My lord, they know!"

"Quickly!" Zero said, between his teeth. "We're too close! They'll burn everything this time!"

"Oi!" I said indignantly. So what if the bodies were burnt? The changelings would be revealed, and serve them right. "The detective!"

"Too late," Zero said, starting forward in haste and dragging me with him. "He'll have to look after himself."

But the detective, his eyes rolling back until they were nearly all white, had stopped, and he swayed as he stood. That wall he was propping himself against looked pretty holey, which meant—

A goblin popped its head out of the wall.

"Don't think he can," I replied, and let go of Zero's pocket.

I heard Zero yelling but I ignored it. He was probably just saying the Behindkind equivalent of *bad pet* at me, anyway.

I'm not sure if they vanished, or if I fell behind, but either way it only took a second before the detective and I were the only ones in the tunnel—well, apart from the goblin leaning out of its tunnel to stab him.

I put my head down and ran for it. I punched the goblin, the needle flashing silver in my peripheral, wicked sharp, and it tumbled from its tunnel, scattering needles as it went.

The detective stared at it in horror, then down at his hand, which was barely scratched by the needle.

"Beauty!" I said, and snatched up the needles. "Hardly a

scratch! It prob'ly won't even affect you. You lot better keep out of my way, goblin, or I'll stab every one of you with your own needles!"

"Drugs?" asked the detective faintly. His eyes, when they weren't rolled back and white, were trying to focus on the needles in my fist. "Shouldn't do that."

"C'mmon," I said, grabbing his collar with my free hand. "You don't wanna stand here. There's too many flamin' goblins around."

"Goblins?" he said, but it was more of a whimper. His eyes were focused on the goblin that was sobbing its woe on the ground. Too small to be a kid, too humanoid to be a dog; there was no way for him to explain that away to himself.

"Yep. Better than being alone around the vampire. Keep moving."

He didn't move really well, so I pulled him along by his collar. I thought I could see Zero's shadow up ahead; not his actual person, but a thin, watery sort of shadow that made me think of light filtering through the top of a pool. Wherever Zero was, it wasn't exactly in the same place as me and the detective.

I followed the shadowy thing anyway, kicking at the odd goblin and pushing through the heaviness that must have been Between, all the way up that cave-like hallway I knew well, until we were at the courtyard again.

When I stepped up onto the flagstones, dragging Detective Tuatu with me, someone grabbed *me* by the collar.

I yelled, but Zero's face swayed before mine and I stopped mid-yell. Good thing I did, because I didn't realise until I saw his face that I was aiming one of the goblin needles at him. I probably wouldn't have managed to hit him, but he could have done a bit of damage to me defending himself.

"Next time you let go of me, I'll leave you to the goblins," he said, and dropped me to the flagstones.

"Oh, that was you leaving a shadow for me to follow."

Zero strode away without answering, and I sighed heavily.

What a pain. I thought I'd got here by myself. Still, there was warmth mixed in with the annoyance. To the detective, I said, "Oi. You okay?"

"No," he said, and threw up.

Jin Yeong made a disgusted noise and hastily shifted his pointy shoes away from the mess, and Athelas sighed, "Pet, was it really necessary to bring along a playmate?"

"Yes," I told him, scowling. "The goblins were gunna get him."

"Surely *one* human less is not an encumbrance, Pet?"

Jin Yeong made a noise that sounded like agreement, and spoke a short, careless sentence.

"I don't care if he was annoying you anyway!" I retorted, heatedly. "You can't let people die because they're annoying you!"

"Good heavens, Pet! Did you understand that?"

I scowled at Jin Yeong this time. "Nah, I just know his pinched little face, now."

"*Yah, Petteu! Nae olgulun—*"

I stuck my tongue out at him.

"Now that you've finished your rescue, perhaps we could go ahead with our ostensible purpose?" suggested Athelas. "One presumes that the bodies are more or less ash by now, but one can always hope."

Zero was already striding toward the glassy windows without waiting for us. It must have taken the other two by surprise as well, because we all scrambled to catch up. Even the detective stumbled after us, raw determination fighting through the confusion and fear in his face.

"Careful," I said, and grabbed his hand. "Yeah, mind the step, it's a big one."

Zero must have really been on the hunt, because he didn't seem to notice that I was attached to his pocket again—or the extra weight from the detective, for that matter.

The step up to the platform wasn't as big as I remembered, but the switch in sound was just as sudden; when I stepped up onto the wooden platform, Zero's voice cut in suddenly above the whining roar of something insecty and very, very loud.

"Pet," he said, his voice crisp, "Stay behind me."

Ah heck. What was it *now*?

"Another ambush?" Athelas' voice wasn't loud, but somehow it cut through the noise to rest, soft and interested, on my ear. "Dear me, we do seem to be having our fair share of excitement at this Waystation!"

"This one isn't for us," Zero said grimly. "That's the sound of devourers."

The sound of what?

JinYeong sniffed a small laugh and made a dismissive remark.

"Yes, I'd venture to think so," agreed Athelas. "The Family has ways of finding out when Behindkind become too free with their affairs. Happily for us, it means we were *not* discovered; the devourers must have tripped the alarms."

"We'll need to fight, regardless," said Zero. "They'll destroy everything at the Waystation; and we're still looking for our human witness who may be the only one to have seen the murderer at his work."

"*Choshimhaeyo*," said JinYeong warningly, his teeth bared. "*Watda, watda!*"

I saw a brief flash of yellow that turned to the gleam of steel; Zero was carrying the umbrella that was a sword.

"Perhaps it wasn't entirely wise to carry that back here," said Athelas.

"We shall see," Zero said, taking a step toward the glass windows.

There was a flutter of drapes or maybe wings, then the glass windows flew open all along the platform. A roar rose in the air; wings, so many wings, bright and loud and buzzing, burst onto the wooden platform. They might have been humans, but humans didn't have wings that looked like they could cut throats; nor did human mouths split half their faces to display rows of two-inch teeth.

Swords flashed between the wings, barely sharper than the wings themselves, and Zero's sword slashed, wide and devastating, to meet them.

I gripped the detective's wrist, pulled painfully between Zero's moving figure and Detective Tuatu's lax one, and saw Athelas dart past, lithe and neat, in a skirl of twin blades that were small and thin enough to have been knitting needles. Jin Yeong, eschewing any other weapon than his teeth, was a bloody nightmare on the other side, his face already dripping gore.

Above the buzz of wings, Zero thundered, "Clear the deck and take the station!" and we pressed forward, locust-people screeching around us.

I stayed behind Zero, kicking out at the locusts that got too close to his flanks or the detective's sluggish body, and wished for an extra hand so that I could use a few of the needles I'd pinched from the goblins.

One of the locusts, ducking low and wicked fast, slid below Zero's sword and slashed a wing at me. I jerked back reflexively, but I saw a spray of dark hair flying, touched with blood, and kicked out instinctively.

The locust kept coming in spite of my assault, gnashing at me with its mouth bloody and bruised. I kicked at it again, panicking, and it screeched its anger, wings shivering.

"Ah heck," I panted.

It wasn't going to stop, and I didn't have enough hands.

It lunged again; lunged and halted abruptly as Zero reached back, plucking it away, and slammed it into the nearest chair. I heard the crack as its neck broke; then Zero hefted the body once again and used it as a shield to plough through the three nearest locusts as he swept their feet from beneath them with his sword.

Jin Yeong fell on their bodies at once, tearing out throats with teeth just as deadly as theirs, and it came to my attention that I could hear the sound of those throats being torn out.

"Ah man, *gross!*" I wailed.

"They're dead, JinYeong," Zero said. "They're all dead. You can stop now."

JinYeong looked up, his eyes dark, but pulled away from the ruined bodies. He wiped his mouth on his sleeve, raising his brows at me as if to say *what?*

"There's something wrong with you," I told him. The silence was very loud, and so was my voice.

"Are all the waystation fae dead?" asked Zero. His eyes flickered over the room, and I saw that there were fae bodies mingled with the locusts; these ones cut apart with locust wings.

"I imagine so," said Athelas. "Good heavens! I belie me. There's one still alive over there, but he is certainly dying."

Zero threw down the locust he had been using as a shield and towed me and the detective over toward the dying fae. "How long?"

"He has a little breath left," Athelas continued in a considering sort of manner, "but not much, I'd say."

I don't know why, but I felt like I should cover the detective's eyes.

"I wouldn't have told," said the fae, in a gasp, looking up glassily in our direction. "I wouldn't have told about the human."

"What human?" Zero asked. "Speak quickly."

"The one that can pass through Between and Behind," he said. "The one that should have died. I wouldn't have told. Not to the Family."

Zero, sharply, asked, "Where is the human?"

The fae laughed breathlessly, and pointed behind us. That laugh must have taken the last of his breath, because his hand dropped and I didn't see his chest rise again.

Poor old bearded bloke. When had they caught him again?

Echoing me, Athelas said, "They must have caught it and put

it in the lock-up since you were last here." He moved back through the room, picking his way through dead bodies to a metal door.

"Ah, Jin Yeong, if you please?"

Jin Yeong smiled lazily and crossed the room after him to open the door. "*Himi obseo!*" he said mockingly, but Athelas only gave a small smile.

"Wait here, Pet," said Zero, but I was already following them.

The first thing I saw was an old, holey t-shirt on the cell floor, half burnt. It was the same sort of shirt I'd seen on the old bearded guy the other day—no, it was the *same* shirt. The exact same shirt, with the big, round hole turning the word *shoot* into *shot*.

A little bit beside and beneath it was a pile of dust—or maybe ashes. Beyond that—

I swayed a bit. I should have guessed from the smell, but the dead locusts were pretty smelly themselves, so maybe it had masked the smell from the cells.

Beyond the pile of ashes on the floor was a small sprinkle of blood, and a hand; then more blood, a deep, dark slick of it that slashed the cell across, top to bottom. Someone's vertebrae, still attached to most of the important bits, gleamed red in one corner.

Even attached to Zero's pocket, I shivered.

"Go outside, Pet," said Zero. "You're in the way."

I cleared my throat and said thickly, "I'm not. Fought my way here, just like you. Brought him along, too."

I held up the detective's limp hand; he stared around at the carnage as if he thought he was still dreaming.

"*Nawa,*" said Jin Yeong. He pinched my ear between his fingers and dragged me back out with as much implacability as I had dragged the detective through Between.

He released my ear when we were back at the platform; smirked, and went back inside.

"Flamin' vampire," I muttered to the detective, but I wasn't shivering anymore so maybe it wasn't a bad thing to be outside.

I found that my face was wet, and wiped a warmth of moisture away that wasn't blood.

Crazy old coot. Why hadn't he run away after he tipped me off? They must have caught him lurking while we were at the library, matching faces and figuring it all out.

I sniffled a bit and used my t-shirt to dab away the rest of the tears. Fine protection I was. Hadn't even been able to stop one old bloke from dying.

My voice was still a bit thick when I said to the detective, "You shouldn't have come here. It's not safe."

He gazed around him in a sick kind of way, and said, "Am I awake yet?"

"Nope, sorry. Hang on for a bit longer, okay? You'll be safe when we get back out."

"Out?" he asked, as though he was trying to figure it out. "But this was a house. A house!"

"Still is," I said. "Don't worry about it. It doesn't make sense if you think about it too much. Just keep quiet and try not to get killed."

Maybe he fainted, or maybe it was that bit of goblin poison working in him. I helped him sit down on the step and he went pretty quiet for a while, eyes closed.

I peered through the window on tiptoes, as if that would help me see any better, glad for the section of wall that hid the worst of the gore from me. JinYeong saw me through the sliver of sight I had of the lockup, and snarled at me, but Zero was only a hulking shadow somewhere near to where the dead Behindkind fae lay. Athelas didn't glance in my direction at all.

"He's dead after all," I said huskily—to the detective or to myself, I wasn't sure which one. Why did they have to burn him, though? It wasn't like they had a changeling of him out there to get rid of: it was as if they'd wanted to make a mockery of human death rites.

I'd gotten used to seeing him out of the corner of my eye whenever my three psychos weren't around, a kind of scruffy guardian angel who shouldn't have existed, or survived, or been possible.

I was glad I hadn't told my psychos about him.

Faintly, I heard Athelas ask, "No telling, I suppose, how long he's been dead?"

"No," Zero said shortly. "Human, Jin Yeong?"

Jin Yeong made a noise of assent, and kicked at the ashes angrily.

"At least we know it's human," remarked Athelas. "I suppose our search for the real human murder victim is now over. He's probably been dead the whole time."

"Well, he hasn't," I said to myself, in a small, angry mutter.

"They must have taken the body down because they didn't want to draw attention to the house," Zero said, nodding. "They wouldn't have expected one of their own to be murdered next."

Athelas surveyed the rest of the cell. "It's quite possible they didn't know who they were dealing with."

"It's no good trying to find anything else here," Zero said abruptly. "Anyone we could have spoken with is dead. We'll deal with the changelings and find a new angle."

"A good idea, I fancy," agreed Athelas. "I wonder if I should mention, Zero, that the waystation seems to be becoming a little...well, condensed."

"I know," said Zero. "Something is pulling this whole area of Between in on itself. We'd better leave while we can. Jin Yeong, take a sample of the ashes just in case."

He came for the door at a lope while Jin Yeong fished something small and plasticky from his pocket to scoop up ashes, and Athelas followed behind.

"What a shame," sighed Athelas, looking over his shoulder. "It might have been nice to see someone play with the Family. They were doing quite well."

"It wouldn't do any good," said Zero, his voice harsh. "This is the way it always turns out. Pet, hold tight. No, *tight*."

"That's as tight as I can hold!" I protested, as Jin Yeong whipped past us and disappeared down into the courtyard. Athelas followed, moving more swiftly than I'd ever seen him move.

Oh man. This was bad.

Zero made a hissing between his teeth, snatched up my hand, and dragged me out from Behind and into Between, the detective trailing behind me as I snagged his collar just in time. The courtyard passed in a flash, the tunnel Between and human by turns, but the detective didn't feel like a drain on me anymore, though my fist was tight around his collar. Maybe Zero was doing that, too.

But above and beyond the pull I should have felt from the detective, there was another feeling entirely. A feeling of pressure, or weight; or maybe it was the feeling that something was trying to turn me inside out.

"Ow, ow, ow!" I said, as I sprinted behind Zero. "Ow, flamin' heck, ow!"

"Faster!" said Zero, between his teeth. I saw him look back at me once, while the hallway flashed past, Between but not Between, and windows winked with vaguely sunny light. Then he swept me off my feet, detective and all, and fairly *hurled* us all through a window.

We should have fallen, but we floated instead. We floated, and then something made a giant *puff* around us, and we blew sideways into a bush.

"Yow!" I mumbled in protest, smothered by leather jacket on one side and stabbed by branches on the other.

Someone stuck an elbow in my ribs, so I jabbed them back.

"What?" said Detective Tuatu's voice, plaintively.

"Don't jab me with your elbow, then," I told him sourly.

"Well, Pet?" asked Athelas' voice, and two slender hands removed me from the dual embrace of Zero and the bush.

"I s'pose," I said gloomily. "Reckon I've lost a bit of skin, though."

I turned to give the detective a hand out of the bush, and he came up still looking a bit dizzy.

"You all right?" I asked Zero, brushing twigs off the detective's shoulders and pinching leaves out of his tightly curled hair.

"Of course." He didn't need anyone's help to climb out of the bush; he brushed himself off slowly, gazing at the house behind us in a considering sort of way. "Not bad," he said.

I turned around to see what he meant, and my mouth dropped open.

"What the *flaming* heck!"

The entire house was gone. Just...gone.

In its place, the overgrown bushes of an empty yard sprawled over the fence and tried to take over the footpath as well, flowers and branches growing in wild abundance.

"Dear me," said Athelas. "It would seem that we managed to get out just in time. I wonder if the Family knew you were in there, Zero?"

"I doubt it," Zero said grimly. "They'd have tried harder, if they had."

"We've got some flamin' bad timing lately," I said, trying not to shiver at the lack of house. That was gunna bring a really cold breeze down from the mountain during winter, that hole in the street. "First that body melts, then some other bodies burn up, and then a hoard of locusts kills your bad guys just before you get there to question them."

"That's a very good point," said Zero. His voice was level and emotionless, but his eyes were twin chips of blue ice. "I would very much like to know who knows enough about our movements and enough about the Family to give them that kind of information. If I find out that it's someone close to me—"

Jin Yeong made a scornful sound and stalked across the road toward the house.

"Stop!" said Detective Tuatu, hazily. "You're all under arrest!"

"Flamin' heck!" I said, jumping. "Forgot you were there, detective. You can't arrest 'em; there's no crime scene. You can't even get 'em for trespass—there's nowhere *to* trespass."

"All of you!" he said, more forcefully. "You're *all* under arrest!"

"Perhaps it's time to see if fae persuasion will do the trick," suggested Athelas.

"No," said Zero, and hit the detective smartly on the side of the head.

Detective Tuatu dropped like a stone. I grabbed him, staggering under his weight, but Zero plucked him effortlessly away from me, and said, "Lunch."

"What?"

"Red meat, I should think," Athelas said, nodding. "Will you take care of the detective, Zero, or shall I?"

"I'll do it," said Zero, hefting the detective up on his shoulders like a lamb. "Potatoes, too. And I want gravy."

"Right," I said, blinking. "You want spuds and steak for lunch. With gravy."

It was gunna be hard to think about cooking for my three psychos when I'd seen bodies and human locusts before lunch time—not to mention a house disappearing in front of my eyes.

"And coffee," said Zero consideringly.

"You want me to make you coffee first?"

"No." Zero fished out a wallet from the inside pocket of his leather jacket. "Have coffee somewhere, and buy the steak fresh. I don't want to see you back at the house yet."

"Oh." I took the wallet. "Okay. You're not gunna kill him, are you?"

Zero's brows rose momentarily. "Of course not. I'm going to put him back at his desk."

"Make sure to get it with sugar," Athelas said over his shoulder, as he started across the road. "You're looking pale. I don't think Zero wants to prop your limp body up against a wall."

"Go see if Jin Yeong needs help," said Zero impatiently, and strode away down the street with the detective across his shoulders. I don't know if my eyes were playing tricks on me, but it was more likely that Zero ducked back Between as a way of shortening his journey, because he grew hazy and then disappeared altogether before the swell in the street would have hidden him from view.

"Take your time, Pet," Athelas called, waving carelessly at me. "There might be a thing or two to clean up at the house. Wash your face and make sure you buy a *lot* of steak, won't you? If Jin Yeong has to clean, he'll be very hungry."

What did they have to clean up? I wondered miserably, kicking at a few bits of gravel as I took the shortcut to my local Woollies. All the bad mess was across the road, and it was already gone for good. No more batty old dude, no more bodies.

I sniffed a bit again, and shoved my hands in my pockets. There was a bit of devourer blood on my hoodie, but it wasn't red enough to look like real blood.

If there was mess at home, I should be cleaning it up. I was the pet. I wanted to clean.

Hang on. Athelas said *a thing or two to clean up*, and that Jin Yeong would be hungry. Did that mean he expected someone to be at the house as well?

"They better not get blood in the carpet," I muttered to myself, sniffing one last time. Was that why Zero wanted me out of the way? He wanted me away from more blood and mess?

I couldn't help smiling at that, and the barista who was watching the counter smiled back at me as I walked through the door.

I said, "Coffee please. One sugar, with milk."

I took it outside with me, feeling a bit more cheerful, and sat down in the sunlight with my feet on the struts underneath the table. Everything was too cold today.

Maybe it was the thought of that poor old bloke dying alone, Between, without the human sun to keep him warm. Maybe the morgue-like frigidity of the body-filled rubbish bin had gotten into my bones. Whatever it was, it was hard to get warm again. Not that the rubbish bin was likely to be frigid anymore; I'd seen it on my way to the café, smoke and flames leaking from the edges of the battered lid.

At least those changelings were gunna have a hard time.

I wrapped my hands around my paper coffee cup and stretched out to take in the most of the sun, yawning until my eyes almost shut; and as I did so, a shadow fell over me.

I opened my eyes, squinting up at the cause of the shadow, and nearly fell off my seat.

The old bearded bloke was right there, his bushy beard sticking out more wildly than ever.

"Oi!" I said. "You're not dead!"

"Aren't I?" He patted his hands across his chest and down to his legs as if to make sure, but he was grinning.

I was, too, if it came to that. The sneaky old duffer! He'd gotten away again!

Hang on, though—was he the real batty man, or a changeling one who was under glamour? It didn't make sense to put a changeling mad man out on the streets, but if the body back at the waystation really wasn't him, who was it? More importantly, should I be telling Zero about it?

He looked at me with crafty, beady eyes, and put a blackened finger up to his lips.

"What, you don't want me to tell?"

He nodded, grinning another gappy grin at me.

"All right," I said. "But only this once."

"Thanks!" he said, and grabbed my coffee.

"Oi!" I protested, but the old duffer was long gone, chortling his way between two shops. "Mucky thief," I muttered, but I might still have been grinning. Unless there was a glamoured fae who knew the old bloke's habit of pinching my coffee, it was really him.

I could have bought myself another coffee—Zero was paying, after all—but it felt like the sunshine had warmed me enough not to need another one. That, or seeing the old bloke alive and as batty as ever in his spare holey shirt.

I went to the butcher's shop and Woollies, then went home. If Zero and the others weren't finished cleaning up any mess around the house, they'd just have to make sure the kitchen was clear.

The curtains were pulled when I got back, letting in the afternoon light. I saw them all through the glass, my three psychos; they were going back and forth through the living room and kitchen. Athelas had a thin, tidy bag on the table, which he was filling with neatly rolled socks and folded blazers. As he did so, Jin Yeong removed his esky full of blood bags from the fridge, and brought it over to him with a request I couldn't hear.

On the other side of the table, Zero turned the umbrella sword over in the air, but I thought he looked a bit more dressed than usual. A moment later, it occurred to me that he was wearing *all* his weapons.

Hang on. They were packing up? They were leaving? I had my house back to myself again?

"Heck yes!" I said, but my voice didn't sound quite right, and there was an empty sort of feeling in the pit of my stomach. I repositioned my plastic bags, shifting from foot to foot.

Weird. I must have got used to having them around the house. It's not like they were family, or something; they were all three of them killers. None of them cared about me, or humans, or anything that wasn't fae.

Except for Zero, who still cared enough about humans getting killed to investigate their deaths.

I looked at him as he checked his weapons, and saw him put a thick, official piece of paper on the kitchen island, beneath the coffee tin. I swallowed against a tight, sore lump in my throat.

He'd said he was going to sign my house over to me when they were done; that must be what the paper was. I actually had my house back properly—I owned it.

Some of the tension left my shoulders.

I had my house, so it was fine, right?

Just it was a pain that Detective Tuatu knew where I lived now. I would have to be really careful about going in an out, now.

That was definitely what was bothering me. It stayed as a small patch of ice at the bottom of my stomach, beneath the relief of having my own house back again—really owning it.

I put my hand on the doorknob, not sure if I wanted to go in straight away. It hadn't seemed like they had a lot of stuff, so how come the house suddenly looked so empty?

It wasn't like they had anything left to do here, right? The whole house they were investigating had disappeared somewhere I didn't think I would ever fully understand, whether or not Athelas condescendingly explained it to me. They couldn't even keep investigating from here.

They were probably going back Behind, or Between, or wherever, while they waited for the next victim to drop.

I wished I hadn't had that coffee. It was dark and acidic at the back of my throat, making me cough and sniff.

I kicked the toe of my boot against the curb, silently debating on whether I should go in, and jumped a mile when someone's hand slapped down on my shoulder.

I dropped my bags.

"There you are!" said Detective Tuatu's voice said, sharp and tight.

"Police aren't meant to assault the public," I said, before I had time to think about it. I gasped a bit to get my breath back, and turned to face him. "I'm the public; what are you grabbing me for?"

I could see his eyes now that I'd turned; they were wild and just slightly too wide.

Uh oh. He wasn't reacting well to his trip Between, was he?

Or maybe it was the hit in the head.

As if that was my fault! He was the one who had pushed his way in when he wasn't wanted!

He looked at me for a hazy moment or two more. Then he said, "You're under arrest."

"Oi! What for?" I protested, as I was dragged away to his car by my collar. Ah man. My good steak was gunna go bad. "What did *I* do?"

"We'll discuss that," he said, more grimly than wildly this time, "at the station."

CHAPTER TWELVE

I DIDN'T EXPECT SMELL OF THE INTERVIEW ROOM: THEY LOOK clean and air-conditioned on T.V. If I did expect to smell anything, it would have been the faint whiff of coffee on the cool air.

There was more of a plasticky, antibacterial sort of smell to it, and it was *icy*. Was he making it colder on purpose?

He left me in there to stew for about an hour, and I sat on the table, legs crossed beneath me. I'm usually polite enough not to put my feet on tabletops, but he was rude first. I put my chin in my palms and wondered gloomily what my three psychos were going to think when they found that steak on the doorstep.

They probably wouldn't care much. They were getting ready to leave, after all. One human more or less didn't much matter to them.

Detective Tuatu gave me a look as he came in but he didn't tell me to get off the table, which was surprising. Okay, then. Not quite the normal arrest.

He sat down, his face hard, and asked, "What are you to them?"

"Ah," I said, drawing out the syllable in understanding. "So that's what this is. Thought I was being arrested for trespassing."

"Those three," he said, his face harder, "What are you to them?"

I sighed. "You're asking the wrong question. You're always asking the wrong questions. It's a flamin' bad habit."

"Just—"

"I mean, okay, I'll answer it; but it's not going to help you. What am I to them? I dunno—a pet. Maybe a mascot, some days."

"A mascot?"

I thought about it. "Nah, pet's right. They mostly remember to feed me and sometimes they pat me on the head, but it's not like they think I'm capable of rational thought. Not the kind of thinking they're capable of, anyway. I'm something that trots around the house and curls up on the couch to sleep while they're talking business."

"Their business," the detective said eagerly, leaning forward. "What is their business? What do they do when they're—"

"Nope, sorry," I said, shaking my head. "I don't pay attention to their business. Couldn't tell you a thing about it."

Plus there was an agreement I made not to chatter about them. I was gunna have my house back.

No, I already had it back—my psychos were all off again.

Funny how there was still that hollow, icy spot in my stomach. I didn't feel as good as I should have felt about having my house back at this point. It was probably the detective's fault for locking me up. It's a bit hard to be joyful when you're in the clink.

"Don't lie to me. I've seen you around town with them."

"Look, how long are you going to keep me here? I don't remember you cautioning me. Am I really under arrest?"

"You're staying here until they come for you."

"Until they *come for me*?" I laughed, but that was somehow

hollow as well. "Sorry, didn't mean to laugh. It's just...you actually think they're going to come for me?"

"I think so," he said coolly. "Even if you are a—" he stopped and grimaced, "—a pet. People have a habit of being fond of their pets."

"Well, yeah," I said. "People. They're not really *people*, though, are they?"

That brought him up short. He opened his mouth and shut it again. Rolled his lips together and back out again.

"What do you mean, they're not really people?"

I grinned at him. He was sparring for time, because he knew exactly what I meant.

"You know," I said. "You've seen it. Isn't that why you turned off the cameras and the microphone before you came in? You don't want your mates to think you're crazy."

"Who says I turned off the equipment?"

"Didn't you? Bet you did."

"You," he said, breathing just a bit too fast, "need to be locked up in the psych ward."

"That's rude."

"Vampires don't exist."

"Didn't say they did," I said, leaning my elbows on my knees and propping my chin back on my palms. "Don't think I even said the word *vampire*. That was you."

He was still breathing too fast, and it looked like his eyes could roll back in his head if he wasn't careful. "Fae don't exist either."

"I didn't say anything about Fae," I reminded him.

He gave me a particularly steely look. "Not now. Earlier. When you dragged my drug-addled backside through that house—place—"

"Between," I reminded him. "It's called Hobart Between. You're lucky you didn't go into Hobart Behind. And you weren't drugged—well, not exactly."

"Then what was *all that*?"

"That?" I looked at him and suddenly I was grinning again. "That's the truth. It's what's there all the time when you can't see it."

"The truth?" He smiled bitterly. Look who's taken a leaf out of my book. "Is that what they told you?"

I shrugged. I didn't really want to talk about my three psychos. They weren't even *my* three psychos anymore. They were gone; packed up; off on another investigation.

"They told me a bit. Mostly we just...I don't know, end up there. Between, mostly. I don't go Behind unless I'm with them. Not on purpose, anyway."

I probably shouldn't have told him that much, but it wasn't like he knew what to do with the information—unless he was a lot more knowledgeable than I thought he was. Not to mention a much better actor.

"And Between is where the fairies live."

He was fairly dripping with sarcasm. Pretty good for a bloke I had to haul through Between with his eyes wide open and rolling whites.

"Fae," I said. "They don't like being called fairies. They reckon it's disrespectful or something. It's not just fae, though; so far I've met fae, vampires, goblins, devourers and a couple of blokes with four arms. Well, I didn't exactly meet them; they met Zero and Jin Yeong instead."

Detective Tuatu looked startled. Maybe I sounded too satisfied about that. He asked, "Where are the bodies?"

"Dunno. Somewhere Between. Oh, wait; you don't believe in Between anymore. Guess you won't be finding the bodies."

"You realise I could hold you on suspicion as an accessory to murder after making a statement like that?"

"Yeah? And what d'you want me to tell your officers when they interview me? That a fae and a vampire killed five four-armed men and left their bodies in a twilight realm known as Between, that borders Behind and the human world?"

He shut his mouth, and this time I was the one who smiled, smugly. Now I knew why Jin Yeong does it so often. It felt good.

"Let's forget about vampires," said the detective, clearing his throat. "And let's forget about fae, and Hobart Between or Behind, or whatever you want to call it."

"If you want," I said, shrugging. It's not like it was going to make a difference to their existence, talking about them or not. I'd like to see anyone's belief—or lack of it—affect Zero's solid, immovable existence by one atom. Or Jin Yeong's self-satisfied, pouty existence, if it comes to that.

"Let's talk about your parents instead."

Oh.

I flashed him an insincere smile. "Let's go back to talking about vampires and fae."

He gave me another of those ironlike looks, his lips pressed together. "How did you escape? There was no trace of you there, no sign you ever lived there—"

Someone laughed tiredly.

Oh. That was me. "You think I killed them."

He traded me look for look. "You were what? Thirteen? I've known thirteen-year-olds who killed their parents."

"I didn't."

"Then how—"

"The home invaders didn't find me," I said baldly. "What? The police didn't find me, either, and I was at home then, too. If I'd been in my right mind I might have come out at the start, but after I'd been hiding for the first few hours it seemed stupid to come out and start crying on someone."

"Say I believe that," he said. "Say I believe you were so well hidden that the police searching your house didn't find you—what about the house? There were no photos of you anywhere. No certificates on the wall, nothing. Like they'd been cleared away by someone who didn't want to be found. There wasn't even a birth certificate, for pity's sake!"

"Dunno. I s'pose we weren't photo takers."

The detective's face almost looked despairing. "Do you know how downright dodgy that sounds?"

"Dodgy?" I grinned. "That a police term? I don't know what to tell you, mate. We didn't take photos. We didn't take photos of our food, either—is that weird too?"

I mean, it's not like there were photos of Mum and Dad and none of me. There were never photos of any of us on the shelves around the house. Just books. Lots of books.

"Anyway, it's not like you ever looked for me. No one did. Don't think you guys even knew I existed."

"You were home-schooled," he said, nodding grimly. I couldn't tell if the grimness was aimed at me, or at his fellow police. "And all your friends are from out of state."

"Yeah." I looked at him curiously. "How'd you know?"

"I did what they should have been— I mean, I made inquiries. All right, if you were there that night, what happened?"

"Don't know," I said briefly. "I don't know what they did to them. Sometimes I see stuff in my nightmares, but...I don't even know why I woke up that night. Maybe I was too hot. Kicked my sheets off and went to get some water but the place smelled funny. They were like that when I turned on the light."

The detective frowned. I couldn't tell if he didn't believe me, or if he just didn't like what he was hearing. It didn't matter either way. It's not like I could change what happened, no matter how much I'd like to.

Anyway, I wasn't the one who insisted on the subject, so if he didn't like it, that was his problem.

"They were already dead when you came out?"

"Yeah."

"*All that* happened without you hearing a thing?"

"Seems like it," I said. I didn't want to talk about it before, and now I really didn't want to talk about it. I was remembering stuff I hadn't remembered in years—stuff you shouldn't have to remember.

I mean, it's not like I didn't know where he was coming from. The state the upstairs living room was in when I came out for my drink of water that night, it was impossible for me not to have heard anything.

I hadn't seen it straight away; it was dark, and the streetlights don't really come through the side windows. I felt something sticky beneath my socks, though.

That was the first thing. Then the stickiness was a wetness that went through the socks, and it came to my mind that all I'd been able to smell since I woke was something heavy and salty and metallic.

The couch was lumpy; there was usually a throw rug there. But between the smell and the wetness underfoot—the weirdness of it all—I couldn't push away the thought that I could see some-one's head in shadow above the backrest of the couch. It creeped me out, even though it could have been Dad, asleep on the couch —or Mum, for that matter. I was so creeped out that I was shaking by the time I was close enough to lunge for the light switch. And when the light flickered and began to brighten, and I saw the scope of it all, the shivers got bigger and bigger until it seemed that my teeth were rattling in my head.

There wasn't a patch of carpet that wasn't red; not a corner of the room that wasn't at least dappled with red stickiness. I looked down at my socks numbly and saw that they were stained red, too, the colour leaching up and over the arch of my foot to the ankle. There was something trailing from my left sock. I whimpered and wiped it on the carpet, but it wouldn't come off, and I couldn't bring myself to reach down and pull it off.

Mum and I had been studying anatomy since the start of last month. That piece of something squishy, I knew, was part of someone's small intestine. And scattered around the living room floor were other parts of things I'd labelled and studied last week, clean and tidy on paper but glistening and weird and out of shape on the carpet. Stuff that wasn't meant to be outside of skin.

The detective sounded sick as he asked, "How could that— that room be like it—how could you not hear anything?"

I hunched my shoulders. "You tell me."

I didn't want to talk about it. Didn't want to think about it, either, but that was impossible, now. It was all right for him to be sick; he didn't even see the room first hand. I did see it first hand, and if I didn't see the murder of my parents I feel like that's something your average person should be glad about.

But sometimes I have the Nightmare, and I wake up thinking that maybe I saw something, after all. Saw something, or heard something, or—I don't know.

Maybe the detective was right.

"Those three," he began, again.

I was glad he wasn't talking about my parents anymore, but I didn't particularly want to go back to talking about my three psychos, either. They were gone, and my parents were gone, and now there was only an empty house with a bit of paper that said it was mine waiting for me when I got out.

"What about 'em?" If he thought he was going to get anything out of me but their names, he was as mad as they are.

"Why are they staying in your house?"

Wait. He didn't know that the house belonged to Zero? That was weird. With all the stuff he'd dug up about me and them, you think he'd know at least that much.

"They needed a place for a while," I said, shrugging. "I wouldn't bother looking for them there any more, though. They're finished what they were doing."

"They're not still at the house?"

"I told you; they don't tell me stuff. I'm the pet." I propped my chin in my palm and said crankily, "Oi. What charges are you holding me on, anyway? Aren't I supposed to be told that I can have a lawyer if I want one?"

The detective looked at me. "Do you want one?"

"Nope. Just thought you ought to know I know my rights." That was rubbish, of course; he'd turned off the camera and the mic, so what did he care about my rights? But I hadn't got the feeling that he was a dodgy cop all the times I'd met him, and I wanted to remind him that he knew me, as well. I didn't want to stay in the cop shop all night. I had a house to go back to.

"You're staying where you are until they come to get you."

"Yeah, you said that before. It's nuts. They're not going to come for me. They're probably half way back to Behind by now."

"We'll see," he said.

We sat in silence for a while; I don't think he quite knew what to ask next.

"Oi," I said at last, tugging at the jean-wrinkles around my knees. "What about you, then?"

He looked wary. "What about me?"

I half-grinned. I didn't really expect him to answer that. I expected him to be all business-like—"Don't ask me questions, I'm asking you"—that kind of thing.

"That thing you can do where you're immune to stuff," I said. "How d'you do that?"

It was creeping JinYeong out, and even if I approved of creeping out JinYeong, I didn't see why anyone else but me should be able to do it.

The detective shrugged, his full lips compressing. This time it wasn't annoyance making him do it. It was more like he didn't know whether or not he should tell me.

I wondered if it would occur to him that if he shared stuff with me, I might share stuff with him?

I wouldn't, but I still wondered if the thought would occur to him.

It did; he pulled a necklace out of his shirtfront and waggled the pendant at me.

"This," he said. "I think. My grandma gave it to me. She told me it would protect me from things that can't be stopped by humans."

"Good for grandma," I said in approval. I don't know why I tried to find out; it's not like Zero and the others are going to come back for me to share it with them. For me, it's useless info.

Habits die hard, I s'pose; even new ones.

The detective looked tired; or maybe just a bit sad. He tucked the pendant back away in his shirt, and I was surprised to find myself feeling sorry for him. After all, who was he going to talk to about this? It wasn't like he could share his suspicions with anyone. Not without people thinking he was bonkers, anyway.

"Why d'you wanna know about them so much, anyway?" I asked him. "Thought you lot were trying to catch the murderer who killed the bloke across the road, but you seem to be pretty interested in me and those three."

"We are," he said grimly. "I am. But I keep getting the feeling that if I can figure out those three, a lot of other mysteries will be solved. I think the murder will, as well."

"Oh." I gazed at him for a long time, and that made him uneasy.

He twitched his collar straight and looked away.

"They didn't do it, y'know."

"I thought you didn't know what they got up to? Thought you were just the pet."

"I am, and I don't," I said firmly. "But I saw 'em arrive, and they've been trying to figure out who did this, too."

"Why? If they're—if they're—"

"Behindkind," I supplied, helpfully.

He closed his eyes briefly, but gave in. "If they're *Behindkind*, why do they care about a human murder?"

"Yeah, well, that's the question, isn't it?"

"What is the go with the murdered bloke, anyway?" he asked, impatiently.

"The go?" I was surprised. A bit because he was finally asking about the actual murder he should have been investigating while he was running around spying on my three psychos, but also a bit because I hadn't wondered about that for a while now. "Dunno. They've been trying to find out who murdered him, but I don't know why."

"Like I said; he's human. They're...something else. Why should they care about him?"

"Don't know that they care about him," I said, thinking it over. There was no need to tell him too much, but that bit wasn't a secret or something important, so I didn't mind telling him. "It's more about the bloke who murdered him. Reckon they've been after him for a while."

"I suppose he's been murdering fairies, too."

"Yeah," I said laconically. It was no use putting him right again —he was doing it on purpose. Sort of a defence against what he knew was true but couldn't bear to believe. "We done yet?"

His eyes narrowed. "Not even close."

I sighed. The more I saw of this room, the uglier it got. It'd be nice to see some Between flickering around the edges; just enough so I could slip away and startle the detective.

I looked around gloomily. Oh well. Even if there was a way Between, I probably wouldn't be able to get through. Not without my psychos.

Well, if I couldn't get outta there, I wanted coffee. "Aren't you supposed to give me coffee or something?" I asked the detective, accusatorily. "I don't care if it's to get my DNA or whatever. I'm having withdrawal."

He gave me a look that was all pressed lips and Dad-level disapproval.

"What? I got you tea when you broke into my place. Least you can do is get me a cup of coffee. It doesn't have to be good."

"Fine," he said. "But when I get back, we're going to talk about what happened in the house across the street from you, and how a whole house—a whole house—"

"Yeah, good luck trying to make that bit normal," I said, grinning.

He gave up. Instead of trying to say it in a way that wouldn't sound crazy, he got up and left the room.

Hopefully he'd get me some coffee while he figured it out.

I waited in the silence of the interview room, batting at the edges of Between that were visible to me; and every now and then I saw a bit of the room that wasn't just room. No matter how hard I tried, I couldn't do more than see a glimmer of it every now and then. I definitely couldn't see enough to walk Between. Not here, anyway.

Looked like I was stuck here until Detective Tuatu decided to let me go.

It was only a few minutes later that I heard his voice outside the door. It was raised; annoyed and disbelieving. I couldn't hear exactly what he was saying, and I didn't know who he was talking to, but whoever it was—whatever it was—it got under his collar.

That meant it was probably about my three psychos.

He slammed into the room after another minute, his phone still in his hand.

"Oi!" I said indignantly. "Where's me coffee?"

"Are you lot playing games with me?"

"Ay?"

"You think you're part of the police force, or something?"

I laughed. "Yeah, that's a good one. Better give me a badge, then. I could use it next time I need to 'trespass'."

"Don't play games with me!" the detective snapped, his voice cracking. "Somehow they've got to the chief commissioner as well —they're a part of the force now! Freelancers! Don't tell me you didn't know that!"

"What?" If my face was as blank as my brain, he had to know I wasn't lying. "They're what?"

He looked like he wanted to punch something. He made a circle around the desk to give him a chance to squash that urge, and then said bitterly, "I had the news from the commander. They're attached to the police force now. Whenever we've got a case with anything weird or difficult about it, they're the ones we're supposed to call. And anything that shows the same M.O. as this case—it goes straight to them. We don't even get a look in."

The room seemed suddenly very cool again. This—none of it —made any sense.

I saw them getting ready to leave. I saw Athelas clearing out cupboards and Jin Yeong emptying the blood stock in the fridge. I saw Zero putting that bit of paper, that important bit of paper, on the kitchen island before the detective arrested me.

"When did you hear that?" I asked. It probably didn't matter, but it could.

"I took the call five minutes ago," he said. "While I was out of the room. You'd better start talking. I can't let this go, not when they're conning their way into the police force."

"They've got a lot of guts," I said. What was going on? They were definitely going when I saw them; it was no use feeling hopeful now. "Gotta hand it to 'em. I don't know what they're up to, but they've got a lot of guts."

I sighed, and hunched down. I really wanted to be out of here. Times like this, it'd be really handy if I could get into Between by myself. If I could get Between by myself, I could just sort of push at that curling edge of Other I could see dividing the interview room, and walk right through the walls.

But I was stuck here for as long as the detective chose to keep me. Or as long as he could do it without getting in trouble, I supposed. Actually, it was kind of insulting: did he think I was going to talk for this?

"Are you listening to me?"

"Yeah, yeah," I said wearily. Everything seemed to be catching up with me now, and I felt that I'd really like to sniffle in a corner somewhere, then go to sleep.

The almost translucent edge of Between space through the interview room was brightening. I smiled at it, wondering if it was responding to me—if maybe I'd managed to influence it by thinking about it and wanting it.

C'mmon. Open up just a bit. Just a little bit. That's all I needed to slip through into Between. And if I was lucky, maybe I could get myself out again, too; like I did the first time.

"What?" said the detective. He sounded wary. "Why are you smiling?"

I glared at him. "Who's smiling?"

"You are. Don't. It creeps me out."

I yawned at him this time.

"I can wait all day," Detective Tuatu said warningly, sitting back with crossed arms. His body language said he wasn't concerned, but I was pretty sure he was sweating. He really thought they were going to come for me. Or maybe that hit on the head was still bothering him. "I can wait all day for them to come for you. Then we'll all have a bit of a talk about this and that."

Completely troppo. Which was worrying, since he'd already admitted he disconnected the camera and audio feeds.

I made more of an effort with the divide I could see between the human world and Between.

See 'em like they are Behind. See 'em as more than just dust bunnies sweeping across the floor on a draught.

Nothing. It did nothing.

I sighed, my shoulders sinking. And then it occurred to me.

The dust bunnies were sweeping across the floor like miniature tumbleweed. Why were they doing that? There was no breeze in here. The aircon was so high up on the wall, with its vents pointing straight across from itself, that it couldn't be that, either.

Opposite me, a crack of light broke across the detective's face, rising in a zigzag above his head on the wall behind him. It split further, bathing his entire face in golden light; and that face was frozen, its eyes wide and white, terror clear in the light of Between.

I couldn't help it. I smiled, wide and glad, and scooted around on the interview table.

There was a huge gap in the wall, soft around the edges, but with a razor sharp Zero at the centre. And as the edges softened still more, I saw the gleam of Athelas' eyes and the sharp point of Jin Yeong's teeth.

"Well, strike me pink!" I said in wonder.

CHAPTER THIRTEEN

"WHAT D'YOU KNOW!" I SAID, TURNING FROM THE WAIST TO grin at the detective. I was probably just as astonished as he was, but I was lucky; the three of them together isn't something that scares me anymore. I wasn't sure when that had happened, but it was true. "They did come! Bet you're glad."

"Not exactly," he said, through clenched teeth. He was doing pretty well; he was stiff, but he could still talk, even with the side of his interview room open to Between.

"Pet," said Zero, twitching one finger at me. "Come."

I touched a finger to my eyebrow in the detective's direction and boosted myself off the table. "See ya."

I saw Detective Tuatu's mouth trying to form the word *stop*, but maybe he thought better of it. At any rate, when I turned again, laughing, toward Zero, he didn't try to stop me.

Zero left without another word, but when I would have slipped my hand in his pocket he reached back and grabbed my hand instead.

I walked through the wall into Between, where it was cool and fresh and unconfined, and felt the lightness of laughter bubbling up in my stomach.

Zero came back for me. He actually came to find me.

I didn't think it would be wise to say that out loud. Instead, my hand warm and my heart light, I asked, "House over the road still gone?"

"Indeed," Athelas agreed from my left side. "Did you suppose it might have grown back?"

"Dunno," I told him. "Wouldn't surprise me, around here."

"Things the Family do tend to stay done," Zero said, without looking over his shoulder at me. "Remember that. And next time, scream when someone tries to steal you."

"Tries to—yeah, I'll do that."

"And if ever you see the devourers again—"

"Those locust things?"

"Yes. If you see them again, run."

"Yeah, I will," I replied, in heartfelt sincerity. "How the heck am I gunna fight giant locusts?"

"You'll have to have some lessons, but you won't be ready to fight them for at least a few years."

"Lessons? A few years? You're stay— I'm having— What lessons? I'm gunna fight? Do I get a sword?"

Zero ignored that barrage of questions, and shouldered his way through a wall I vaguely recognised.

I stepped down suddenly, jarring my teeth, and found myself in the kitchen, Between a vague muddying of the wall behind me. I beamed around at the kitchen in general, and the cracked tile over the sink in particular, and let the questions go for later.

To Zero, I said, "Thanks for coming for me. Thought I'd never get out."

"You'll have to learn to take care of yourself," said Zero briefly. "We won't always be here."

"'Zat right?"

I flicked a look up at him, and maybe it annoyed him. At any rate, he stalked on through the kitchen and down into the living room, ignoring me. Jin Yeong shot me an amused, somewhat malicious look, and sauntered after Zero.

"How come you lot came for me?" I asked Athelas, since he was the only one left. "Thought you'd all left."

"No one makes me tea when you're not here," he said, settling himself at the table. He crossed one leg over the other in his usual manner and gazed pleasantly at me. "I appreciate my tea. Jin Yeong is a savage who cares only for coffee, and Zero doesn't care enough about either to make a tolerable effort. You make an effort."

"'S'pose that's a hint," I said cheerfully, and put the kettle on. "Want a biscuit?"

"Oh, I think so," he said. "It's been a busy day, after all."

"Yeah," I said. "I thought you lot were finished and gone—you were packing and everything. What's the go?"

"We've got some changelings to round up," said Athelas. "Now that we know what they're going to look like."

"Oh," I said, and there was a deeper relief running beneath the sparkling feeling of happiness that had come when I saw all three of them. "You mean you weren't going for good?"

"Certainly not," Athelas said. "We've still got four more murders to come. We're best waiting for them here; they'll happen close to home."

I stopped with my hand on the kettle handle. "What, the other murders will happen here, around this house, I mean?"

"Every one of them," Zero said, from the living room. "We can guess where, but we can't be sure. Bring the coffee in here, Pet."

"But you're still going off to catch the changelings?" I asked, loading the teapot and coffee mugs on a tray with the biscuits.

"Certainly. There won't be another murder for a little while yet," Athelas said, and took the tray from me. "It could be one year, or five; we won't know until it happens. We might as well clean up what we can."

"That's all you know?"

Zero's brows went up.

"For Investigators, you lot are pretty rubbish!" I said. I took my cup of coffee and plopped down on my end of the couch. I was heady and bright, and probably not too wise, but I couldn't help it. "You solved the wrong case, and you didn't even find the murderer!"

JinYeong scowled at me, but Athelas' eyes crinkled at the edges.

"Are you unhappy with the uncovering of an otherworldly kidnapping plot, Pet?"

Zero, expressionlessly, said, "We've been chasing this murderer all the way from Behind, and for the last fifteen years. It's not to be expected that we'll find him at once. And now that the house is gone we've only blood and ash with which to investigate the first murder further."

"Yeah, but—"

"Quiet, Pet," said Zero, and lofted a white box at me from his desk. "You'll need this, in future."

I caught it by reflex, but I didn't realise what it was until I felt the smooth weight of it in my hand.

"You're giving me a phone?"

"It's tiresome to communicate with humans who don't have the means to speak in other ways," said Athelas.

"You can take pictures with it next time," said Zero, and left the room.

"Cool!" I said, hugging the phone box to my chest happily. I hadn't ever had my own phone.

JinYeong looked at me sourly, and I stuck my tongue out at him.

"What?" I demanded. "Zero probably hasn't given you one 'cos he doesn't want to talk to you."

"*Choshimhae, Petteu,*" said JinYeong through his teeth, and rose liquidly to his feet to stalk away to the kitchen.

Probably needed to suck on a blood bag.

I chuckled happily to myself and turned the box over to open it. "Hang on, is it okay for him to give me free things? Like phones and stuff?"

Stuff, most importantly, being the house when it was no longer needed.

That reminded me. What was the piece of paper Zero had put on the kitchen island, if it wasn't something to do with signing over the house to me?

"Those aren't free things," Athelas said, sipping his tea. "You're our pet. We feed you and keep you clothed, and sometimes we give you a treat. The balance of power is different. Now, if you give one of us something, it's incumbent upon us to give you something back for it."

"I see," I said; and I really did. I'd guessed it, if it came to that.

"Now, Pet," said Athelas, lifting his teacup, "in light of that fact, you have until the moment I finish my tea to ask questions. I should point out that it is a fair exchange, and it is unlikely that I will ever be so open again; so use your exchange wisely."

I wanted badly to ask exactly what I'd done to put him into my debt, and as I hesitated on the question, between the blink of my eyes and their opening, his tea was half gone. Across from me, Athelas smiled, his teacup still poised.

I asked, in a rush, "Who is the Family?"

"Interesting," Athelas said. "The Family is Zero's birth family, if somewhat illegitimately."

"But they're trying to kill him."

"Another interesting thing."

A second blink, and his tea was almost gone: he obviously didn't want to answer those particular questions. What a cheater.

Since I wouldn't get any proper answers for those questions, I asked another instead. "I thought—well, Jin Yeong is always so angry at Zero, and it always looks like he's on the verge of killing him. But they still fight together against everyone else, and last night I saw him tear out the throats of a couple of devourers who got too close to killing Zero."

Athelas' eyes gleamed at me above the rim of his teacup. He was laughing at me. Why?

"They fought together in the war," he said.

"Which war?"

"Not one that humankind ever heard about."

"Does Jin Yeong hate or love Zero?"

There was a thoughtful pause before Athelas answered. "I don't think even Jin Yeong could tell you that. They fought together through several wars, and were as close as brothers. Then Jin Yeong's sister was bitten and he went home to make sure she turned safely. Unfortunately, there were...complications. She went rabid and Jin Yeong couldn't bring himself to kill her. So Zero did it."

"Oh," I said. That explained the feeling I'd gotten from the two of them. "So Jin Yeong wants to make sure that if anyone kills Zero, it's him."

"Something like that," said Athelas, and put down his teacup. There was the slightest gleam of liquid there, taunting me.

Could I ask another question, or would he drain it before I got the question out?

That was the game, I realised, as the amusement in Athelas' eyes grew. If he didn't want to answer the next question I asked, he would simply drink the rest of the tea. If he felt like answering it, he would.

The question was, what should I ask? What before about my question had amused him?

I thought about that, and said experimentally, "Athelas."

"Mm?"

"Why are you always telling me what Jin Yeong says? You don't have to do that."

"I find it interesting. It's a new development in Jin Yeong's psychopathy."

"His what?"

"His manner of thinking and his habits," Athelas said, and sipped delicately. When he put down his cup, it was completely empty, but he still added, "There seems to be a slight shift, which interests me immensely."

"Oh," I said gloomily. Well, that was a wasted question: I didn't understand a single thing Athelas had just said.

"Now," he said silkily, "I have a few questions of my own."

"Thought you were paying *me* back," I said, before I could stop myself.

"Humour me, Pet," said Athelas, though he smiled. "Has it never occurred to you to wonder about your affinity with this house?"

"What do you mean?"

"Has it never occurred to you to leave? There are other—"

"No."

"Other easier places—"

"No."

"More comfortable places."

"This is *my* house," I said, stubbornly.

"I see," said Athelas, and his eyes creased very slightly. "Then if it hasn't occurred to you to live elsewhere, perhaps it has occurred to you to wonder exactly why the power and water were left on when it wasn't being occupied?"

"That's—" I stopped. Now that I thought about the reason, it seemed a bit ridiculous. I said it anyway. "They had to leave it on to show the house to buyers and renters."

"And exactly how many people have been brought through the house?"

His voice was light and unconcerned, but I had the feeling he was listening very closely to my answer.

"None," I said.

I was still frowning about that when Athelas asked, "What is it about this house that keeps you here, Pet?"

"I lived here with my parents," I said. I hadn't really thought about it—about that burning necessity that was always somewhere in the back of my mind, reminding me at every moment that I had to keep striving to keep this place for myself.

"Mm," murmured Athelas. "However, your parents were murdered here."

"I've gotta stay," I said sharply, but it wasn't exactly what I'd meant to say. If it came to that, I didn't know what I did mean to say.

Athelas gazed at me for some time. "From what I understand of humans, when their parents are murdered, it's an important thing."

"Isn't it an important thing with Fae?"

"I killed my parents," Athelas said casually, pouring himself another cup of tea from the pot. "My mother sold me off to the Family to pay the debts she and my father owed. It doesn't pay to be very attached to parents Behind."

"You killed—"

"It doesn't pay to be too attached to Fae, either," said Athelas, and his eyes looked at me through the multi-coloured tea steam, as impossible to fathom as the steam itself. "Do you understand me, Pet?"

I did understand him. But if I didn't fully grasp the ways of the Fae, I was pretty sure that none of my three psychos understood humans fully, either. I said, "I don't work like that. And Zero is—Zero is different."

His head bent forward in acknowledgement. "Zero *is* different. He's got that human strain in him. But it would be a mistake to think that his Fae side won't overcome that during his lifetime. It's unwise to trust the Fae."

"I only have to stay behind him," I said. There was a stubborn bit of me that knew exactly what Athelas was getting at, but refused to believe it. "And trust that he won't let me be killed. That's all I need."

"Is it? Well, that's safe enough, I suppose. And what if Jin Yeong decides one day that you do smell like dinner?"

"I'll stand behind Zero," I said.

"And me?"

"You can stand behind Zero, too."

Athelas' face lit with the smile that went all the way to his eyes. "You don't fancy yourself in any danger from me, Pet?"

"No," I said.

"You should," he said.

I waited until Athelas fell into a reflective mood, sipping his third cup of tea, and went back into the kitchen. Zero was there, reading one of his mouldy old books that was probably a spell book, and the piece of paper I'd seen earlier was still there on the kitchen island, too.

I crossed the kitchen to put my coffee mug in the sink, and drifted a little closer to the island. It was definitely expensive paper, but there was nothing printed on there—just handwriting.

I leaned over to get a better look, and saw the word 'Pet' written there.

It said, 'Pet. We'll be back. Make dinner tomorrow—'

A large hand swiped the paper from beneath my nose before I could read it all. "That's not necessary anymore," said Zero, crumpling the paper carelessly in one hand. When he unclenched his hand, there was no paper there anymore.

"Thought it was my house deed," I said.

"No," said Zero. "You get that when we're finished with the house."

I looked up at him, shoving my hands in my pockets. "How long's that gunna be, then?" I asked, and it felt like I couldn't breathe, waiting for the answer.

"As long as it takes," he said.

"All right," I said. "But if you go back on it, there'll be trouble. Got friends in the police now, you know."

Zero's eyes narrowed very slightly in amusement. "I'll remember that," he said.

"All right," I said, and grinned. "Just so long as you know."